MW00618976

DONATED BY CHRISTOPHER RAPP

"Ohboy, when y___ ___ a__ you don't
take noth___ ___th you,
but your soul - *THINK!*

Homo Sovieticus

Books by Alexander Zinoviev
(in English translation)

THE YAWNING HEIGHTS

THE RADIANT FUTURE

THE REALITY OF COMMUNISM

HOMO SOVIETICUS

Homo Sovieticus

ALEXANDER ZINOVIEV

translated by Charles Janson

The Atlantic Monthly Press

BOSTON / NEW YORK

Copyright © 1982 by Editions l'Age d'Homme
Translation copyright © 1985 by Victor Gollancz Ltd

ALL RIGHTS RESERVED. NO PART OF THIS BOOK MAY BE REPRODUCED
IN ANY FORM OR BY ANY ELECTRONIC OR MECHANICAL MEANS IN-
CLUDING INFORMATION STORAGE AND RETRIEVAL SYSTEMS WITHOUT
PERMISSION IN WRITING FROM THE PUBLISHER, EXCEPT BY A REVIEWER
WHO MAY QUOTE BRIEF PASSAGES IN A REVIEW.

FIRST AMERICAN EDITION

BP

PRINTED IN THE UNITED STATES OF AMERICA

AUTHOR'S FOREWORD

This book is about Soviet Man. He is a new type of man, *Homo Sovieticus*. We will shorten him to Homosos. I have a dual relationship with this new being: I love him and at the same time I hate him; I respect him and I despise him. I am delighted with him and I am appalled by him. I myself am a Homosos. Therefore I am merciless and cruel when I describe him. Judge us, because you yourselves will be judged by us.

A.Z.

The course of true love does not run
smoothly
  (Western folk-saying)

If he didn't like me, he wouldn't
strike me
  (Russian folk-saying)

We will fight for peace until there
isn't one stone left standing on another
  (Soviet folk-saying)

THE FIRST ALARM

I came to during the night and immediately sank into a delirium. It was as though I was being dragged along somewhere.

"Where are we going?" I asked soundlessly.

"To the Court of Judgement," the Voice soundlessly began to thunder.

"Which one?"

"The Last One."

"What should I be judged for, if every moment of my life was preordained by you?"

"For your life."

"What can I pay for it with?"

"The payment for life is death. Your time has come. Pay up!"

"Don't hurry me. Perhaps I can still pull through. I haven't yet drained life's bitter cup to the dregs."

And They let me go. And I sort of got over it, and began to think about all sorts of nonsense.

TO WISH OR NOT TO WISH

I often have a wish to get something done; but I very rarely have the wish actually to do what I want to get done. Don't imagine that this is a piece of dead sophistry. It is living dialectics. Now I'll formulate my thought in a different way, so that you will even be disappointed by its banal clarity: I want to do something, but I don't want to make the effort to accomplish what I want. You see how simple it is? Incidentally, it's the same with all the "eternal problems", classed as the deepest and most complex by the greatest thinkers of the past and their miserable regurgitators of the present. One has only to put the thing in a rather different way and at once it turns out to be all uselessness and futility. For instance, take the eternal Problem Number One: "to be or not to be?". For the Russian it comes out in the form: to b[ooz]e or not to b[ooz]e?". And there can't be two opinions about that: of course, b[ooz]e. And seriously, by God! Then start boozing again. Then some more. And then begin all over again. In the Russian language one can also formulate this Problem Number One in another way: "to be[at] or not to be[at]?". And again

9

there are no two ways about that: be[at]. Of course one must beat. And above all, in the face! In the West, of course, they don't understand this, because you can't translate Russian problems into Western languages. If you try to do that, all the romantic nuances disappear, and all the psychological profundity.

The wish to do nothing arises in me even more often. But then I make titanic efforts to accomplish my wish. And I always succeed. Western thinkers see in this "typical Russian laziness". And they are wrong, as always.

A POLITICAL NOVEL

Now I have the wish to write a novel. And indeed why not? All Russian émigrés write something. Am I any worse than them? And so, a novel, a romance. Moreover, in the original sense of the word "romance": about love. But about a special kind of love: between the Soviet Union (Moscow, in short) and the West. But what kind of love could that be, you wonder indignantly, if . . . ? Yet this "if" also allows one to discern genuine love. Love until death do us part, one could say. If you read the epigraphs at the beginning you ought to understand what it's about. And if you missed them, read them without fail. It will only take a minute, and you will pick up enough wisdom for the rest of your life.

The love between my heroes is not only genuine love, it is also contemporary love: the homosexual kind. Moreover, Moscow is the active partner. Ask any Soviet man what Moscow is doing to the West, and you will hear something that supports my previous statement. Citizens of Western countries will say the same thing, they just use less indecent expressions. But our attitude to this union is radically different. The West thinks it's a healthy one and experiences the most voluptuous satisfaction. We have feelings of shame and disgust. True, not for ourselves, but for the West.

EVIDENCE OF AN EYE-WITNESS

An acquaintance of mine worked for ten years in a Western country as a spy. Not long ago they found him out, by accident. When he was drunk he made a bet with his boon-companion, a local journalist, that he could organize a protest-demonstration on any subject whatsoever that the

10

journalist cared to choose. The incident received publicity and they asked my friend to leave the country. They did this reluctantly and in a languid kind of way, because the country wanted to stay friendly with Moscow. When he reached Moscow my friend said (naturally, he was drunk again) that "all those defectives" (he was referring to Western leftists, pacifists, neutralists and intellectuals) "should have their. . . ." And he went on to use the very words which I was ashamed to spell out earlier.

PHILOSOPHICAL CONVICTIONS AND BEHAVIOURAL STEREOTYPES

And here's yet another mystery for you: what I'm saying here doesn't express my convictions. And, what is more, it's only an apparent mystery: I haven't got any convictions. I've only got a more or less stable reaction to everything I bump up against: a behavioural stereotype. Convictions are something Western man has, not Soviet man. Instead of having convictions the latter has a "stereotype of behaviour". This doesn't presuppose any convictions, and so it's compatible with every sort of conviction. When you confuse convictions with behavioural stereotypes without convictions, you get many misunderstandings, and strange ideas arise among Westerners about Soviet behaviour. If somebody else were to say what I am saying, I would start arguing with him. If you want to get at the truth, the first thing to do is to get into an argument with yourself. But I say this not from conviction, but in order to be witty, because I am not concerned with the truth either.

If a man has convictions it is a sign that he is not intellectually mature. Convictions are only a compensation for not being able to understand a given phenomenon quickly and accurately in its concrete manifestation. They are *a priori* guides to how one should behave in a concrete situation without understanding its concreteness. A man with convictions is rigid, dogmatic, tedious and, as a rule, stupid. But more often convictions have no effect on people's behaviour. They merely beautify vanity, relieve unclear consciences and cover up stupidity.

I AND MOSCOW

I am a Soviet émigré in the West. The words "in the West" could really be left out, because a Soviet émigré in the East is a logical impossibility:

11

we are always in the East and don't need to emigrate there. But all the same I'll leave these words in because many Western people, afraid that the Soviet Army will arrive in their midst, are doing a bunk to the East. They imagine that we too can do that.

I now live in the West; and I feel as if I had been cast out into a Russian province at the back of beyond. That gives one something to think about. For me only one place in the world is a capital: Moscow. Everything else seems provincial. Moscow is the capital not only of a state. It's the capital of history. So when I left it I made a real bloomer: I fell out of history.

I AND THE WEST

"Why do you want Western Europe?" a local asked me. "You've got too much land already. Get all you can out of Siberia, but leave us in peace." "We wish we could," I said, "but look at it from our angle. In Siberia it's cold, slushy, empty and there are swarms of midges; while you have beauty, comfort and wealth. Which is better? Don't shunt us off into Siberia, we are fed up to the back teeth with it. We want to come here, to Europe. And then in time we'll send *you* to Siberia."

"But we won't let you in here," he cries, frightened and indignant.

"You're the first and perhaps the only person to talk like that," I say. "But you're too late, alas! We're already here."

DENUNCIATIONS

The mechanism of my wishes is very cunningly constructed. As soon as I began to think of writing a novel my *arrière-pensée* whispered: why a novel? Perhaps it would be better to write a denunciation? That's more like it, you'll say. After all, it's more your style. But here I must disappoint you: I have never written a denunciation in my life. You don't believe me? An acquaintance of mine (not the one I mentioned earlier, but another), never wrote denunciations either. But then he was a KGB officer and people wrote denunciations to him. I wasn't a KGB officer. But I had occasion to study denunciations as part of my work, so I have some experience of them. I'm a specialist in denunciations, but not a denouncer. I am a theorist in the field, not a practitioner.

It is undeniable that we have lost the reverent and tremulous attitude to denunciations that we used to have. They have lost their revolutionary-romantic tinge. And it's no longer possible to say what their role in the history of our times has been. But the denunciation has retained a very great epistemological significance. It is the only branch of human culture in which people can achieve some competence without any training or literary ability. To write denunciations there is no need to be a member of the Soviet Writers' Union. And, as they sing in a popular opera, all ages are susceptible to denunciation.*

At one time there was such a spate of denunciations to the KGB that its officers couldn't keep up with them on their own. They had to call in outside specialists to help. Hundreds of them, including myself, were brought in. You cannot imagine the size of the piles of *unread* denunciations alone in the central offices of the organs of State security, nor how many had piled up in the republics, provinces and districts and in the files and safes of individual operatives. And how many had been readied for action! How many perished in the war! How many were destroyed! What a mighty amount of human energy, feeling and thought went into the whole business of denunciation!

My task was to select from many thousands the ones which deserved attention and chuck away the rest; or, as it was then called, "write them off". I read the denunciations of innocent children in the morning of their lives; of decrepit old men wise with experience; of sober young careerists; of alcoholics out of their mind in their hopelessness; of prominent academics, of housewives, of young and pure virgins, of old debauchees, of Party officials, illiterate cretins, professors, pensioners and artists. They were all as alike as coins of the same value, or bugs. It was just as if denunciation was lodged in our genes from the start, instead of being, as we know, the most elevated product of human history. And then I realized that the denunciation is the most profound, comprehensive and sincere form of personal self-expression.

It is a pity that thousands of tons of denunciations were destroyed during the years of liberalism. The *oeuvre* of a vast population in its most interesting historical period disappeared without trace. Of course, denunciations will continue to be written in the future. But not on the same scale, nor with such an expenditure of intellect and passion, nor with such ingenuity of invention as there was then; it is sad indeed that this will never be repeated!

---

*This is a reference to Gremin's famous aria in the last act of Tchaikovsky's *Eugene Onegin*, based on Pushkin's novel in verse. Pushkin wrote, "All ages are susceptible to love."

DOUBTS

But why write in the form of the now morally discredited denunciation if we've invented another crystal-pure literary genre: the Official Report? Here we have no need to wrestle with our consciences and suffer (if we ever did suffer) when they politely ask us to write a Report about a journey, a meeting, a conversation. And there's no need even to ask us, because we all know that to write Reports about everything is our sacred duty. Why on earth didn't they get round to this in Stalin's time? There is an unusually simple explanation: there weren't enough typewriters and paper. One can write denunciations on scraps of paper with pencil-stubs. Reports are unthinkable without decent paper and typewriters.

WE AND THE WEST

That acquaintance of mine who was thrown out of a Western capital wrote in his Report, after ten years' residence in the West, that after Western Europe had been occupied by the Soviet Army the first thing to do would be to liquidate all those who voluntarily give us their help: the Communists, the leftists, the pacifists, the neutralists, the intellectuals, the liberal writers, the professors, the youths with beards, and all that kind of filth. Why? Because they will then come to their senses and start to rebel against us. And in general, may the Lord deliver us from our friends: we can get rid of our enemies ourselves! Besides, advised my friend, there is some point in preserving your enemies, inasmuch as you can get some use out of them. But let us rather return to the theory of the Report.

THE REPORT

Soviet people are trained to write Reports about everything. It is an indispensable element of the Communist organization of work. Monthly Reports, Quarterly Reports, Yearly Reports, Five-yearly Reports. One old Bolshevik on the books of our institute wrote a Report about his entire life since the revolution. Three thousand pages in very small type. He trundled his epoch-making Report round to the Party office in two battered old shopping bags, and asked the officials to study it and

14

draw lessons from it. The Secretary of the Party bureau entrusted me with this noble mission. In half an hour I wrote my Report on the Report of the old Bolshevik without even looking at it. In the years of Soviet power (so I wrote in my Report) he had consumed so many tons of bread and porridge, drunk so many kegs of vodka, written so many secret denunciations and made so many oral ones, sat for so many years of time at meetings and stood for so many years in queues. "You are laughing at him," said Secretary. "No, I'm crying," I said. "What shall we do?" asked Secretary. "We'll write to the author on official paper telling him that his manuscript has been transmitted to the Secret Division of the Central Party Archives," I said. "Why on official paper?" asked Secretary. "So that the author can frame it and hang it on the wall next to the fifty or so official testimonials that he has received in the course of his inordinately long and stupid life," I said. "But why to the Secret Division?" asked Secretary. "So that he won't torment us any more with his reminiscences," I answered. "But where does this go?" asked Secretary, motioning towards the battered shopping bags that contained the priceless experience of the life of a whole generation. "To the rubbish dump," I said. "Go ahead," said Secretary, "and then write me a short Report about what you've done."

On another occasion they gave me the task of "polishing" the Reports of the members of one of our scientific delegations at an international congress. The delegation consisted of 50 people, but there were 60 Reports. Some distinguished scholars, wishing to demonstrate their devotion, had written two Reports each. Each Report was 50 typewritten pages. And what didn't the scholars tell their beloved Organs about! For example, that they could get one Western professor over on to our side by publishing his book in Moscow; that one should invite the director of a secret laboratory to Moscow and fix him up with a reliable girl . . .

These Reports of the delegation were true and instructive. But we usually write Reports not in order to do a summing-up or extract lessons, but by virtue of certain higher, mystical considerations. For the sake of ordered formality. Therefore we put all we've got into them as a rule, so that it's practically impossible to sift the truth from invention. And indeed there is no need to do this. Nobody reads our Reports anyway. In my Quarterly Report I once wrote that I had discovered ten new elementary particles. I did this with the purely cognitive intention of checking my theory of Reports. The director of the section sent for me. I was on the point of thinking that my theory was mistaken, but I needn't have worried. My Report, Director said, was too short. Would I add a couple of pages? I made a demagogic declaration: the value, I said, of a

15

Report lay not in the number of its pages but in what, according to the Report, had been done. "Read what I have done," I said, "and compare it with what the others did." "Don't try to fool me," said Director calmly. "Do you think the others have done less than you?" And so I added a couple of pages to the Report in which I communicated the news that I had discovered a method of converting the contents of Moscow's rubbish-bins into first-class foodstuffs. "Well done!" said Director, filing my Report in the bundle of other unread Reports by my colleagues. "The man who can write a good Report is a good worker."

But don't imagine that the Report is a superfluous bureaucratic operation. It is a powerful way of integrating people into the Communist system. The important thing is not the contents, just the fact that the Report exists.

TOWARDS A PSYCHOLOGY OF REPORTS

If you haven't done anything it is easy to write a Report. You're entitled to draw on everything that happened in your collective during the Report period as well as on everything in the country and the cosmos. You have that right because you are indeed a co-participant in everything that has happened in the universe. It is harder to write a Report if you've actually done something. And if you've done a lot, then to write a Report will be beyond your powers because your mind will concentrate exclusively on what *you* have done, which seems to be the centre of creation to you, which to your colleagues seems to be rubbish and which gives the Report, as a linguistic phenomenon, nothing whatsoever. But even in the first case virtuoso Report-writing is not an innate skill. Many years of training are required before a man becomes a qualified Reporter and begins to draft Reports of Mozartian fluency.

Anyway, the fiction I am about to write can be taken as my Report on the rules of the art of Soviet Reporting. And please regard it as just that; don't look for truth in it, but at the same time don't accuse it of error. A Report is a Report and nothing more. It is only a milestone in life. My Report will be about one piece of work which I should have done but didn't do, because my work consisted of not doing it. So I'll talk of everything on earth except what I should be talking about. I will talk, for example, of the attempt on the life of the American President, of the bomb explosion in Bologna, of a peace demonstration in Bonn and the rebellion of young people in London just as if they were the work of my own hands. And the most amusing thing is that this isn't entirely without foundation, inasmuch as I belong to the organization which in one way or another did have a hand in all this: that is, the KGB. In other words, it will be a psychological Report of a being with no psychology of his own, about his sojourn in an alien milieu. He was cast into this milieu in the interests of some great Scheme, and then he and the Scheme were forgotten.

TOWARDS A METHODOLOGY OF REPORTS

Do not look for any concealed meaning in my words. I always talk without hints or allegories, and I never leave anything unsaid or only partially said. In general I have no time for thoughts between the lines or for literary icebergs. When people have nothing to say they mask the nullity of what they do say with a mendacious veneer, as if there were a hidden and powerful foundation and a secret depth of thought. Not only writers but also film-producers offer brilliant examples of this. We had a colleague in our institute who was considered a very great thinker just because he was a master of the "iceberg" and of "between the lines". When he had developed his art to the limit, i.e., managed to do without the lines between which his deep thoughts resided and without the visible, supermarine parts of his "icebergs", then we realized that he was nothing but an ordinary parasite and a fool. But the reputation of this great thinker has remained intact right up to the present day. My own position has an advantage over such thinkers: my "icebergs" have no submarine section, and there are no unnecessary intervals between the lines.

As a man of experience I know that my Report will never be read. So the way in which I address myself to the reader is only a result of our Soviet custom. That old Bolshevik whose Report I threw into the rubbish bin also addressed himself to an imaginary reader: to "the Leninist Central Committee"; to "My Dear Party"; and to "the Whole of Progressive Humanity". And who recognized or utilized his priceless life experience? So what is one to say about a little man who *didn't* languish in Tsarist prisons, *didn't* shed his blood on the barricades, *didn't* take Perekop* by storm, *didn't* build Komsomolsk,** *didn't* hurl himself against the enemy's bullets and *didn't* pave the way to a single new venture?***

* A famous battle in the Civil War.
** Built by young people on the River Amur in the 1930s.
*** A Soviet cliché about the need to innovate.

THE CREATIVE APPROACH

We Soviet people are also trained to take a creative approach to everything. I remember, in this connection, a very instructive happening. Our spies in the West stole the drawings of a machine-tool that was intended for very complex and sophisticated operations. At the same time they picked up the machine tool's component parts. A special group was formed to get the hang of the machine-tool. The high-ups were interested in it because the machine-tool was necessary for tank-production. They ordered the group to approach their task in a creative and innovatory spirit and in the most economical manner possible. And they certainly innovated. At the first assembly of the machine-tool they found that five of the components were superfluous. The machine-tool worked without them. Once more they took it to bits and put it together again. Now there were ten unnecessary parts. And still the machine-tool worked. Once more they dismantled and reassembled it. Twenty parts too many. But the machine-tool worked. Ho! Ho! How they made fun of the much-vaunted Western technology.

Somebody voiced the proposition that, after five more dismantlings and reassemblies, the machine-tool would work without any components at all. What a discovery that would be! The members of the group looked suspiciously at this super-economizer and decided to rest on their laurels. They reported to the management that, as a result of the creative approach, the group had substantially simplified the excessively complicated construction of the machine-tool. From then on the machine-tool began to perform the most elementary and crude operations. After a month it broke down completely, and for good. But by this time the government had lost interest in it. Western firms had begun to sell us parts of tanks ready-made, and so the machine-tool was superfluous.

An even more instructive case occurred in the "Lenin School" where they train our spies, the leaders of Communist parties and future pro-Soviet government officials for Western countries. One of the pupils who wished to please our government took the demand for a creative approach seriously and began to gibber such nonsense that they wanted to close down the School as a hotbed of Eurocommunism. This Western Communist, although he was a Communist, was also a Westerner, and didn't grasp the real meaning of the "creative approach". At a closed meeting of the Central Committee at which the incorrect behaviour of Western Communists was being analysed, the secretary for ideology said that the reason for their mistakes was their inability to approach the concept of the "creative approach" creatively.

When they had sent me here, the responsible comrades from the Organs ordered me, among other parting words, to adopt a creative approach to my mission. As a Soviet man I understood the real meaning of this farewell: sit quiet and don't make a nuisance of yourself. And as regards creativity, that is needed only for the Report. The worst possible Report is more interesting than the greatest conceivable achievements if it's executed with expertise not in the matter which the Report is about, but in the really important matter, which is the technique of writing a Report. Here my real life is boredom and grey depression in comparison with a whole heap of things I could say about it. You can imagine what would happen in *this* world if we all began to write Reports about our sojourn in the *other* one!

THE SCIENTIFIC TRACT

But perhaps it would be better to write a scientific tract? After all, I am a professional scholar. True, I and my colleagues were servicing the completely unscientific aims of the Central Committee and the KGB. But we did it in a scientific way. For example, they took the decision to snuff out the dissident movement. But that wasn't so simple. Our task was to establish a theoretical justification for the asphyxiation of the dissidents and work out effective measures to achieve this. You shouldn't imagine that this was easy, or that it was done without conflict. In this field too, serious scientific discoveries forge ahead via cruel struggles. The project to discredit our dissidents in the eyes of the West by sending them into exile in the West at first encountered opposition with fixed bayonets. And then the highest leadership made the idea its own. In the long run it turned into the idea of the Politburo itself. But how much effort was needed for this! How many sacrificial victims! By the way, the number of casualties in the conflict over the most effective ways of stifling the dissidents was many times higher than the number of victims among the dissidents themselves.

And how much effort and talent I myself spent working out ideas of this sort! I drew graphs, made tables, came up with formulae and proved theorems. According to these formulae, for instance, it emerged that one critic of the Soviet regime was bad for the regime, but not very. Two critics were worse than one. But not twice as bad; only one and eight-tenths. And 20 critics are better for the regime than five. Then you can partly leave it to the dissidents themselves to conduct the struggle against dissidents. When you've got even three critics they already start

19

gnawing away at each other. With ten critics the regime is already becoming merely a motive for bashing each other in the face. At least one out of three is helping the KGB. And at least five out of ten can be regarded as voluntary assistants of the Organs and even as their supernumerary staff. And I don't need to add how many full-time operatives can be infiltrated into such groups.

True, as the number of critics of the regime grows, unforeseen consequences occur. The most important is that the critics of the regime begin to compete with the apologists of the regime in understanding the regime itself. The Ideological Secretary of the Central Committee wept tears of vitriol when the news reached him that one émigré critic in the West had said that the Soviet system was stable. "There's a scoundrel for you!" shouted Secretary. "It is *we*, the genuine Marxist-Leninists, who claim that the Soviet system is stable. And here's this disgusting traitor having the impudence to assert that our Soviet system is stable!"

Our rulers hate critics of the regime not because they undermine the regime (no criticism can do that, it can only strengthen it), but because the regime's critics usurp the inalienable prerogative of the highest Soviet leadership: to criticize the Soviet way of life.

Of course for me in my position a scientific tract would be best of all. But I've no money for graphs and tables: in Moscow I drew them at government expense.

DOUBTS

But what shall I call my novel-denunciation-Report-tract? You shouldn't think that this is a secondary matter. Here again we have an instructive example. A certain Muscovite specialist in Scientific Communism suddenly decided to show what it's really like. But he couldn't start it because he had used up all his strength on the problem of whether it would be better called "Sky and Stone" or "Stone and Sky". So he came to the West without his book of revelations, which did him a lot of damage. He still hasn't found a permanent job, even though everyone knows for sure that he's working for the KGB. Odd, isn't it? A Soviet agent, and no job. The West is beginning to behave incorrectly. It's time to call it to order.

Remembering the sad fate of the man who wanted to take the lid off Scientific Communism, I decided to postpone the problem of the title. Who knows, perhaps I won't write anything at all, in which case this thorny problem will automatically lapse. But another no less thorny problem has arisen: to whom will I dedicate my still unwritten work? To my late mother or to the thriving Party? To the Party's latest congress or to the forthcoming plenum of the Central Committee? To the beloved people or to my hateful former wife? To the regime's rare victims or to my countless boon-companions? I finally chose a patriotic variant: "I dedicate this book to Us, Soviet intelligence officers, working far from the Motherland."

A beautiful dedication. Very sincere. But what if they should misinterpret me? Doubt is our State (not our national) characteristic. Doubt hampers us when we begin anything or, if we've begun it, while we are carrying it through to the end and trying to do it properly, and once we've got to the end, doubt prevents us from stopping in time.

This is why, for example, we aim for the Indian Ocean but get stuck half-way in Afghanistan, pretending that we want to terminate the machinations of American imperialists and help the legal government to bring some order to the country. And we do it so badly that the machinations of the imperialists and the disorders increase there from one day to the next. And there's no way of getting out of this terrible mess.

My late mother tried three times to have an abortion; she ate a kilogram of quinine, scalded her legs five times with boiling water and much else, all in the vain attempt to prevent my coming into the world. When she became convinced that her efforts were in vain, she declared that motherhood was the highest blessing in life. Afterwards, to her dying day, she never tired of saying that if she had known that I would grow up into such a callous egoist she would have had an abortion.

Moreover, the West too is now infected with our disease: it has been literally worn out by its suspicions that the promises and appeals of the crafty Soviet government about disarmament are quite sincere.

With all these considerations in mind I made my decision: let them misinterpret my dedication, because it will be worse if they interpret it correctly. Can you imagine what would happen in the world if the West were to interpret Soviet intentions in Afghanistan correctly? Everyone would do it in their trousers, and outside them, with such frightful force that there would be no way of living because of the suffocating stink. So, away with doubt. The West won't interpret your dedication correctly anyway: it won't dare to. And our people know what's what without having to interpret it.

The problem of what I shall dedicate to us, the Homososes, is easily

21

solved. As my step-father loved to say (he was the director of a large cemetery in the suburbs of Moscow), if there's an epitaph, a dead body will be found to fit it.*

ABOUT ACCESS TO THE OCEAN

We were already tackling the problem of access to the Indian Ocean in Khrushchev's time. True, in a dreamy rather than a practical way. After all, in Peter's time we forced our way through to the sea;** so now it's time to force our way through to the ocean. We have forgotten that we have access to oceans along a sea-board stretching for tens of thousands of kilometres. But that doesn't count, because it's cold and uncomfortable up there. We need a warm ocean, the Indian one. The British made use of India and other countries in the East; and that's gone on long enough. Now it's our turn. We didn't know then that the problem was much simpler than we supposed because none of us had taken the trouble to look at a map. We thought that the way to this ocean lay through the Altai, Pamir and the Himalayas. But it turned out it was only a bit further than Sochi, and much easier than going to Sochi. Oh, if only someone then had shoved a school atlas in front of us! There would have been no crisis in Iran. And there wouldn't have been any Arabs around either. Where on earth did they suddenly come from?

We did at long last reach the warm ocean. But a little bit farther off, on the very shores of America; in Cuba.

WE AND THE WEST

Some years ago an employee of a Western embassy was constantly on duty near the Kremlin. His duties included observing government cars as they entered and left it. Western specialists in Kremlinology processed his information and made portentous pronouncements about the policy of "the Kremlin". And there was a KGB employee whose job it was to hoodwink the Western observer. His job was to programme the en-

---

* A reference to the popular saying, "If there's an article [in the criminal code], a person will be found to fit it."
** Peter the Great, who founded St Petersburg on the Baltic in the early eighteenth century.

trances and exits of phoney "Brezhnevs", "Suslovs", "Gromykos" and other members of the Soviet leadership; at such and such a time and in such and such an order. This KGB man laughed until he cried when he told people about his manipulations of the Soviet "leaders". Once he let in three "Brezhnevs" and let out five. I wonder how Western Kremlinologists solved that riddle.

MORNING

The first to look in on me was Cynic, one of the lodgers in the *Pension*.

"What's wrong? Shall I call a doctor?"

"Don't bother, I'll pull through on my own."

"Shall I tell the police? Nasty things do happen here."

"But what good will that do?"

"You're right. None at all. One bloke here admitted that he sent two of our fellows to Kingdom Come with the aid of some germs. But the police didn't believe him. They said he didn't have enough proof. That's what they call democracy. Right, then. Don't expect too much, but I'll bring you a butterbread."

Cynic went out. I thought that this butterbread might be my last thing on earth. All right. This time as well, at least I haven't got to take a decision—Soviet people are not trained to take decisions by themselves.

Then Joker arrived, another inhabitant of our *Pension*. He sacrificed a packet of cigarettes for me. Recently he was in Spain and Italy on business for an anti-Soviet organization which pays him a pittance but covers all his travelling expenses. Otherwise he would have had to save up for at least five years to go on a trip to Spain.

"How are things there?"

"Same as ever. In England, you know, they drive on the left. In Italy diagonally. In Spain straight at you. There isn't one undamaged car in the country. Rubbish; government crises; murders; bombs going off. Children and politicians kidnapped. Burglaries. Swindles. Strikes. But they eat very well. And they're great hands at making love. In a word, freedom. I met one of your friends from Moscow. He said you were a Soviet agent."

When he had gone I began to reflect on a problem that is a very real one for us Soviet émigrés: what *is* a Soviet agent?

A SOVIET AGENT

The concept "KGB agent" is bureaucratic, not scientific. It's too narrow, too indefinite, too evocative of negative emotion. I would propose a term that was more general and more precise, as well as scientifically dispassionate: the sociological concept "Soviet agent" or "Agent of the Soviet State"; in short, "ASS". This is an absolutely precise concept. In respect of any man in the world one can say with complete confidence whether he is, or is not, an ASS. Whereas, even with an obvious agent of the KGB, it is sometimes impossible to state with confidence that he *is* an agent of the KGB. And it's dangerous too: he will take you to court. He will sue you for slanderous insinuations. To be an agent of the KGB is reprehensible; but to be an Agent of the Soviet State, an ASS, isn't reprehensible in the least. If a man is an ASS, it doesn't follow that you will not shake him by the hand. But if he isn't one, it doesn't follow that you will throw yourself on his neck. You can see what advantages there are in using "ASS" instead of "agent for the KGB". And notice how the problem is resolved on a purely semantic level.

The relationship between the two concepts under examination is as follows: not every ASS is a KGB agent. You can be an ASS even if the KGB doesn't know of your existence; even if it has struck you off its list of agents; and even if it refuses to have anything to do with you or touch you with a barge pole. I omit people who've never heard of the KGB because such cases are not known to nature. A man can be an ASS without knowing that he is one. Not every KGB agent in his turn is an ASS. I've met parasites living in the West who were officers of the KGB and received plenty of money, decorations and promotion for their parasitism, and who never raised a finger on behalf of their organization or their country, and sometimes even did it appreciable harm. There you can see with your own eyes the difference between the nominal-official and the sociological approaches towards the understanding of real life.

ASSES can be subdivided into categories, ranks, levels, profiles and other groups. I won't weigh you down with fine points that are of interest only to professionals. The difference between a junior and a senior ASS, for example, is like the difference between a junior and senior research officer; while Honoured and People's ASSES are like Honoured and People's Artistes and Painters. To describe properly what an ASS is, one would have to develop a whole new science. But for people who are incapable of understanding theoretical constructs (and that means the overwhelming majority of mankind, including scholars), one can stick to concrete examples which will enable them to learn quickly how to distinguish ASSES from other mortals.

I will now give you some examples from my present circle and from the people they talk about.

EXPLANATORY SAMPLES

Writer is a senior ASS who left the USSR in the guise of a Jew and a writer of genius. Soon it was discovered he wasn't a Jew. There was no need for anyone to expose the fact that he wasn't a genius. His wife is a junior ASS who came here (and nips back) in the guise of faithful-wife-of-a-writer-of-genius. She really is faithful to him, inasmuch as not one man has been found in the West who wanted to seduce her. (This is a clear sign of the weakness of the West.)

Professor is a People's ASS who in his time had headed some Party delegation to the West and stayed here (having "chosen freedom"). At the moment he's in charge of Soviet activities in the part of Europe where, for the time being, I live. It's put about that he was a member of the Central Committee, although he wasn't even in the bureau of a primary Party organization. With the knowledge of the KGB he had become an agent of some Western spy-ring in Moscow. After he turned up in the West he became an agent of the KGB with the knowledge of the same Western spy-ring. Lady, an Honoured ASS, is Professor's deputy. Lady's husband is a People's ASS and the head of Soviet intelligence in this part of Europe.

Enthusiast, Whiner, Joker, Cynic, Dissident and his wife and Artist and his wife are all Soviet émigrés and junior ASSES.

As I developed my idea I included in the company of ASSES the landlord of our *Pension* (he gives shelter to émigrés from the Socialist camp), the landlord's wife (she sleeps with unattached inhabitants of the *Pension* and doesn't take money for it) and the charlady (she also sleeps with the same people but charges a bit). Here I use the word "sleep" in the pure spirit of Soviet chastity. Our landlady doesn't take money not because of the goodness of her soul (you won't find fools like that here in a month of Sundays) but because nobody would give her a pfennig anyway. She is old, frightful and a trollop, and we have to watch every pfennig. The charlady takes money because she's young and quite attractive. And she has a couple of children. And her husband has nothing against her putting in a bit of extra work: they're saving up to buy their own house.

Next I included in the company of ASSES the head of a very respected church who turned it into a source of self-advertisement; the brother of a president who provides a lot of grist for the Soviet propaganda-mill; the head of a political party who is always shuffling off to Moscow in the guise of a peace-maker, but in fact to receive fresh instructions. I added the Sovietologues, the Kremlinologues and other logues or (as we say in Russian) rogues, for the reason that they understand nothing about the Soviet system, but imagine that they understand everything. I put in Western journalists, professors, politicians, businessmen—all honest servants of the Soviet leadership while claiming all the time to be getting the better of it. I included the soldiers of the Special Amphibious Battalion who help Moscow if only by spitting on the complex international situation and refusing to make any serious preparations for a future war.

Lastly, it would be unjust if I failed to mention another two persons. One is Chief, an honoured ASS, a member of some intelligence group or other, but of which one even he isn't very sure. He began his services as an ASS in a Western intelligence organization which turned out to be only a cover for Soviet espionage. And then there's Mrs Anti, an honoured ASS who has rendered priceless service to the USSR by publishing an unusually stupid anti-Soviet journal and spreading around slanderous rumours to the effect that I'm an agent of Moscow who is in the West with the aim of establishing a Communist regime here.

CYNIC

Cynic came back with some butter . . . I must get used to the Western way of life . . . with some sandwiches. He told me the latest news: another couple has arrived from Moscow. Obvious clinical schizos. And old ones. Why do they let people like that out? "Precisely because they are old, stupid and schizo," I said. "To muddle things up; to set an example." "They slipped in here illegally from Austria," said Cynic. "Why did they do that?" "Because," I said, "it is easier to catch fish in troubled waters. One clever man surrounded by a mass of stupid schizos can do great things." "But who is the clever man?" asked Cynic. "Who can tell?" I said. "Perhaps me. Perhaps you." "I'm afraid that such a tasty morsel is not for you or me," he said. "You know that there's a law of time. If a man doesn't fix himself up by the end of the critical period, then you can put a cross on him. We have exceeded the critical period by at least twice. But we still have to report to the police. Just in case. And for their statistics. When they've got fifty cases like ours they may suspect there's something wrong."

A FRANK CONFESSION

Naturally, I am an ASS too. True, only a very junior grade, a beginner; or rather someone who wants to be a beginner, because I haven't yet managed even to begin. Meanwhile my ASS functions are most elementary: to play the role of observation point and guinea-pig in an alien environment. The KGB officer who instructed me said straight out: "Regard yourself as being our binoculars and guinea-pig on another, unknown, planet. We need to know everything that you see there as well as your relations with the environment and your own experiences. Great Things are ahead of us. We are making a Great Attack on the West. You are a particle of these Great Things, of the Great Attack. Do you understand?" I understood, of course. But I agreed to become a particle of these Great Things not because of them but . . . But because of something that I myself don't understand to this very day. I haven't yet chosen a suitable justification of my agreement to become a particle of Great Things.

But don't rush to the conclusion that I'm an evil fellow. In every Great Thing there are unforeseen and uncontrolled consequences. That's what happened with our revolution, which was intended to establish an earthly paradise, but instead . . . Well, you know what it established instead. Something similar may happen with our Great Attack. It can give a result opposite to the one desired because of its excessive scope and excessive audacity. Besides, I know only too well the people on the staff of the Great Attack. It's a surprising phenomenon: all great events and processes in human history are generated, stimulated and directed by dilettantes and charlatans.

AFTERNOON

Enthusiast came running in. He ran in because he moves in space only at a run, like a recruit, although he's just on sixty and never served in the army because of his flat feet, shortsightedness and a squint. On the threshold he began to yell (his normal manner of speech) that They (but who are They?) only gave me a scare just in case, while They will try to remove *him* for good at the earliest opportunity. They had been after him for a long time. So he had prepared a list of people, societies and newspapers with whom I should get in touch at once should anything serious happen to him. He had already warned the police and the security services to be on the alert. I asked him what I should do if he had diarrhoea. He was offended and ran out of the house, taking with him the packet of edibles he had brought for me, the poor invalid. A pity.

AN AGONIZING QUESTION

Enthusiast thinks he's a genuine Marxist. I wonder whether Marx would have bothered to have a conversation with him. Or with Brezhnev. I think he would have. And even with the head of the KGB. Marx would have given him a lot of useful advice about the demoralization of the West. And a list of Russian Marxists in the West. And Engels would have been perfectly capable of becoming a Soviet agent in England.

But Marx and Engels wouldn't talk to me. They would think I was an agent of the KGB even if I wasn't. And they would hound me just as they hounded Düring. After Engels's public denunciation (*vide* the "Anti-Düring") he was sacked from his university and withered away in the provinces. And what denunciations Marx himself scribbled against the Russian revolutionaries! And Lenin handed over all the revolutionaries competing with him to the Tsarist government. There is a rumour that Stalin himself was an agent of the Tsarist secret police. But, you know, there's some doubt about that: could Stalin have been just an *ordinary* agent? Surely not! *Head* of the secret service, that's another matter. But even if the rumour is true, it can only mean one thing: the October Revolution was not simply a natural development, it was inevitable. If Tsarism didn't believe the denunciations of Stalin himself, then clearly its days were numbered. When Enthusiast told me that "even Stalin was an informer", his eyes looked strangely askance.

And what language would Marx talk to Enthusiast in if the latter can't string two words of German or English together? Well, damn it all, they would talk in Russian. Not long before his death Marx began to study Russian in order to read the leading lights of Marxism, such as Enthusiast, in the original. But he only managed to learn the Russian swear words. There's foresight for you! Enthusiast himself has declared that German is a difficult language. As he puts it: "Das deutscher sprache ist ein schwerer sprache", and when he talks to the locals he does so in international sign-language.

28

WE AND SEX

I remembered the existence of women; a sure sign that I was on my way to recovery. But my thoughts took a theoretical rather than a practical direction.

The practical situation with sex in the Soviet Union isn't really so bad. In any case we have solved brilliantly the problem of copulation in bad weather and bad living conditions and in the absence of decent food, decent lavatories, cosmetics and contraceptives. There we are a whole century ahead of the West. But, on the other hand, we are a century behind the West as far as theory is concerned.

The most sophisticated level of sexology reached by Soviet science was the advice given to men to wash the crockery and launder the nappies. The leading Soviet sex-theorist, who had spent a creative sojourn in the West, wrote a brochure in which he fulminated against the so-called "sexual revolution" as a sign of the final collapse of capitalism. However, he did admit that we cannot entirely reject a certain positive role played by ladies' intimate clothing. First they slightly criticized him in the *Literary Gazette*; and then they really tore him to bits in *Communist* for his "under-estimation", his "over-estimation", his "concessions", his "uncritical attitude", his "lack of vigilance" and many other things too. For a whole year Theorist was regarded as one of the "victims of the regime". The dissidents tried to get hold of his signature under some exposé of something or other, and foreign journalists wanted to interview him. But he resisted all these blandishments, so they allowed him to make another journey to the West. And this time he brought back a whole heap of finery for his mistress and an entire trunkful of contraceptives for his superiors. In his new brochure he didn't repeat his previous mistakes. Then the *Gazette* rather criticized him for being behind the times, while *Communist* somewhat reproached him for his lack of a creative approach. After that Theorist began going to the West every month and furnishing the top ranks of the administration and the cream of the Soviet intelligentsia with all the accessories of contemporary sex. As far as theory is concerned, that was the end of our sexual revolution. But in practice, I repeat, we. . . .

Here in the West we solve our sexual problems in nearly the same way as in Moscow, but at a lower level. This is quite understandable. Here our social position is on the whole lower than it was in the USSR. Enthusiast is an exception. In Moscow he's got an old wife and a mass of relatives. The authorities promised him they would let them all out to join him once he had got himself fixed up. Meanwhile he has been satisfying his fleshly needs with the charlady. He can permit himself this luxury since he sometimes receives some modest fees. He doesn't hide his liaison and is even proud of it, because the charlady is twice as young as his wife and in all probability five times as attractive. Cynic said that if he were in Enthusiast's place he wouldn't send for his wife. He would marry the charlady: it would be a sin to lose such a gorgeous woman. Enthusiast sighed and said that unfortunately the charlady had a husband and children. And she had one serious shortcoming besides: she was morally unstable. And as a former old Communist he had to condemn her for this.

The position of Whiner is at the other extreme. He hasn't got any money for the charlady, and begrudges paying for that sort of thing anyway; and Landlady ignores him as a man. Other "bachelors" here hold their tongues about their escapades. But as a theorist I know that they cannot go beyond these two extremes: the mad success of Enthusiast and the miserable failure of Whiner.

EVENING

A gloomy Whiner drifted in. And he did literally drift in because, unlike Enthusiast, he doesn't run, he just wanders around in space. On the table he saw the last sandwich that Cynic had brought. He gobbled it up. In whining tones he told me that some periodical had published an article by a well-known Western writer in which the latter boasted that in the course of his life he had copulated with ten thousand women. Now all the inhabitants of the *Pension* are talking about it. At first I decided that the writer was lying. But then I remembered that this writer teaches Westerners morality, which means that he can't be lying. And so I fell into an even deeper gloom than Whiner. "In our Soviet conditions," said Whiner, "one would have to live for no less than five hundred years to get results like that. No, whatever people say, the fact remains that civilization is civilization. In our district all the men taken together haven't had as many women as that in the course of the entire Soviet period. The food's too bad. Ten thousand! And here you can't even get a single shop-soiled old woman. No, it's high time we got this properly sorted out. By the way, find me a woman. You know how to chat them up in their own language."

In Moscow I was considered to be a powerful ladies' man. Many of my colleagues thought that the main reason for my emigration was the desire to "try the Western tarts". Having learnt of the modest sexual experience of that Western writer-cum-moralist, I registered my own complete sexual insignificance and switched over to social themes. There we can give any Western scribbler a hundred points and still beat him. I advised Whiner to calculate how many copulations there are on average *per capita* in the Soviet Union, and how many women an average Soviet man enters into sexual relations with. And then compare this with the corresponding data in the West. You won't get better *agitprop* against Communism than that.

THE EMIGRATION MIRACLE

I am almost well. It's time to get down to basic business. But the most basic thing for us can be defined in one word: emigration. For Western people the word sounds quite ordinary. For us Soviet people it sounds like an alarm-bell, like the roar of a hurricane, like peals of thunder, like a volley of cannon-fire. We ourselves still haven't fathomed with our minds or our emotions the causes, essence and consequences of this historical hurricane. It is an unprecedented hurricane. The phenomenon is only outwardly like an emigration. It bears the name of emigration, but in essence it is something else.

Take the dictionary and open it at the letter "e". Find the word "emigration". Read: "emigration is the forced or voluntary re-settlement from one's own country to another country, for political, economic or other reasons". The authors of the dictionary, in giving such a definition, imagine that they have exhausted all possible cases of emigration.

But how was it in my case? Nobody forced me to abandon my country. And it didn't happen of my own free will either. I had no political, economic or other reasons of any kind to abandon my country. And I didn't turn up in another country but in another world, another epoch, another section of space, in another continuum of time. But all the same I'm an émigré. How can there be such a logical absurdity? Why, because I'm a Soviet man, for whom only the semblance of emigration is possible.

WHAT I'M HERE FOR

Why am I here? Well, if only to shatter a widespread myth that Soviet man is a bamboozled and intimidated being. Those who chucked me over here wanted their action to mean this: look at this man; he is intelligent and educated. Nobody was bamboozling or intimidating him, nobody was corrupting him. Quite the contrary, he did this himself to other people, who do not, however, regard themselves as bamboozled, intimidated or corrupted. There is no need for Soviet people to be subjected to that kind of treatment because they are quite capable themselves of bamboozling, intimidating and corrupting anyone they want to. It is their nature; and therefore they enjoy doing it both to themselves and to others. They represent a new, more advanced type of thinking being and offer this model to others. Beware!

There are many like him in the Soviet Union. In our society they have their share of the good things of life, power and freedom. Not such a big share that one can place them in the privileged strata, but not such a small one that you have to lump them together with the lower strata. You can't count them as success stories; at the same time they are not sacrificial victims. They have a special role in society. They are the kernel of it; they are its salt, its yeast, its vitamins, its inspiration, its catalysts. They are the bearers and apologists of this society. And they are its suffering tissue as well. They accept this society and try to make themselves a niche in it for ever, without any *arrière-pensées* or provisos. When they are chucked out into the West they regard themselves as being on a mission from the Soviet Union and as having a rest from it at the same time, although with their reason they know that this is the end. They do not strive for either truth or virtue. They simply live in a manner appropriate to the time with their share of its errors and vices. But then people and historical epochs are characterized not so much by truth and virtue, which are general and abstract things, as by errors and vices, which are individual and concrete. Take a look at this creature and marvel: he is what you call Soviet Man!

THE HOMOSOS

In the West clever and educated people call us *Homo Sovieticus*. They are proud to have discovered the existence of this type of man and thought up such a beautiful name for him. Moreover they use this term in what is for us a derogatory and contemptuous sense. It has never occurred to them that we have actually done something, more than simply finding a name for ourselves, that we were the first to develop this type of man, while it took the West 50 years after this to invent a new little term for it; and the West reckons that its contribution to history was infinitely greater than ours. The conceit of the West deserves our mockery.

Well, there it is. If they call us *Homo Sovieticus* we'll use *Homo Sovieticus*. I will go a bit further in this direction and outdo the West. I will introduce a more convenient abbreviation of this long expression: *Homosos*. At least it sounds Soviet.

The Homosos is a fairly disgusting creature. I know that because I know myself. When I lived in the Soviet Union I dreamed of living in a democratic country where you could join any party or form one of your own; go out and demonstrate, take part in strikes, expose every sort of fraud and lies. More like heaven than life on earth. Now that I have lived in the West for a while I have swivelled my dreams round 180 degrees. Now I dream of living in a good old police state in which Leftist parties are forbidden, demonstrations are broken up and strikes suppressed. In a word, down with democracy!

Why am I dreaming of this? Because I am a Homosos. I am an extreme reactionary marching in the van of extreme progress. How can this be? For the Homosos, nothing is impossible. In the West even the most rabid reactionaries struggle for democracy because for them democracy offers the last chance of struggling against democracy. We are against democracy because it prevents us from struggling for democracy honestly and without the use of lies and play-acting. And so, down with democracy!

We are beginning a new history. But we are beginning it not from the beginning, but from the end. We will reach the beginning only at the end. And so, once again: down with democracy!

NIGHT

Before I went to sleep Cynic came in to enquire after my health. "You're a fine chap," he said, "a real Ivan. Other people give up the ghost to God after tricks like that. But Russian Ivans only get stronger. Do you want to hear the latest joke from Moscow? The Soviet dissidents turned to some Western philistines and appealed to them: Set up a Soviet regime of your own and then we'll join you in fighting against it. Funny? You were a dissident, I think?" "A bit of one," I said. "Why did you have to do that?" he asked. "To get out," I answered. "Oh," he said. "I see there's a very simple explanation."

THOUGHTS ABOUT THE FUTURE

In honour of my recovery I took the decision to read no more newspapers and journals. I don't mean Soviet newspapers and journals, but local ones: i.e., Western ones. Western; and suddenly they are local! It's impossible to get used to such a thing. When someone says "local" the words "Tambov", "Saratov" and "Ryazan" swim into my mind, not "German", "French" and "English". Only by an effort of will, which I managed to exhibit only a short time ago, can I stifle these flesh-and-blood associations. "Remember," I say to myself, "you are living in the West now. Now Russia is abroad for you. And you'll have to live here until your last breath. Yes, you'll peg out here in the West. They will bury you in Western soil, not in Russian. As a matter of curiosity, where *will* they bury you? They are very short of earth here. There's nowhere to bury their own people. It's more likely that they'll cremate you. But they will save your ashes to use as fertilizer, because there will be nobody to whom they can give the urn to preserve for ever."

Of course one could provide oneself with a more optimistic future after death. For this it is enough to declare yourself Orthodox, begin to go to church and take part in all kinds of church activities. Now many Soviet émigrés do this. Not long ago a very important Lady from Moscow arrived here. In Moscow she was in charge of the secret section of a top-secret institute. A Member of the Party. She was even elected to the bureau of the province committee of the Party. You should have seen how every imaginable kind of secret service fell upon her. My word, what attention they gave her! They got her a passport, a flat and sources of income immediately. Can you understand anything about all this? No? Nor can I. But that isn't the point. Who knows, perhaps Lady brought with her the secret protocol of the last session of the bureau of the province committee of the Party at which it was decided to put an end to all oppositional tendencies in the area. Lady immediately declared herself to be a fervent Christian; naturally, Russian Orthodox. Then Lady set up a committee to struggle for the conferment of the title "Honoured Saint of the Republic" on Tsar Nicholas the Second for outstanding services as a martyr of the Bolsheviks. (This is my own formulation of the tasks of the committee. But Lady's formulation was even stupider.) Lady tried to involve me in this noble task and even suggested I became secretary to the committee. Then I made my proposal to amend the formula about the aims of the committee. Then Lady declared that I would be as likely to get a permanent job in this country as to see my own ears. She is a person with real Party steel in her;

she will keep her word. When she kicks the bucket and is buried with all the formalities in the local Orthodox cemetery, it will be interesting to see whether they inscribe all the titles and awards she won in Moscow on her gravestone.

In a word, I didn't join up as an Orthodox despite the obvious blessings it would have brought me. Perhaps this was my first mistake in a series of mistakes I've made here in the West. My instructing officer in the KGB said I mustn't let slip even the tiniest chance of getting a foothold, however absurd it might seem at the first glance. "If there's a chance of becoming a church worker, become one," he said. "If you have to be circumcised in order to land a good job, get yourself circumcised." I didn't follow his advice. Why? Because I'm a convinced atheist. Better that my ashes be used as fertilizer than that I should hang about at Matins in the company of old Russian émigrés, their Western-born offspring and newly fledged Christians like Lady, the former member of an *Obkom* bureau. To absorb the results of history's greatest revolution and the achievements of world science in order at the end of the road to become a son of the misbegotten Orthodox Church? Anything you like, but *not that*!

ABOUT KNEELING

The main thing is that I despise people who kneel voluntarily. I have never knelt before anybody. And I won't. By the way, this isn't just me. It's a quality of Soviet man. It's the product and result of our revolution. This is what Westerners simply can't understand. When they look at our behaviour they interpret it in the terms and forms they are accustomed to. And among their convictions is the one that the Soviet people kneels before its own authorities. Our behaviour is anything you like, but not kneeling before the authorities. One can kneel before pop clerics, before emperors, before bosses. Moreover, one can kneel without there being any external signs of kneeling. But to kneel before our government is quite impossible, even if we wanted to, because this government is: US! Communism liberates people from kneeling; there's the psychological heart of the matter. Even if we wanted to kneel before our powers-that-be, they simply wouldn't allow us to do so. They'd give us such a crack on the head if we did that we wouldn't even think of such liberties as kneeling. It is forbidden to kneel under Communism. Under Communism the human being is obliged to stand at attention: that is, heels together, toes apart, hands on trouser-seams, eyes gaping wide and gazing fawningly at the authorities.

I couldn't overcome the Soviet man in myself and follow Lady's example. If I had been more active in the Party network in Moscow, perhaps I might have conquered this weakness.

THE PRESS

But let's get back to newspapers and journals. My decision to finish with them has been ripening in me from the first day of my sojourn in the West. The more so since I had many years' experience behind me of ignoring the Soviet Press. Having broken out of the torture-chamber of Bolshevism into the free world (this is how the representative of one anti-Soviet organisation greeted me when I arrived here), the first thing I did was to go full pelt for the local Press. Naturally I began with the most intriguing section of it by looking at naked women and sexual escapades. But I quickly became sated and I was soon running an indifferent eye over them. Sometimes I heckled the pictures in terms which I should be ashamed to mention here even to myself. All in all I concluded that these things were for impotents, sex maniacs, corrupted children and bored idlers. That was how I summed up my observations. As for us Soviet men, just give us a woman and we'll be able to work out what to do with her, and how, without any Western prompting. Incidentally, à propos the above-mentioned anti-Soviet organization. The representative of another anti-Soviet organization whispered to me on the same day that I should treat the representative of the first one with great caution because he was a Soviet agent. A little later the representative of the first organization said exactly the same thing to me in the very same words about the representative of the other anti-Soviet organization. What is this: a piece of local etiquette or Soviet inertia? The whole thing is a scene from a surrealist film: a Soviet agent disguised as a critic of the Soviet regime comes to the West, where he is met by other Soviet agents in the guise of members of all the Western anti-Soviet organizations and émigré societies. Well, one may ask, what next? It isn't hard to say what will come next; a typical Soviet struggle between the individual and the collective. Lady said as much about my case (rumours circulate here just as they do in Moscow): "'We' (who are these 'we'?) will break him in a jiffy. He's not in the Soviet Union now. We won't let him get out of line." Notice the manner of speaking. Evidently it comes from Lady's Komsomol past.

In the end I got to the articles in the Press which expressed Western society's social and political intellect. From the very first lines I began to notice that the West wasn't going where it should be going according to my ideas of it; and that people weren't behaving at all as they should behave according to my image of them. Here's another paradox for you about Soviet man. I came here as a Soviet agent anxious in theory for the West to behave badly from the standpoint of its own interests, and well from the viewpoint of Soviet interests. I came with the purpose of weakening and destroying the West. But no sooner had I crossed the frontier than I began to live and think the other way round. The conduct of Westerners and the West began to irritate me precisely because of its pro-Soviet orientation.

Every day the incorrect behaviour of the West irritated me more and more. This morning I read that one prominent Western politician thinks it would be possible to make the Soviet leadership change its mind about something which the Soviet leadership cannot change its mind about in any circumstances whatever. "That's too much," I said to myself. I flung the newspaper away and swore to myself that I would never spend another pfennig on it. But in the next paper, one considered here to be highly intellectual, I read a conversation between a Western sovietologist and a Soviet "critic of the regime". The critic, who had been expelled during his third year as a student at a down-at-heel provincial technical institute and spent five years in prison (this is considered to be the necessary and sufficient qualification for understanding Soviet society), declared that the Soviet leaders had betrayed Marxism. The Sovietologue, who had studied Marxism for 20 years in libraries, and Soviet society along with it, added that the social system in the USSR wasn't Socialism at all. "Oh, the idiots," I cried. "If there's one thing in the Soviet Union that is done correctly and properly, then it's Socialism. And that's the only thing they can do there." And I took the decision which I told you of at the beginning of this section.

THE HEALTHY HOMOSOS

I didn't go to be circumcised either, because I hate any kind of nationalism. There is one Russian writer here who publishes his hopelessly mediocre books on Jewish themes under a Jewish pseudonym. They make a great fuss of him, because of that. And there is another even less talented scribbler who poses as a representative of Russian culture even though he's a Jew. He too is made much of, because of that. I am a

37

healthy Homosos: that is, a supranational creature. And a healthy Homosos is glad whenever any nation comes to grief. Did the Buddhists slaughter a million Moslems in Pakistan? Well, it serves them right; there are quite enough of them as it is. Did they castrate two million men in India? Jolly good! There's enough of them too. Were three million people murdered in Cambodia? Fine! That'll show them what Communism brings you. Is it true that twenty million Soviet people perished in the war? Well, it serves them right too. We'll know better next time. Why is this? Well, because a healthy Homosos is a genuine internationalist and regards all men as brothers. And there's no need to stand on ceremony with one's brothers, is there?

There's a Tartar living here who collaborated with the Germans during the war. They brought some sort of charge of anti-semitism against him. "Why are they so steamed up?" he asked. "I didn't only kill Jews. I shot Russians as well." He's a sound Homosos. And, by the way, he isn't a Russian at all; those who think Sovietism is a Russian national characteristic, please note. For in this new emigration, which consists exclusively of the most colourful and thorough-going Homososes, there is hardly a Russian to be seen. From that it doesn't follow that Russians are not Homososes. We Russians, after all, served as the original raw material from which the great Communist-breeders reared the contemporary Homosos. But we stopped half-way to the fully-fledged Homosos and got bogged down in petty details of self-analysis. In this too, other peoples got ahead of us.

WE AND THE WEST

I live in a *Pension*, and a certain organization pays for me. Although I occupy a tiny little room without a telephone or a desk, the organization pays a crazy sum. I suggested a change of procedure; why shouldn't they give me the money directly and let me rent a room privately? It would be three times cheaper and I could spend the rest of the money on food, clothing and paper. But for some reason they couldn't do that.

Joker, who has already found his way around the finer points of Western life, affirms that the reasons for this "we can't" are exactly the same as in the Soviet Union. And on the whole many things in the West remind me very closely of our life in the USSR.

The inhabitants of the *Pension* are divided into short-term and long-term ones. Of the short-termers, Professor was here before I moved in, followed during my long period of residence by Lady and her colourless

Husband. I had only to take a single look at her rickety Husband to realize what sort of a bird *he* was. I am sure that the local intelligence service knows that Husband is KGB. But they think that if he's their man (and he's their man too for sure), then his KGB affiliations are a secondary matter. To sell oneself to all the espionage agencies of the world is the professional (and even the civic) duty of every Soviet spy. And the point isn't that on balance his work helps the KGB more than it harms it. The point is that even the harm it causes also works to the advantage of the KGB. If the very head of the KGB defected to the West bringing with him all the secrets known to the KGB, his flight would, in the last reckoning, work to the advantage of the Soviet Union. The Soviet intelligence agency and the Western ones have different criteria for evaluating what they do. The so-called mutually advantageous relationships between the KGB and the Western services always act to the advantage of the KGB because the very fact of any kind of relationship always works to the advantage of the KGB. If it were possible to measure what damage the West suffered from the efforts of its Intelligence to pump information out of Lady, that would be enough to make certain people's hair begin to stand on end. And this assumes that all the information she provided was valuable and correct. But how much of the stuff she revealed is disinformation, padding, invention and sheer nonsense? And how does one measure the psychological consequences of such contacts? I've been told that the Western espionage services had built up for themselves a clear picture of Soviet man on the basis of conversations with many thousands of Soviet people. I will tell you something with a hundred per cent confidence in what I say: if the West loses the future war to the USSR, then the most important reason for its defeat will be nothing else than the image of Soviet man created by Western special services and sovietologists on the basis of their contacts with Soviet people.

WHINER AND ENTHUSIAST

Whiner and Enthusiast suggested taking me to a café where "everything is twice as cheap". I said that at the moment I would prefer a café where everything was ten times as cheap. They said that such a thing existed, but for the moment it wasn't the season.

Whiner and Enthusiast provide a shining example of the expression of one and the same essence in diametrically opposite forms. Whiner's principles are: "nobody needs us here; it's no better here than it is at home; we shan't get anywhere here". Enthusiast's principles are: "they can't take a single step without us; it's paradise here compared with the Union; we shall move mountains". Whiner waits humbly until the West throws him a crumb from its rich banquet. Enthusiast rants and raves, pokes his nose in everywhere and is quite ready to tear the tit-bit intended for him from the West's mouth. Whiner himself doesn't know why he's here. Enthusiast came with a great mission: to teach the West what's what and to lead the dissident movement in the Soviet Union from here. He is dying to publish a periodical, better still a newspaper. He thinks that this is "the fundamental link. When we've grasped it we (who?) will draw out the whole chain. Lenin started this way too."

The thing they have in common is that they both come drifting into my roomlet, without knocking and at all hours of the day and night, always ask me for a loan and always try to borrow something "for a little while". In order to stop these tendencies I wrote a declaration on a large sheet of paper: ABANDON HOPE, ALL YE WHO ENTER HERE. The next day Landlord took the declaration down: he didn't want to be reminded of his country's shameful past. Somebody must have reported the matter to him and translated my declaration.

When he arrived in Vienna, the first thing Enthusiast looked into was the question of why the President of the United States hadn't flown in to meet him. He was told the President was busy. Enthusiast said that the President could have sent his representative instead. They told him there were lots of Presidential representatives there and they would soon have the honour of talking to Enthusiast. Enthusiast paid no attention to the somewhat humorous nuance in these words, calmed down and began to scan the throng of all sorts and conditions of men that had gathered at the airport: he was looking for the leaders of the West European Communist parties. They at least must have thrown all business aside and rushed to meet the leading (and for the time being the only) representative of Soviet Eurocommunism. But there was nobody there of that sort either. As a former old Communist, this upset Enthusiast most of all. "The swine," he said, referring to the Eurocommunists, the Americans and everyone else. "We did everything for them there and all they do here is . . . The swine! But just you wait: I'll show you . . ."

Whiner left his country thanks to a fictitious marriage, which cost him a pretty penny or two. As soon as he got to Vienna his first concern was to find the "black market". He had brought out a very valuable icon which he expected to live off comfortably for at least five years. However, the icon turned out to be a fake. When he heard this, Whiner also said "the swine". He spent the remainder of his former riches on the "annulment" of his marriage; that is, on getting forged documents that turned out

40

to be unnecessary. After that he acquired the psychology of a ruined millionaire and became a whiner, ditherer and driveller.

But on the other hand, the intelligence services for some reason showed quite an interest in Whiner. They re-directed him here at once. I asked Whiner why they were taking such an interest in him. Whiner said they seemed to think that he knew a lot of things that he didn't know. What could this mean? I told him that he, like every other Soviet person, had a rich subconscious, especially if he had worked in a military factory. He himself didn't know his own subconscious, but "these cretins" were obviously pumping out valuable information from it. "You're joking," he said. "What can they pump out from there? A bit of sharp practice? Drinking bouts? Escapades with women?" I said there was nothing laughable about that. And perhaps they suspected that he was a big shot in the KGB. "If only I were just a small one," he sighed. "If I were, I could move mountains. There's grace abounding for Soviet agents here. But it's all the same to those cretins who one is. The only thing they mind about is who *they* are."

JOKER

On the way to the café Joker joined us. He said that everything was twice as cheap at the café simply because everything was three times worse. That was why practical Germans didn't think it was a good idea to go to it. Only low-down Soviet émigrés are clever enough to save money by wasting it.

I called him "Joker" after he had had a collision in the doorway with Landlady as she was going out of my room. "It's a bad thing, dear comrade, to break up a sound Capitalist family," he said. "But you're a Soviet man. The moral corruption of the West is our sacred duty," I answered.

He arrived here before I did and exercised his rights as an old inhabitant to show me the beauties of the town. The weather was superb. This was doubly enjoyable for us because the weather in Moscow just then was appalling. When we had had our fill of the monuments of architecture and the luxurious windows of the shops, we went into an enchanting little café. The charming young waitress immediately came up to us. We hadn't had time to marvel at this and compare this heavenly creature with the witch-waitresses of Moscow when she brought our order. "If only there had been a tenth part of such service in the Soviet Union, I wouldn't have left for anything in the world. You know what my

41

main reason was for emigrating? The dream of sitting just once in such a café and being served in the style we've been served in now. What's your impression of the city?"

"Too much past in it. The West in general is weighed down by its past. It can't hold on to it any longer. It's slipping away. And it's taking the West's future with it."

"But then we haven't got a past. For us everything is in the future. And the West's past is our future."

"And what do you think of the people?"

"Freedom and prosperity don't make people intelligent. There are four million foreign workers here. But they've got a million and a half unemployed of their own. Moreover, the unemployed aren't willing to work in the same conditions as the foreigners. Or they don't want to work at all. They prefer to be parasites on society. Some charitable institution or other decided to arrange a competition in which the winner would be given a job. Nobody wanted to enter. As to the young people, don't talk to me about them. Racial problems. Terrorism. Drugs. Crime. It'll be a pity if Capitalism collapses too quickly. I want a little bit of Capitalist life. I want to go to a few more cafés and night-clubs. To bathe in warm seas. To have a go at all kinds of women. Have you tried negresses yet? I have. Nothing special. It's a fairy tale that they have a very high sexual potential. Our women are just as good. But it's an interesting experience all the same. Would you like me to fix you up with a negress?"

"No, I haven't tried everything European yet."

THE ROLE OF THE UMBRELLA IN HISTORY

In the *Pension* there are also émigrés from other countries in the Socialist camp. They are still hoping for a "third way" and "free trade-unions". They accuse us of "dogmatism" and "Great Russian chauvinism". From time to time they return to their Socialist Fatherlands and print articles that unmask the West. They are always signed by a State security official with the rank of captain at least. The West takes no notice of these articles. This offends the pride of our friendly intelligence agencies. And then they begin frantically arranging attempts on the lives of their former citizens, mainly with the aid of umbrellas, tubes of toothpaste, shampoo and other everyday objects. At one time it was umbrellas that caused a sensation. And the East European émigrés were very proud of this. Even in sunny weather the Bulgarians went about carrying umbrellas. Everyone shied off as they passed. To tell the truth, I too wasn't quite myself. I am ready to die in the jaws of a shark or a crocodile. I am prepared at worst for a sticky end from the sting of a tsetse fly. But to die from the bite of a mere umbrella? B-r-r-r-r!

The umbrella sensation blew over and was forgotten, like all sensations in the West. Now our brothers in Socialism and in the emigration are savouring the argument: "Well, what about Poland?" On the surface the Western philistines wax ecstatic about this Polish business as it fortifies their hope that the USSR will soon collapse of itself, so that they, the Western philistines, will be able to save an extra pfennig or two a week. But below the surface they are trembling with horror because, as a result of the Polish emigration, they are losing at least ten marks per week. And that's only the beginning.

WE AND THE WEST

At the *Pension* in the evenings there are conversations about high politics. This is the sort of thing we say:

"The Iranian students have seized the American and not the Soviet embassy. Why's that?"

"If they had forced their way into the Soviet embassy the Soviet army would have occupied Iran at once. Whereas the Americans are weaklings."

"They have a democracy."

"That's what I said, they are weaklings."

"What a mess! We'll need half a litre to get to the bottom of it."

"Forget about the half-litre. It's expensive. And there's nowhere to throw up."

"This miserable Iran is terrorizing a mighty superpower. The Arabs are raping Western Europe. My God, what *is* going on?"

"The West has gone rotten."

"Don't be too eager to bury the West. It has a hidden pig-quality which will still show itself."

"There's piggery in it all right; but more idiocy. If there were less idiocy and more piggery things might be better."

In Moscow such conversations always ended with one idea: to get drunk. Here even the alcoholics don't advance such ideas. They prefer to drink on the sly. And we, having spat at the Iranian revolution and the Arabs and pulled Western politicians to pieces, slink off to our box-sized rooms.

43

MODEST JOYS

The media have reported that one of the officials in the Soviet embassy is a KGB agent. All day in the *Pension* there was a mood of great hilarity. One! Is there even one official in the embassy who *isn't* a KGB agent?

MY WAY

Next to the *Pension* there is a grand newspaper-kiosk. A little further on there's a magnificent shop where they sell the same newspapers and periodicals. Further still there is an ever grander kiosk. In between them there are containers from which you can take newspapers and stick the requisite amount of money into a hole. I used to buy the newspapers from the containers. This was twice as cheap because I only put in half the price. Joker puts a quarter in! This shows that his conscience is only half as great as mine. And Cynic doesn't put in anything at all. He just pretends to, moving his fingers a few times towards the slit. You can reckon for yourselves how much conscience *he* has.

My way lies past this journalistic temptation. From the magazine covers female behinds in full colour look enticingly towards me. Breasts and other tempting parts of the body do the same. Salacious newspaper headlines announce the fact that a sex maniac has thrown his twentieth victim from a tenth-storey window; that terrorists have kidnapped a millionaire; that a princess is being divorced from her current husband. "Oh no, my darlings," I said with metal in my voice, "you won't buy me with that sort of thing this time." And I walked past with a fine indifference. And there it was for the first time in my life that I discovered I had some will-power after all. I discovered it and I wept tears of . . . bitterness. "Where were you earlier?" I whispered, addressing my will-power. "If you had appeared twenty years back I shouldn't be hanging about here now in a free society looking for something bearable to eat. I should be lying on a sofa, like my most successful friends, in a five-room flat in Rublyovo, or walking around a Central Committee country villa near Moscow, or tanning myself in a Central Committee resort in the south, or sitting decorously in state in my office on *Old Square** or in the Lubyanka. And no problems about life after

*i.e., in the HQ of the Central Committee of the CPSU.

death would be troubling me at all. And I shouldn't be experiencing this disenchantment with the Western Press. And I wouldn't realize that the West should long ago have been awarded the Order of Lenin or the October Revolution for services rendered towards the preservation and strengthening of Soviet power."

But what's past is gone forever. We are used to consoling ourselves with the saying: better late than never. Now that my will-power has awoken, I must use it. I shall be as firm as a rock. I shall have things my way, however long this period of "screening" drags on. Forward!

ABOUT OLD MEN

I go to an institution where people who are interested in the Soviet Union talk to me; or, to speak candidly, where they interrogate me. I go there on foot because public transport here, unlike Moscow, is expensive and inconvenient. Besides, I have nothing else to do. I walk along looking at the well-fed and well-dressed passers-by. Most of them are old people. There's also a lot of idle youth about. The young people deliberately dress untidily. The boys are covered with hair. The girls look as dirty as unwashed gypsies. The kind that sometimes appear on the streets of Moscow. The main danger for mankind, I think, isn't the bomb, but unarmed human beings; that is, too many people who live too long. People have violated certain socio-biological laws. Sickly children survive. Ill people drag out their existence for decades. Old men live an uncustomarily long time. Old men have taken over the planet. There is nothing more dangerous in the world than old men. They are stupid and totally lacking in talent. But they have inordinate self-confidence and self-esteem. All the vileness of the contemporary world is the work of old men. Until the world's population is at least halved and life-expectancy reduced by at least 20 years, there will be no solution. Things will only get even worse. And in the end, all those inventions of old men which are alone able to halve the population and cut down life-expectancy will go into action. However, youth is now beginning to compete with age in the danger stakes. It is discontented with everything. It doesn't want to work, but it wants to have everything without working for it, and at once. Its apparent contempt for material goods and hatred of the rich are only a negatively concealed thirst for the good things of life. And when it comes to stupidity and lack of talent, youth is in no way inferior to age.

45

ABOUT ÉMIGRÉS

But to hell with Westerners, both old and young! There is a danger which affects me personally. The flood of our émigrés to the West. Being in the vanguard of the Great Soviet Army's offensive against the West, I ought to have been rather happy about the emigration. But as an ordinary inhabitant who must eat, drink, dress myself, have women and enjoy culture, I find myself in despair at this joyous phenomenon. My chances of arranging my life nicely diminish every day. All the time new Soviet scoundrels keep pouring in. They bring the Western security services more and more valuable information, disinformation and weightier and weightier proofs of their affiliations to the KGB. I feel like roaring at the whole world: "Come to your senses. Whom are you letting in? Can't you see that it's the beginning of our (Soviet) invasion of the West?" Do get me right: I want to shout out loud about this, not in order to save the West, but to make myself a nice little nest in the West at last. And for that, of course, one has to save the West a bit. Once I've got nicely fixed up, I'll stop the shouting. On the other hand, perhaps it will be the other way round: if I get settled in nicely it would be a pity to lose a good niche. The Soviet émigrés who've got themselves cushy jobs—and especially the KGB agents among them—are the main opponents in the West of the arrival here of Communism. There's another example for you of the despised, but eternally triumphant, dialectic.

WHO I AM

Sometimes I am asked how it was that I, a Russian national and former member of the CPSU who belonged to the highest circles of the Party and the KGB and who had taken part in secret research projects, managed to get out to the West. I always answer sincerely that I came here on a job for the Central Committee of the CPSU, the KGB, and the entire Soviet people. But they don't believe me. They think I am playing the fool or want to put a higher value on myself so as to get an offer of a nice little job somewhere. Repentant Soviet spies are always popular in the West. They are given political asylum at once, as well as the means of subsistence. But for some reason or other I'm not making any headway.

"You'll still have to prove that you're a genuine Soviet spy and not a fake," said one of the men on the panel during my interrogation. "If you're a real spy," he said, "you ought to have brought us some valuable information that we would have believed and assessed according to its worth." "Or disinformation, which you would have believed even more," I added, completing his thought myself. As a result of that remark of mine I acquired the reputation of being a man who pretends to be an agent of the KGB but isn't. It's odd, isn't it? All this is happening in the *Soviet* emigration, where everyone speaks of everyone else's being a member of the KGB. But about me they usually advance the unanswerable argument: what kind of agent is he if he doesn't know a single secret about the Soviet Union? I retort: "What if I was sent here to *ferret out* secrets?" "Then why do you admit that you're an ASS?" My opponents hack at the roots of my logic: "Besides, it's completely pointless to try to *ferret out* secrets over here. We haven't got any, everything's on show. No, my friend, it'll be better if you don't try to be too crafty. It's better you admit you're trying to take us in." I admit it. The people I'm talking to exchange glances; they take my admission that I am trying to take them in as an attempt to try to take them in. Where's the way out of that?

I'm an ASS. And I don't see anything bad in that. Or good either, for that matter. It's simply an objective fact. A rather sad and rather comical fact, but in no way tragic. It's banal rather than anything else. Today there are so many tons of agents that even the KGB doesn't remember them all. Today they fling agents into the ocean of life like puppies into a dirty village pond. If you want to live, survive. If you don't, go to the bottom. And the sole reward we get for everything we've done is to be kicked out into the West. Not all agents, of course, are like that. I have in mind only the mass type to which I belong. And we are not so much real as potential agents. The situation is like the one in which junior officers were trained in the last war. They picked milksops straight from school and after a few months they spat them out on to the front as second lieutenants. Most of them were killed in their first battle. But most of them were needed only for one battle. And most of us are needed only for one operation.

To be a potential agent is really agonizing; you have all the disadvantages of being an agent, but none of the advantages. There are two roads ahead of us: to leave the corps of agents altogether or to become a real agent. The first road is not open to us. Only a few lucky people manage to take the second. Now that my will-power has plainly shown itself, I will definitely turn myself into a real agent.

47

It was in this combative, optimistic mood that I approached the river. Or riverlet, as one might call it. On very rainy days the water comes up to your knees. And it is so narrow that one can spit across it. In general, the West is very weak in rivers, not at all like us in Russia. Even real Western rivers are somehow pretty laughable things. They flow up to the level of their banks and sometimes higher. They hide under houses and reappear from under them in the most surprising places. Sometimes they flow upstream. I drew Cynic's attention to this phenomenon of nature. He said that this happens only on a small section of the river, and that beyond the bend the river flows downstream again, but twice as fast as usual.

On the banks of the little river, not far from the bridge named after some outstanding man of action (was it worth his while taking so much trouble for such a meagre reward?), there are some barracks belonging to a special army unit trained to master all the techniques required in aquatic warfare. Every morning the soldiers put on bright orange safety-jackets, drag out inflatable dinghies, lower them into the water and get into them with shouts and screams. And with cans of beer, but without weapons. The crossing to the other bank begins. But the boat runs aground. Some of the soldiers get out to push the boat into deeper water. Again the boat gets stuck. This time everybody has to get out except for one man and carry the boat to the shore in their arms. The man left in the boat plays the fool. The soldiers roar with laughter. They drop the boat. The clown falls into the water. There is wild jubilation. A crowd of idlers gathers on the bank and gives a running commentary. The basic theme of the commentary is this: the army costs a lot; it should be demobbed, leaving only a residue. To look at and listen to all this is comical and at the same time somewhat terrifying. You won't stop the Soviet troops with a pitiful army such as this. And even on *it* they grudge spending every pfennig.

Having got to the other bank the soldiers settle down for a rest. They shout, pester women, guffaw, drink beer and sing. They have well-fed faces. They are so well-dressed they don't even look like soldiers. Just before lunch they negotiate the billowing depths again, and then the river sees them no more. "All right, my dears," I think, looking at these well-fed and self-satisfied lads, "get your sun-tan, bawl out your songs, drink your beer, pinch the girls. Enjoy yourselves. You won't have it for long. I can tell you this as the representative of a mighty army of badly fed, badly dressed, untanned, womenless young men: an army which has long been ready to march. Once upon a time our fathers sang: "If there's a war to-morrow, if we have to march tomorrow, we must be ready to march today." When the last war started it turned out that they weren't ready to march. We've learned the lesson from their mistakes. Immediately after the end of their frightful campaign we began to prepare for another even more frightful one. And we are ready now. And if people are ready for war today, tomorrow they will certainly plunge into it: you can't remain at the ready for too long. For a long time we've been on the defensive. But remember this: continual defence is attack. Premature defence is attack too. And excessive defence is also attack."

I did my military service in fairly good conditions, as things go in our army. Once an officer from Moscow gave us a lecture about how the Americans train special units for operations in difficult conditions. These "difficult conditions" seemed to us like a holiday in a health resort compared with our normal ones. That's the point. What's normal life for us is from the Western viewpoint life in nightmarishly difficult conditions. This is where our superiority lies. What we have is not some pathetic pre-war training for "difficult conditions", but a gigantic historical experience of real life in ultra-difficult conditions. We have no need to prepare for war because we are always prepared for it.

AN INTELLECTUAL DUEL

I am now facing what in spy stories is known as an intellectual duel. I will tell my opponents that I am an ASS. I will tell them about other ASSES who work here and about the latest methods of Soviet penetration in the West. They won't believe a single word I say. They'll catch me out contradicting myself and set traps. Why? Well, in order to unmask me as an ASS. Can you resolve this situation? It defeats me. We are too far apart. For me, the unfolding of history has profoundly tragic implications; for *them*, history is of no more consequence than a musical comedy. But they view our roles completely the other way round. And I make no objection. I myself play the fool. And I think they are fools, just as they do me.

I go out to these duels as though to work. My interrogators pay no attention to what I consider important, and what is indeed important; they listen to me with an air of mocking boredom, interrupt me continually and soon get bogged down in trivia. Therefore I will put our conversations into edited literary form and boil them down to what I think is essential. Their Reports on our conversations doubtless look quite different. In their Reports I appear as a dim-witted, slippery, lying type of person, while they are clever and penetrating investigators, continually forcing me into a corner, tearing the mask from my face and showing me up as an impostor. For me there's nothing new in all that; I have been trained in such things in Moscow since my childhood.

"Last time you mentioned some Committee of Intellectual Advisers [CIA] under the direction of the KGB. What sort of an organization is that?"

"It's an unofficial group. Its members are not KGB people. They work in other institutions and represent a wide variety of professions. They are not paid extra for belonging to the CIA. It's a hobby for them. They enjoy playing intellectual games for their own sake. They like the feeling that they belong to the highest circles and can be of some use. They are interested in forming a true picture of the country's situation in the minds of the top leadership, and a true image of the international situation too. They also want to find effective measures to improve the country's position. The organizer and inspirer of the CIA was my friend . . ."

"Were you also a member of the CIA?"

"I was friendly with Inspirer and other members of the CIA. I discussed various problems with them. But I wasn't a member."

"Why not?"

"It just happened that way. I made no effort to join. I didn't need it. Besides, I was a collection point for information, which excluded membership of the CIA."

"What do you mean?"

"The members of the CIA had a network of specially selected informants through whom they gathered the data they needed for their intellectual activity."

"You mean informers and stool-pigeons?"

"Not at all. It's simply that the members of the CIA were confronted with questions which they wanted to have answered with the help of empirical sociology. The informants were selected for their competence and truthfulness. For example, Brezhnev was invested with the title of Marshal. I get a telephone call. It's Inspirer. What do I think of this event? Well, I come from a certain social circle and my opinion is characteristic of it. Inspirer knows that I won't put on an 'honest Communist' act, and that I will tell him what I really think. I know that I will suffer absolutely no punishment for my reply. And so I answer: 'these idiots'—I am referring to the members of the Politburo—'have simply gone off their heads'. Questions like that cropped up about Brezhnev's speeches, resolutions of the Central Committee, and dissidents. But the fulfilment of such tasks was a secondary matter for the Committee."

"What was its primary task?"

"Thinking about political problems at a strategic level. For example, the plan to convert the recent emigration into an Operation was hatched by the CIA."

"What did the plan actually amount to?"

"Turning a trickle of emigrants into a flood."

"By compulsion?"

"No, by provoking voluntary mass emigration. To arrange things so that hundreds of thousands of people would want to emigrate."

"With what object?"

"To cleanse the country of unhealthy elements. To deprive them of a social base within the USSR. To infiltrate agents into the West. To increase the number of carriers of Sovietism in the West. This was to be a form of penetration of the enemy. To show the West what the opposition is really like. To sow dissension among the dissidents. To arouse the West's irritation. To inculcate false ideas about Soviet society. To muddy the waters and catch fish in them. Very convenient from many angles."

"To what extent has this plan paid off?"

"One hundred per cent, plus some indirect benefits that weren't part of the original calculations at all. For example, the West is at a loss in the face of the flood of Soviet émigrés. The Western security services are at a loss in their struggle with Soviet operations in the West."

"How large an operation were they envisaging?"

"We advised the authorities to chuck out at least one million people to the West, mainly Jews. But the high-ups got frightened at this figure and, as usual, stopped half-way."

After our talk about the CIA the conversation sank to its usual banal level.

"When did you begin your service in the KGB?"

"It hasn't begun yet. For many years I worked *for* the KGB, as do many other Soviet people. But I never worked *in* the KGB. I agreed to become a Soviet agent in order to get permission to emigrate."

"You were a KGB informer? What was your code-name?"

"I've never been an informer."

"That can't be true."

"Not all Soviet people are KGB informers. But in principle any Soviet person may be used by the KGB as a source of information or for some operation or other. But that's a different matter. For instance, the KGB uses Western intelligence services for its own purposes. According to your way of thinking that means that they too . . ."

"Did they ask you to become an informer?"

"I find it hard to answer that. Sometimes it's done in such a veiled form that it isn't a formal proposition. In any case, I refused."

"That's impossible."

"Agreement or refusal doesn't play the role that you in the West imagine. I know people who agreed to become informers but actually didn't; and people who refused but actually did do work for the KGB. Nowadays there are many people carrying out KGB instructions but not working for them formally. For example, I wrote Reports for the Presidium of the Academy of Sciences which went automatically to the KGB."

"So that means that you were, all the same, a collaborator with the KGB. You are not being one hundred per cent honest with us."

"Define 'one hundred per cent honesty' for me and I promise to keep to it unswervingly and even to go over the top."

But they didn't understand the ambiguity of my request.

ABOUT SINCERITY

Am I being sincere with the people I talk to or not? I am and I am not. The very concept of sincerity has no meaning when applied to the ideological consciousness of the Homosos. When I decided to emigrate, an old friend of mine said: "that means you will now become our enemy". And he isn't a fool either. And he didn't say this at a Party meeting. But another acquaintance, after the Party meeting at which they branded me as a traitor, warmly shook my hand. When there was nobody looking, of course. Which of the two was being sincere? Everything depends on the circumstances in which the Homosos exhibits his qualities. He is supple and situational. His reactions come naturally, but they are not the only possible ones. There is nothing in him which could be called genuine, because "genuineness" is only one of a number of historical possibilities which people in their imagination elevate into an absolute. But everything in him is natural in the sense that it corresponds with the concrete conditions of his life.

My first friend treated me as an enemy not because he was worried about the Soviet system but because I had transgressed the accepted norm and behaved in a non-Soviet manner. He merely dressed the concept of "enemy" in ideological clothing. He didn't feel towards me what one is meant to feel towards an enemy. My second friend, on the other hand, sympathized with me without feeling any real sympathy. He merely chose that way to express one of his own varied attitudes to the Soviet system. In fact both of them felt about me what the mass of people feels about a member of the collective who behaves in a non-standard way: they felt bewilderment, curiosity, irritation, envy, ill-will and self-pity. One can't define this reaction with the help of any one standard linguistic expression. And so it is with everything.

So it's ridiculous to expect a Homosos to be sincere towards you. He would be glad to be, but he can't, because he considers that he is always sincere in one respect or another. So if he is ready to change one sincerity into another from one minute to the next, this isn't a sign of insincerity. The KGB-men who instructed me never once suggested that I should deceive the people who would de-brief me here. These KGB types are experienced Homososes. They know there's no need to give us such advice, inasmuch as we've been trained from childhood not to deceive people, but to lead them into confusion by using the truth. When my interrogators here started hinting about the use of lie-detectors, I burst out laughing. This time they did understand me, and realized that their idea was senseless.

ABOUT COLLABORATION WITH THE AUTHORITIES

Was I a collaborator with the KGB? To be scientifically accurate, I didn't collaborate with them. In fact the Homosos doesn't collaborate with the powers-that-be. He himself participates in power. That's the essence of the matter. He is merely exercising his own potential and actual power-functions. The Reports of KGB informers, the denunciations of volunteers and aficionados, the communications of official personages, public unmaskings and other phenomena of Soviet life are merely the forms of participation by Homososes in the system of power.

For example, I went abroad several times. When I got back I used to write Reports about these trips. I did this according to instructions which in particular included the following: "When talking to foreign scholars widely propagandize the achievements of Soviet science, the successes of Socialist construction in the USSR and the peace-loving policies of our State. Explain and popularize the ideas of the new constitution of the USSR; when the question of 'human rights' comes up, proceed from our position of principle as expounded in the national Press. On returning from your journey present a Report on your assignment to the Presidium of the Academy of Sciences of the USSR within a fortnight."

I would sign the paper which contained these words without reading it.

I knew in advance that my Report would go to the KGB. But what's the difference? How is the Presidium of the Academy of Sciences of the USSR different from the KGB? I simply did my duty as a Homosos who was allowed to go on a journey abroad. I tried to do my duty as well as I could. And I see nothing immoral in this whatever. I despised then, and I despise to this day, all those who pretend they did such things unwillingly or under duress. I don't believe them. Either they were so lazy they didn't want to write any Reports, or they weren't clever enough to do them well.

A SPEECH ADDRESSED TO MORALISTS

There was nobody in the park, only ducks. They clustered around me hoping for breadcrumbs. There arose within me a keen desire to make a statement, so I delivered a lecture to the ducks. The amusing thing was that they didn't go off. They listened patiently and quacked in an encouraging way, or so it seemed to me. No doubt they were lonely, and bored too.

"You, of course, will think that my behaviour and the behaviour of other Homososes in such a situation is amoral. But we look at it differently. It is easy to be moral if you live in conditions which do not force you into morally reprehensible actions. You are well fed and clothed; you have a nice house with books and other ways of enjoying yourselves. And it seems to you that to be moral is natural and not in the least bit difficult. And indeed, why be an informer for the KGB, for example, if nobody forces you to be one and if in fact there *is* no KGB? Everything is simple and clear-cut. But if a man finds himself below the bread-line, beneath the minimum that is indispensable if moral norms are to be considered applicable in real life, then it is senseless to apply moral criteria to his behaviour. A man in such a position is not only freed *ipso facto* from normal norms, he is freed from them by these moral concepts themselves. It is immoral to expect a man to be moral if he lacks the minimum living conditions that permit society to demand morality of him."

At this point the ducks quacked more animatedly than usual, as though they had understood my words. Only it was not clear whether they endorsed or rejected my proposition.

"Homososes are born, are educated and live in such conditions that it is just as ridiculous to accuse them of immorality or to attribute moral virtues to them as it would be to regard the behaviour of the hordes of

54

Genghis Khan from a moral viewpoint; or the ancient Egyptians, the Incas or other similar phenomena from the past.

"Once they did actually propose that I should become an informer; and I refused. I didn't feel that I was a hero engaged in a struggle with some evil or criminal power. And I am not proud of my refusal today. At that time there was simply no reason for me to become an informer. I had nothing to gain from becoming one. And there was absolutely no danger in my refusing. There was no need for the officer who was trying to recruit me to recruit me personally. He didn't insist. I had no special value for him as an informer. And everything he needed to know from me I could tell him even without being an informer. Which is what I did. And I suffered no pangs of conscience from that. And I don't suffer any now.

"My dealings with the KGB were pure Soviet routine, which cannot be subject to moral evaluations. I agreed to work for the KGB before my departure for the West. Why? I could have had the intention of working honestly for the good of my Motherland. Is that moral or not? I could have pretended to agree to be an agent in order to get myself out of the Communist torture-chamber and then act against the KGB. Is that moral or not? I could deceive the KGB *and* the Western intelligence services which are reckoned *a priori* to be amoral organizations, in order to begin to lead a life worthy of a human being. Is that moral or not? These are only a few of the possible variants of rational calculation. And in the consciousness of the Homosos all possible variants coexist, actually or potentially, at one and the same time. They are mixed up with one another and displace one another. As a function of the actual situation one or other combination of them begins to predominate, and it comes to be taken as the 'genuine nature' of the Homosos. And indeed it is genuine, but only for a given situation, not in general.

"The Homosos thinks in blocks of thoughts and feels in blocks of feelings, for which (meaning blocks as a whole) there is as yet no adequate terminology. Consequently the Homosos is psychologically and intellectually plastic, supple and adaptive. Behaviour that is bad in itself is not experienced by the Homosos as bad, inasmuch as it is experienced not on its own but merely as an element in a more complex whole (block) which doesn't appear bad as a complete entity. A drop of poison in a complicated life-saving medicine doesn't act as a poison.

"You will think that to be a Homosos means degradation. This is what the well-bred representatives of the animal world, the elephants, the lions, the tigers, thought about our restless, dirty ancestors. But what was the outcome? Homosos doesn't mean degradation. He is only

55

making a temporary retreat to the basics of human existence while he prepares a new and grandiose leap forward in evolution. Is that clear?"

The ducks were disturbed and muttered something, but didn't go away. Clearly my idea interested them. Inspired by their quacking I passed to the following section of my lecture.

"If a man's conduct is not determined by moral principles that doesn't mean that it isn't regulated by any other principles. And this, in turn, doesn't mean that the conduct of a man regulated by these other principles is worse than conduct determined by morality. The means whereby the behaviour of the popular masses is governed, e.g., the power of the collective over the individual, a State ideology, or forced labour, or other means, are much more effective in our time than the nebulous and hypocritical methods of morality. Incidentally, these latter methods have also been preserved by us; they are merely subordinated to the former. For instance, it is immoral to deceive people; and so when we denounce our neighbours we only write the truth about them.

"You think, perhaps, that Westerners are more moral than we are? But I can name numerous aspects of life in which Westerners seem far worse than Homososes. For example, Homososes are much more concerned with the destiny of their fellow beings. And, incidentally, they are not so stingy. But the Homosos is more concerned with his fellows than the Westerner is, not because of moral principles but because of the higher level of collectivism. Which is better: to be indifferent to your neighbour's fate in a moral society or to be concerned about it in an amoral society?"

The ducks listened to the end of my peroration absent-mindedly, moving from one foot to the other and looking about in all directions. Evidently my critical remarks about the West didn't appeal to them at all. They realized that there were no tasty breadcrumbs to be had from me, so they abandoned me as soon as they saw an old-age pensioner approaching with a bag.

I AND CYNIC

"The Soviet authorities should show restraint and patience with regard to the gradual build up of the émigré invasion of the West; then the West will begin to howl. What a shattering effect it would have if the Soviet authorities offered to let all the Jews in the USSR go to the West! Two million of them! I would like to see the expression then on the faces of Western politicians and champions of human rights."

"They discussed that plan in Moscow ten years ago, and wrote it off as being unsuitable. So the secret dream of the Soviet anti-semite will never be realized. Why? First, because the West can't take such a lot of Soviet people. Second, because the USSR can't chuck out such a large number of people to the West."

"Nonsense! Only permit it and half the Soviet population would do a bunk to the West."

"Now that *is* utter nonsense. The number of people dying to leave and able to leave in actual fact depends on the number of people who are convinced that they will be better off in the West and who can wrench themselves away from their native surroundings. Such people are not so thick on the ground; we've been calculating it. Besides, there are laws governing mass phenomena which emigrations too are bound to obey. Emigration is already on the decline. It has to be given an artificial fillip. How? For instance, by limiting it."

"I don't understand whether you're joking or not. What is your own position?"

"I don't know how to joke. I haven't got a position of my own. And if I do have one, I don't agree with it, as in the old anecdote."

"I don't understand."

"Don't try to understand. There are things that by their very nature can't be understood. Just bide your time. And when you've had a lot of cases of this kind you'll develop the habit of looking at events in this way. And you will never make a mistake."

"A marvellous method! And what is it called?"

"Dialectics. Dialectics, my dear comrade, is not only something to be scoffed at by those who know it only by hearsay. Dialectics is a way of moving blindfold in an unknown empty space filled with imaginary obstacles; of moving without support and without resistance. And without an objective."

"You talk like Christ."

"You've guessed it. At one time I had to give anti-religious lectures for the Society of Knowledge."

"Are you a Jew too? No? Then why . . . ?"

"Because Daddy and Mummy . . ."

"Why did you emigrate?"

"It's too late to look for a reason. It's time to look for a justification."

"I don't see the difference."

"Reasons operate before, justifications after."

57

I AND WHINER

Cynic's bewilderment about my nationality is understandable; anybody at all can represent the Russian people in the West except the Russians themselves. This suits the Central Committee and the KGB perfectly. One of the officials of the Central Committee who was giving me my instructions said that "we will not countenance the idea of any national Russian culture in the West"; and that "our general guidelines are to reduce the national Russian element to nil in everything which appears in the West in the Russian language".

Here comes Whiner. He's half Russian and half Jewish. The Jewish half allowed him to get out to the West; the Russian half prevents him from settling down here. The result is that he feels not half-Russian, but doubly Russian. "Why do *they* complain?" sighs Whiner, nodding at the Pope's portrait in the newspaper. "They choose *them* to be Popes while we go flat out and then can't even get any cardinals." This bit of heckling by Whiner is very characteristic. According to the strictly private convictions of the Homosos, a Soviet citizen should be made Pope first, and only later somebody from one of the fraternal Socialist countries. It isn't a matter of being religious: if need be the Central Committee will appoint anybody to be a Catholic. Whiner wouldn't be in the least surprised if they nominated (really nominated) a member of the Central Committee as Pope. It would be perfectly all right to have the CC's Secretary for Ideology exercising the functions of Pope at the same time. But instead we've got a Pole. Absolutely scandalous! What does the KGB think it's doing?

FRIENDS AND ENEMIES

"Over there you'll find yourself in rabidly anti-Soviet and anti-Communist circles," Inspirer used to say. "Here's what they have produced in the last five years. Take a look at it, it's utter sh-t. But it's useful to get to know it. One must know one's enemy."

I remembered this conversation after Lady had rung me up. She said there was a post of consultant-sociologist going in one of the institutes. He should be a specialist in Soviet society. The pay wouldn't be large, but for a single Soviet man it would be more than sufficient. Enough to afford a cosy little flat. "The first thing I'll do is to invite you round," I said. "I accept in advance," she giggled. "I'll recommend you for the job" (already she was using the intimate form of 'you'), "so make sure you don't let me down." "I'll do my very best," I assured her.

Having leafed through the "literature" that Inspirer had given me, I noticed from the very first pages that, for these people, openly expressed anti-Sovietism and anti-Communism play a purely pragmatic role: it is the way in which they express their willingness to serve their new masters. As to what is actually harmful or advantageous to Moscow, they couldn't care less about that. If they reckon that the truth "two plus two equals four" is useful to Moscow, they will regard anyone who says it as a Muscovite agent. Is it really the case, I pondered, that I have got away from that swamp of the idiocies, vulgarity and lies that is Soviet ideology, only to be forced to plunge head first into the even more idiotic, vulgar and lying marsh of anti-Sovietism? Anything, anything but that!

But all the same I went round to the institute whose address Lady had given me. The little man who received me was very like the deputy head of the propaganda department of the Central Committee. I even shuddered when I saw him. Could it really be He? The little fellow straight away read me a lecture about what I was obliged to do in order to smash "our common enemy". It was exactly our own dear CC. I patiently heard Homunculus out. I agreed with his slogans. I said I was ready to begin my active struggle against Moscow that very minute. But I said I wasn't a politician; I was a scholar. And the position of science couldn't always be aligned with current politics.

"For instance, you are criticizing the Soviet Union and calling on the West to impose sanctions against Moscow. You think you're causing Moscow some sort of damage. But science tells a different story. The Soviet attack on the West misfired because of lack of strength within the country. The Soviet leadership should have called a halt and even retreated, in order to avoid a catastrophe and prepare for a better attack in the future. Criticism of the shortcomings of the Soviet system and a firmer Western position will force the Soviet leadership into a more supple policy both outside and within the country. Do you think the Soviet leadership doesn't draw lessons from what is happening? I assure you that even the dissident movement has, to a huge degree, contributed to the strengthening of the Soviet regime. Communism in general and the Soviet Union in particular are your enemies. One must know one's enemies objectively and dispassionately. I am a scholar, I repeat, not a politician. I can help you to know your enemy on the plane of serious science."

"In our business," he said, "one cannot be dispassionate. We know our enemy just as well as you do. We need an active struggle. We need

59

executives. This isn't the Academy of Sciences. But we will think about your application."

A few days later I learned that they had given the job I'd applied for to a mathematician, a recent émigré from Leningrad, who had put his signature under some clamorous little articles in an illegal dissident journal. Lady took umbrage at what I had done. She said it was no good my "acting like a smart Alec"; that if one wanted to live with wolves one had to howl with them. She's right of course. But I just don't want to live with wolves.

WRITER

Our former writer lives in this city. Not a former writer, but formerly ours. It was only on arrival here that I learned of the existence of this Soviet writer. His story was simple and sad. They printed him in Moscow, but he didn't meet with the success he wanted. He composed something of the "revelatory" type and printed it in the West. There he got a few favourable notices. He took this to be worldwide renown. He began to make scenes.

He was summoned for interrogation. The authorities suggested that he should go to Israel, although he was a Russian. He agreed. So now he's dragging out a pitiful existence here (not in Israel, of course). He consoles himself with the thought that at least the KGB isn't keeping an eye on him here, although in fact it is precisely here that he is under the strictest KGB supervision. He gets pleasure from the fact that "there's not a bite to eat in the USSR". In a Press interview he stated that only here had he got the possibility of writing everything he wanted and in the way he wanted. However, to judge by what he produces he himself doesn't yet know what he wants to write about or how to write it. He is in the position of a deaf mute pushed on to the stage of an opera house and told: "Sing anything you like and how you like." It's a good job that the auditorium was empty. Nobody wants to read Writer's books. And they are beginning not to want to print them any more.

Generally speaking, there are quite a lot of our former writers living in this town, including one famous one. But I can't get to him because he's afraid that I am going to ask him for money. And I myself don't want to see the others, because I am afraid that they are going to ask me for money.

CHIEF

Writer invited me to a restaurant. Chief came with him. Chief paid, otherwise Writer wouldn't have dreamed of inviting me. Chief started up a conversation about the difference between the Soviet and the Western ways of life. "Take a restaurant like this one," I said. "It and the service in it are a common phenomenon in the West. As soon as you have been conquered by Communism, restaurants of this standard will disappear completely, and the number of restaurants in general will go down many times. It will be difficult to get into a restaurant. The cooking will be bad and the service even worse. There will be five or even ten times as many waiters and waitresses, but the service will be many times slower. They will be insolent, they will cheat you, they will . . ."

"But why?" cried Chief. "Surely we'll be able to keep what we've got now?" "No," I said, "because such institutions will be organized and will function according to the general principles governing all institutions in a Communist society. A specific establishment of restaurant workers will be instituted, and a specific system of management. Incidentally, working conditions will be a lot easier than they are here now. This is the main blandishment of Communism. There will be a fixed scale of pay for the workers and a work-plan for the enterprise; a fixed allocation of food-stuffs, a fixed source of supply and a fixed way of running the restaurant. There will be no more competition. The employees' income will no longer depend on their personal initiative or risk, or the quality of the food, or the choice available, or the quality of the service. Every sort of illegal kick-back will bring in far more profit than conscientious work and high standards of food and service. Try to put yourself in the position of a manager working in such conditions, or of a waiter, and you will easily draw all the consequences that have become habitual in the Soviet Union. And something similar will emerge in all the other factors of everyday life."

"It wouldn't do any harm to explain things like that to Westerners a bit more frequently," said Chief. "Perhaps the threat of losing a tasty beefsteak would make them think more seriously about the implications of Communism than the threat of losing their civil rights does."

DIALECTICS AS A METHOD OF DECEPTION

I feel I am opposed by an intellect, but one of quite another type than my own. It isn't concentrated in one personality; it is scattered throughout all the surrounding space. It is not embellished by any emotions. It is a pedantic intellect, and a primitive one. And at the same time grandiose. It is as if people were totting me up on computers. And suppose they really are?

When I was a student I was fascinated by this problem: can a man deceive a "thinking" machine which is cleverer than he is? I came to the conclusion that in any combination of given conditions one can find a way of deceiving a "thinking" machine. Under the term "deceiving" I had in mind the capacity to foist upon the machine deductions from the given information which the deceiver himself regards as false. But there is one difficulty in this. In order to deceive a mechanically-minded opponent, I must myself know which deductions follow from what I do and which mistaken deductions I wish to foist upon him; that is to say, mistaken from my point of view. But what if I myself am not very clear about my intentions? Then my opponent doesn't compute me, but a fictitious version of me. And I shall be instilling in him only the fiction of a mistake. Logically there is only one way of surmounting this difficulty: to formulate a certain number of statements in such a way that they implicitly contain within themselves their own negation; and to execute a certain number of actions in such a way that they permit contradictory interpretations.

INTERROGATION

My conversations with the people who are screening me could scarcely be called a duel because in all about ten people are talking to me. They usually do this in various combinations of two or three. I might have been able to humour them by playing the dim-witted and immoral rogue, but then they would have lost interest in me. Then I would have had to go away to some place where my emigration would have lost all its purpose. I think I've chosen the right line of behaviour. I must stick to it all the way until I get political asylum. And this depends on my interrogators.

"Who are your parents?"

"Engineer and housewife."

"Are they Communists?"

"My father was a member of the Party; my mother wasn't."

"He *was*? Was he expelled?"

"He's dead. My mother too."

"And your grandparents?"

"Peasants. My great-grandparents were peasants too. According to Soviet ideology their forebears were monkeys, but according to Western doctrine they were Adam and Eve."

"Were they Jewish?"

"Peasants in Russia couldn't be Jewish."

"That's true. In Tsarist Russia peasants were actually forbidden to be Jews."

"And now under the Soviet regime it's the other way round: Jews are forbidden to be peasants. Or workers."

"Yes, anti-semitism is thriving over there."

"But then all dissidents are obliged to be Jews."

"Yes, national conflicts are destroying the Soviet regime, especially those rebellions among the Muslim peoples. They'll soon be a majority in the USSR and then . . ."

"Then the Russians will have to rebel against the domination of the Muslim and other peoples."

"Your father was a member of the Communist Party of the Soviet Union. When did he join the Party? What were his functions in it?"

This is the kind of way in which our conversation drags out into four, six or even eight hours. I keep on repeating that I went to school and joined the Komsomol. Of my own free will, of course. People do join the Komsomol of their own free will. And it doesn't accept everybody. My interrogators don't believe this. To get into an institute you need a Komsomol reference, so you joined the Komsomol for career reasons. I mentioned casually that they had come in wearing ties and jackets, although it was hot outside. Why did they do this? For career reasons? They didn't get the point, but they took offence, just in case.

The same problem of "free will" or "career reasons" arose in connection with my Party membership. All my efforts to explain to my interrogators the essence of the Party and its position in Soviet society, what it means to be a member, and the relationship between ideology and morality in Soviet society met with total failure. Everything would have been clear to them if I had said that I joined the CPSU for career reasons. But I never made a career and never tried to. Party membership didn't hinder me in any way. On the contrary, it made life just a bit more interesting. And there was no "double-think" about it. In general, "double-think" is an invention of Westerners who don't understand anything about the Soviet way of life or Soviet people. I'm a Communist not in the sense that I believe in Marxist fairy-tales (very few people in the Soviet Union believe in them), but in the sense that I was born, reared and educated in a Communist society and have all the essential characteristics of Soviet man. And what are these qualities? Well, for instance, if they go on plying me with questions about my Party membership, I'll tell them to . . . off. They burst out laughing because they knew this four-letter word very well indeed. But they laughed not because I used it but because we consider it indecent.

WHERE IT ALL BEGAN

They asked me to tell them about the training for Soviet agents like me. "The ordinary Soviet man," I said, "learns from the whole course of his life, without any special training, how to do three things: to administrate, to criticize the regime, and to be a KGB agent." The interrogators laughed a little at that but asked me all the same to tell them how I was recruited and instructed. I do what they ask.

"It was," I said, "an ordinary working day, that is, a weekday on which I was obliged to appear at my institute and sign the in-and-out book. If there were no meetings that day I would leave the institute immediately and occupy myself with anything I needed to, whatever it was. Usually I went home and wrote something. I did this from vanity (this accounted for ten per cent of the motivation), from habit and from having nothing else to do (fifty per cent), and in order to fulfil my individual plan of work for the institute and hold on to my cushy position as senior scientific research officer (forty per cent). I only took up this position three years ago and I valued it greatly because my salary rose steeply and I got two 'library' days a week; these are days when I was not even obliged to sign the in-and-out book. On those days I usually slept until noon and then used my time at my own discretion. I still had to spend a certain number of days per month at the institute. These were days when there were working sessions, Party and trade-union meetings, academic councils, summonses to see the director and other nonsense. A couple of evenings a month were wasted on 'social work', and one day on 'special occasions', such as meetings and send-offs of important people, work in the vegetable depot or unpaid voluntary work on my day off. It was, in short, a very pleasant life; almost paradise. It was only when I was deprived of it that I realized what I had lost. If I were now to get a chair, or even a whole institute, I wouldn't be within miles of the blissful situation I was in in Moscow. And you keep on asking me why the people supports the Soviet regime.

"Anyway, it was an ordinary working day. I arrived at the institute and signed both the in-column and the out-column. I decided to take a turn in the town. I began to look for a companion. But all my usual drinking-partners had disappeared, and I didn't want to spend the day with just anybody. I rang up Inspirer. 'I'm bored,' I said. 'Couldn't we meet?' 'OK,' he said. 'In half an hour at the National.'"

MY COMPANION

There, by the way, is one more great blessing of the Soviet way of life; if you have nothing to do (and that often happens) and you want to find a companion-in-idleness (it's hard to be idle by oneself), you will always find some idler and bletherer like yourself who is ready to pass the whole day chatting with you. This can't happen in the West. If you want to talk to somebody here, make an exact appointment. After half an hour or an hour it's goodbye. In the West idle people are somehow terribly busy. In all my time here I haven't once managed to have a potter-chatter with a local idler. Only with my compatriots. And, under the influence of the West, they too have begun to pretend to be terribly booked-up. It's boring, gentlemen. What kind of life is this? What is it all in aid of?

I settled down with Inspirer at the National. We had a drink. Then we had a little food. Then we ordered some more. Once again it was our Soviet phenomenon; to go on the booze to the last rouble—and beyond, into debt. Here, in the West, they drink a little glass of something, gobble down a steak and it's goodbye. But there we do it until closing time, until our pockets are turned inside out. And it's only now that I have begun to realize the blessings of Soviet life. Then I didn't give tuppence for them. As the saying goes, what we have we don't appreciate; when we lose it we are sorry.

"Isn't life a bore?" I said. "Some people are wandering about in Paris, guzzling oysters, sleeping with negresses and looking through *Playboy*. But here? Unrelieved black boredom. And no light ahead of us. You couldn't send me abroad for a couple of weeks, could you? By the way, why have they stopped letting me out? I know some foreign languages. I can turn out Reports by the kilometre. I won't defect."

"Somebody has put in a denunciation on you. But I've got an idea. And the fact that they've stopped letting you out will help you on your way. You will be taken for a dissident."

"But I don't want to be a dissident."

"Don't be an idiot. You'll be a dissident if you have to. There's a rumour going around that you are half-Jewish."

"Rubbish!"

"I know. It's just a rumour. But it's a good one. How would it be if you were longing for the land of your ancestors?"

"Not on your life!"

"Israel is only for the application form. You'll settle in Europe. See the world. Guzzle oysters. Sleep with negresses. Freedom. Beauty. Romance. What more do you want?"

"Who will invite me? Who'll believe that I'm a Jew?"

"You'll get the invitation in a couple of days."

"My ex-wife won't permit it. She'll ask for all her alimony in advance."

"We'll settle all that."

"But they'll arrest me at once over there."

"Don't count on it!"

"But what's the point of all this?"

"Here's a telephone number. Give them a ring tomorrow morning."

THE DECISIVE CONVERSATION

The next morning I rang the number Inspirer had given me. Within an hour I was sitting in a KGB flat earmarked for meetings between KGB officers and people who are of interest to them as well as informers. I was talking to . . . Let me call this man "General".

"We've had an eye on you for a long time. Your candidature has been endorsed by . . . himself. What do we need from you now? Get to know so-and-so and so-and-so. (He gave me the names of a number of dissidents who were bringing out some illegal journal.) Give them a critical article for their next issue. Sign a letter or appeal exposing something or other. You'll be kicked out of the Party and sacked from your job. There will be a search and an interrogation; in a word, everything you need to get a reputation as a dissident. We can't tell you your exact place of residence in the West; that will depend on a combination of circumstances. Your task is to get a foothold somewhere, settle down to a pretty secure way of life and find yourself the means of subsistence. Live and keep your eyes open. Get to know people. In brief, act according to the circumstances. You must get this into your head once and for all: the world will soon experience life-and-death battles such as have never been seen before. Our duty is to be ready for them at any minute and before the others are. Therefore we must penetrate all the pores of the West immediately. We must know everything about it. We must make use of every chance to weaken and demoralize the West, to loosen it up, to divide it and spread chaos and confusion. We have to intimidate it. We must take everything we need from it for our own existence and for our future conflicts with it. You are a soldier of our Great Army that is marching on the West; the vanguard of our attacking army." Then General ordered his assistant to arrange a meeting for me with a former Soviet spy who had worked in West Germany for many years.

CONVERSATION WITH A FORMER SPY

"Why did you work in West Germany? You are a Russian. Surely there are enough East German spies there?"

"There are, but we use them mainly as red herrings and for political actions. We do the most important things ourselves."

"That's odd. I would have thought that . . ."

"The way people imagine our spies work in the West has nothing to do with reality."

"Oh well, don't exaggerate. There must be some resemblance."

"Of course there is a similarity in certain small matters. But, as to the substance of the work, I repeat and I insist, there is no resemblance. After all, I worked in West Germany for more than ten years."

"And where were you?"

"I lived in M. A relatively small town. But do you know how many professional spies of ours there were there? More than ten in my group alone. And for all anyone knows there may have been more. And at least twenty other people performed various services for us."

"Fantastic! Such a huge network of spies for a little town like that! It must be very expensive."

"Who told you it was expensive? It didn't cost our State a kopek. We all worked in German organizations and firms and got good wages. So Germany itself kept us going. Moreover, many of us even gave part of our earnings to the State. *Our* State, of course. For example, one of our agents worked as a professor in the university. He got five thousand marks a month. After he had paid his taxes, insurance and rent he was left with a good two and a half thousand. So he handed over a thousand. Another of our agents even got a management post in a big firm and gave three thousand marks a month to our authorities."

67

"But what about the twenty assistants? Were they volunteers or were they forced into it?"

"It depends. Partly volunteers, partly under compulsion. Some didn't even know what they were doing."

"And how did you happen to be there?"

"I accompanied a group of our scholars to a congress and, as the saying goes, I chose freedom."

"But surely the Germans aren't such fools? They should have guessed what you were?"

"But I didn't hide it. You read all our books and look at our films and so you think in your simple way that you have to hide your membership of the KGB. It's exactly the other way round. In the West they like people who have links to intelligence more than those who are in the clear. They don't believe the clean ones *are* clean. Look, suppose you're a member of their counter-espionage. I arrive and say: 'I'm a KGB officer. I want to stay here. I'm ready to tell you everything I know.' What will you do? Check up? All right, check up! All my information will be authentic and even pretty valuable. Perhaps you will suspect me and follow me around. All right, do so. What will that give you? All the time I was in M. the Germans were convinced that I remained on the job. But it was better for them to have a Soviet spy like me than a spy whom they had to uncover. Besides, from time to time I rendered them services too, and they closed their eyes to some of my little games. They're human beings too, and they too have to chalk up a few successes for their bosses."

"But why did you come back? Did they catch you out?"

"No. Failures are virtually impossible. I came to Moscow to have a rest and see my family. And then somebody turned up who wanted my job. He wanted to live in the West for a time and that way make a big leap forward in his career here. It turned out he had powerful protectors. And they sent him instead of me. They picked on a small drinking scandal I caused here and used that as a pretext."

"And so this man simply replaced you?"

"Of course not. There's a special technique in these matters. I returned to Germany. On some suitable pretext I resigned from my firm. I moved first to England and then to Moscow. They simply switched my post to the town where my successor had managed to get a toe-hold. In the West this is no problem."

"Were you afraid of having your cover blown?"

"In the West now that's always a special political decision. If they'd picked on me to become an unmasked spy, that would have got me a prison sentence. But prisons over there are what sanatoria are like here.

Later they would have exchanged me for one of their own spies; or they would have proposed that I should work for them and let me out. The epoch of romantic spying is over."

"And what about clandestinity?"

"You can shout aloud all over Europe that you are a Soviet spy. You can carry a placard saying, 'I am a Soviet spy'. They will laugh a bit and maybe put it in the newspapers. Not in the serious ones, of course; only in the tabloids. And that's all. It's insulting, even."

"So there's no risk? No difficulties? A regular holiday?"

"Risks there are. And difficulties. But they are quite different from what you think. You have to experience all that on your own hide to know what it's like."

"But, all in all, is the thing worth my while?"

"Of course it's worthwhile. If there's the slightest chance, go ahead and agree to any conditions. It's better to kick the bucket there than become a vegetable here."

AT THE HIGHEST LEVEL

Before I left, an extremely highly-placed person had a conversation with me. I will call him Secretary. In Secretary's office hung an enormous portrait of Brezhnev, a smaller one of Lenin and a still smaller one of Marx. The portrait of Marx looked totally out of place. It seemed that Marx was squinting at me in a conspiratorial way; he understood my position and sympathized with me. "Agree to absolutely anything," said his expression. "Whatever your circumstances, it's better to live in the West than in the country that has put my ideas into practice. And try to persuade those idiots in the West to forget my stupid ideas."

Secretary went on with the usual banalities, then he wished me good luck and left me alone with his assistant.

"Does he wish *bon voyage* to everyone?"

"No, only in exceptional cases."

"Please decipher the meaning of the goodbye for me."

"Try to muddy the waters when you get there. Talk in such a way that nobody can understand what's true and what's false. When there's complete confusion in the minds of the majority it's easy to push them in the direction we want."

"But then this confusion may also work to the enemy's advantage."

"It will. But only to his own advantage, not to our disadvantage. And the other thing you must do every day is impress on Westerners that we are omnipotent.''

"But this could arouse fear and increase their vigilance.''

"True, but it demoralizes people far more and makes our work easier. People are more ready to help an omnipotent enemy than a weak friend. And feel free to talk any kind of nonsense. The more sensational the better. The West has a liking for superficial and primitive sensations. For instance, you know the case of the half-baked Soviet student who churned out the most incredible rubbish to the effect that the Soviet Union would soon fall apart and cease to exist. Predictions about the speedy demise of the USSR have been made from the first day of its existence. Many of the predicters themselves have been crushed and destroyed by this 'colossus with feet of clay'. But the West still hasn't drawn any lessons from this. There was a real hullabaloo in the West over the Soviet student's prophecy. They still can't get over it. And no wonder! It's simply marvellous. The Soviet Union will soon cease to exist without the West's making any special effort at all. The Chinese will see to that, for the good of the West. So they can go on living in the West as before with all their mod. cons. There's no need for them to spend money on defence. They needn't deny themselves anything or even do any military service . . .

"By now everyone can see that the idea of this half-baked Soviet student is utter rubbish. West Europeans are now afraid that in the very year in which this Soviet student predicted the Soviet Union would collapse Europe itself may not survive in its present form. But his idea played its role. It made its contribution to the pacifist state of mind in the West. Sensations like these are very useful to us. We must think of something like that in the future and provoke others to do it. At the moment another of our 'unmaskers' is preparing a sensational book about our psychological and bacteriological weapons. Good luck to him. We'll slip him some nice little bits of evidence ourselves. You can imagine what a panic there'll be when the book appears! Naturally, you have to choose the right moment.''

"And Number One Himself knows about this line?''

"Of course. It was authorized at the highest level. You've got what's regarded as a very important mission ahead of you. I congratulate you and wish you all success.''

THE PRINCIPLES OF SELECTION

I am often asked why the KGB's choice fell on me. I shrug my shoulders. I am tired of trying to explain things that are tediously obvious to me but incomprehensible to my interrogators. If the choice had fallen only on me, then perhaps I could have given an answer to their question. But many were chosen. There are general criteria for selection which apply to a mass of individuals. But they cannot all be applied directly to each and every candidate. Some member of the Committee of Intellectual Advisers could have remembered something about me. That would have been enough to include me in a list of candidates to be sent to the West on some operation or other. And sometimes a man's fate is decided on the joke-level. For example, they look at a crook like Enthusiast. "Suppose we send that Eurocommunist paranoiac to the West," says one member of the Special Commission with a humorous disposition. "Just imagine how he'll start mucking everyone up over there. They'll start howling in agony. Ha, ha, ha, ha!" "That's it," says another member of the Commission, bursting with laughter. "And let him take out all his 'documents'. Let them feast their eyes on that load of rubbish! Ha, ha, ha!" "I approve," says the chairman of the Commission, grinning broadly. "Let him buzz off to his beloved West. The air will be sweeter here."

And people who want to understand the KGB's general principles of selection when it comes to chucking people out to the West and dumping them there should consider who in fact emigrated, where they went, where and how they found jobs, what they are doing, whom they are playing dirty tricks on and whom they're assisting.

HOMOSOS

When I was talking to my interrogators and telling them that Homososes are born administrators, critics of the regime and secret service agents, I wasn't joking. I never had lessons in any of these activities but I could do any one of them. Some officials of the Central Committee and the KGB began their careers as critics of the regime. In his youth Inspirer was a member of a "terrorist" group. The investigator who was in charge of their case noted Inspirer's abilities and invited him to work in the Organs. For some time his speciality was internal terrorism. After his post-graduate studies were over they transferred him to the department organizing terrorism in the West. He left this department "on moral grounds", which harmed his career. I believe that bit about "moral grounds". He's a Homosos, and a Homosos is capable of even greater things than that.

Inspirer really did leave the Western terrorism department on moral grounds. But it wasn't the methods of terrorism he condemned but his colleagues, who worked badly, squabbled with each other and went in for eyewash.

He dreamed of creating an effective service for the systematic (as distinct from sporadic) elimination of prominent Western personalities. To begin with, he thought, one would liquidate one of them a month. Gradually one could increase one's productivity to four persons a month. After a few years the West would be numb with fright and horror. Every year one could shoot an American president. "This," he said, "would be the training for beginners." "But why shoot them?" I asked. "Why not," he said, "if it's possible? Just clear them out of the way and we'll get some advantage from it." "Who was responsible for Kennedy's assassination?" I asked. "We don't have any direct connection with that kind of thing ourselves," he said. "But whenever any important assassination takes place anywhere in the world, we are in it somewhere. You remember Oswald? Well, he was a screen. There had to be someone like Oswald for the assassination plan to get off the ground. It was he who put it into the minds of those who wanted to rub Kennedy out that the assassination could be represented as being 'the hand of Moscow'. And that stimulated the plotters to prepare the assassination. To give the plotters the hope of putting all the blame on Moscow (while excluding the possibility of doing this officially)—that was a task for specialists of the front rank. There are always plenty of people in the world who want to commit political murders. But a serious scientific method is needed in order to be able to spot them, direct them, and make sure one doesn't get caught oneself."

WE

The Pensionnaires don't read the local newspapers and periodicals. They don't know Western languages and they're saving as much money as they can. For the same reason they don't understand radio and television. But that doesn't prevent them from knowing everything and knowing it better and earlier than everyone else, because they are Homososes. Epithets such as "cretin", "monstrosity", "blockhead", "scoundrel" and suchlike come to their lips as a matter of course whenever they're discussing Western personalities. For instance, they're looking at television. A well-known politician is making a speech. Whiner comes in looking apathetic. "You're listening to *that* degenerate?" he remarks with contempt, although he cannot even distinguish which language "that degenerate" is speaking in. Soon Enthusiast flies in, very excited. "Ah," he roars, "so you're looking at *that* chatterbox! What's he blethering on about? Relations with Moscow? Oh, ha, ha, ha, ha! Even our rulers couldn't think up nonsense like that!"

The most amazing thing is that the Pensionnaires are rarely mistaken in these *a priori* evaluations.

Another essential feature of our judgements is their categorical nature. A revolution in Iran. It's the West's own fault. The idiots should have seen it coming! Of course the Soviet Union did it. There are mad mullahs leading it? Well, what of that? It's a Communist revolution all the same. Sock them in the face and it'll all be over. The Iranian students have seized the American Embassy? Well, they had it coming to them, the idiots! Sock them! The theme of "socking them" is usually the Leitmotiv. Sock the USSR. Sock the Arabs. Sock the blacks. Sock the Iranian mullahs. Sock the terrorists. Sock everyone, and everything will be okay. These Westerners have developed such a line of whining drivel it's shameful to watch them.

All this, as if we didn't know that the West isn't homogeneous. The West is weak; the West hasn't the strength to do this; the West is sinking; the West has gone crazy; the West has too much of everything; the West is capitulating; the West is incompetent. There isn't a single conversation that is free of these expressions.

And in spite of that we never stop admiring the West. On it alone we pin our hopes. "The West is a force to be reckoned with!" says Whiner. "They are definitely going to think up something and bash us [he means Moscow] in the face!" "The West will still say 'No'," roars Enthusiast. "It will still show us how real Socialism ought to be built!"

INTERROGATION

Today they are asking me to tell them what I know about the training given to Soviet agents for work in the West. I tell them about the special schools for Western Communists, terrorists, Leftists, pacifists and other such scum. I tell them how, not long before my departure, Inspirer mentioned in passing the possibility of trying to assassinate a particular prominent politician. My questioners don't react to this in the slightest. I wonder whether this politician is going to be rubbed out or not? They wake up somewhat only when I begin to tell them about a special diversionary group whose members are being instructed in methods of disrupting the Western banking system. At this point they adjourn the interrogation. Someone else is invited to join us. They ask me to repeat what I have said. Money, of course, is more important than the life of some politician or other.

"The place to study the organization and training of Moscow's agents is here in the West," I say in conclusion. "This is where they work. Everything that happens in secret institutions in Moscow is reflected in one way or another over here."

THE WAY HOME

The soldiers of the Special Amphibious Battalion had paddled up to the bridge and were chatting to the girls. Soldiers and girls are always and everywhere the same in peacetime, but they become qualitatively different when war begins.

It wouldn't be a bad idea to have a drink. But I banish this dream. I've no money. And I shan't get my few kopeks of aid until the day after tomorrow. Tomorrow is going to be a hungry day in the full sense of the word. I must give Writer a ring. He might offer me a meal. I shall have to begin telling him some fairy-tales about Soviet life so that I have some practical value for him. It's funny, he hasn't been out of the Soviet Union for all that long but he has already forgotten everything about it. And he views the facts of Soviet life as a foreigner does.

Then my thoughts jump to today's interrogation. I feel that my interrogators are simply unable to form a firm opinion about me. Why is this? As a professional I know that indeterminacy, fluidity, mutability, block- and multi-think are a peculiarity of Soviet society. It consists of jelly-like units and these form a jelly-like whole. It is a society of chameleons; and so the whole resembles a kind of gigantic chameleon. Yet the Homosos finds something stable and specific in his social environment and in the conjuncture of circumstances. I am a riddle not only for my interrogators, but also for myself, a riddle that is insoluble for the moment because its solution lies in the aggregate of events that will take place over a period of time. I am only a potential, but I have a wide range of possibilities. Comrades and Gentlemen, compete with one another! Who I am depends first of all on *you*!

74

To compare us with chameleons is all right for reassuring sovieto-logues, but nonetheless it's superficial. We have a firm base all the same: our historical mania. And pay attention to this: nothing in history is so durable as something which has no inner foundations, such as a myth, a religion or popular prejudice . . .

ABOUT TERROR

"The Bolsheviks were against individual terrorism," said Inspirer. "Why was that? Because terror had already taken place and done its job: it loosened up the Tsarist regime and prepared the masses for mass terror. When we talk about social revolution, you can't dispense with acts of terror by individuals. Technically, a social coup d'état begins with the elimination of certain kinds of people. Once the West has switched over to Communism we ourselves will stop individual terror and destroy the terrorists. And then we'll arrange our own mass terror. Technically speaking, revolution is the conversion of individual, illegal terrorism into legalized mass terror."

When I remember these little conversations with Inspirer, I am visited by iridescent ideas of developing terrorism in the Soviet Union. For example, what if we sent a couple of qualified specialists from the "Red Brigades" to Moscow? They would quickly be able to get our terrorist training right up to European standards. However, I hadn't managed to think this idea through when, from a distance, I sensed the homeric laughter of Inspirer.

"You are suffering from galloping stupidity," he croaked, almost asphyxiated with laughter. "You've forgotten where these specialists from the Red Brigades and other such organizations get their training! We've got any amount of these specialists. It's just that we don't need them at home. Do you know how many of our own important people die every day just from drink and over-eating? What good are terrorists to us? Take an extreme example: an assassination attempt on Brezhnev. You can put a hundred bullets into him, but that'll get you absolutely nowhere at all. If you like you can skin him and stretch it out over the most primitive robot. It will operate even better than Brezhnev did. Nobody would even notice that he had been assassinated. Things would be just the same as if he hadn't been."

MRS ANTI

Mrs Anti rang and suggested a meeting in a café some ten minutes walk from the *Pension*. I agreed, hoping that she would treat me to something, if only tea or coffee.

Externally Mrs Anti looks very like a well-known Muscovite championess against anti-Communism. But in her convictions she turned out to be the very opposite; a championess *of* anti-Communism. It's an amazing phenomenon: every Soviet crook has his counterpart or mirror-image in the West. And, like that self-important Homunculus in the institute, she began to give me a lecture.

For some time I put up with it. But then I told her that I wasn't used to being talked to like that, that even the KGB showed greater respect towards me, and asked her to shut up. She began to yell at me: now I had shown myself in my true colours (nobody before had ever suggested that I had any). I was simply an agent of Moscow. I asked her to convey that to the people who were interrogating me, because the credulous officials from the counter-espionage services didn't believe that I was an agent of the KGB. And she could add on her own account that I came here not so much to establish Communism, which I don't like (because I've experienced its effect on my own skin), as to destroy capitalism, which I would like to experience, not on my own skin this time but on somebody else's. She understood nothing that I said and promised to expose me in the Press.

Although the tea was steaming enticingly on the little table, I left Mrs Anti in silence, swearing that I would never again have anything to do with genuine anti-Communists. They differ from genuine Communists only by switching round the targets of their malice and stupidity. I wandered about the deserted streets of the well-kept town until midnight. Sometimes I remembered the warnings of my former compatriots that in the West it was dangerous to go out in the evenings because of robbers and murderers. But nobody paid any attention to me. "Where are you, robbers and murderers?" I vainly called. "Come and rob me and cut my throat! If you don't I shall go and cut somebody else's out of sheer misery."

AGENTS REAL AND IMAGINARY

Mrs Anti's threat to expose me publicly as a Soviet agent made me laugh. I knew very well she would never do such a thing because she thinks I am a real agent and not a phoney one. I knew this because I had already discovered a most surprising phenomenon here. For some reason or other they never told me about this in the KGB. Had they really not noticed it? If so, then I had exaggerated their intellectual competence. The phenomenon is this: here they publicly expose as Soviet agents only those people who are guilty of nothing whatsoever. But they don't expose the real agents at all, or they expose them only when they are arrested and brought to trial (which is very rarely); or when, having diplomatic immunity, they are expelled. Why? Because innocent people are more like agents than real agents are. The latter quickly get into the game and begin to behave as their would-be unmaskers would have them behave. The innocent folk go on trying to paddle their own canoe, and this really annoys their unmaskers. It is a dangerous thing to expose real agents, but not to expose innocent people. Cases have been known when real agents sued their unmaskers for libel and won. There are practically no known instances of innocent people taking their "unmaskers" to court. They say there was just one case of this sort, and then the victim of the slander lost.

INTERROGATION

The house where I go from time to time to have a conversation was built in Hitler's time. That's why it's very like the Moscow buildings of the Stalin period. There are three sculptured figures on the façade: a worker, a peasant and a woman with a child. The worker has a hammer, the peasant a scythe. If he'd had a sickle the likeness to Moscow would have been complete. The woman and child symbolize the Motherland. She is cutting corn. Both her hands are full. She doesn't hold her infant at all. The latter clings on to the carotid artery of its mother with its tiny hands. The impression is terrifying.

"What do you think of Western propaganda activity in the Soviet Union?"

"It's done so as to provoke events in the Soviet Union which can be interpreted in the West in a way that justifies the expenditure on the propaganda. So basically the propaganda works in aid of itself."

"But in what way, in your view, should the real effectiveness of our propaganda in the USSR be demonstrated?"

"In events right inside Soviet life, by which I mean unsensational happenings that are often inaccessible to Western observers. The people who have succumbed to the influence of Western propaganda should remain in the Soviet Union; they should live and work in the depths of Soviet society; and they shouldn't count on being noticed or helped by the West."

"Then it won't be possible to assess the work of the people who are involved in the propaganda."

"Shrewd and educated people should take care of that problem; I mean real and trustworthy connoisseurs of Soviet life."

"But where could you get hold of people like that?"

"One could find a few people who are ready to do it now; others can be trained."

"But that's only a handful; at most a few dozen. We need thousands of them."

"To do this work properly, quality is more important that quantity. It's better to have one sensible article read over the radio several times than dozens of rubbishy scripts flashing by and not making any real impact. It's better to send in one book that means something, but really to send it in, and in large quantities, than dozens of wretched products of graphomaniacs that are fit only for the pulping machine."

"This means a tremendous reorganization . . ."

"I don't suggest any reorganization. I am only suggesting that beyond what you've got already, you institute a serious study of Soviet society. In order to inflict some damaging blows on your enemy you must know his authentic nature. Your business is to inflict your blows on your enemy. My business is to study your enemy."

"Which is also your enemy."

"Soviet society is not my enemy. It's only my object of study."

IN THE *PENSION*

In the evening the Pensionnaires gather in front of the TV and look at all the programmes one after another. They think it's the best way of studying a foreign language. You enjoy it and don't need to make any effort. The language goes into you of its own accord. This opinion is only partly true: it is only the language of gestures, mumblings and wails that one assimilates as easily as that. That is why our Pensionnaires are still

78

explaining themselves to the local inhabitants on their fingers. The cleverest ones add all kinds of "ekhs", "ikhs" and "mikhs" and other mooing sounds. Enthusiast, who is the cleverest of all, goes further than the others; he even gestures with his feet in his interesting conversations. What is seen and heard but not understood on the television gives the Pensionnaires subjects for conversations such as the simplistic and sterile Westerner is incapable of. At the moment *Don Giovanni* is on the screen.

"This crap was written donkey's years ago and they're still showing it today," says Whiner.

"Haven't they got sick of it yet?"

"He seduced a couple of girls and there's no end to the fuss," says Cynic. "At school we had a PT instructor. He seduced the whole Staff Committee (in our school almost all the teachers were women). But that sort of thing doesn't matter at all. He also seduced more than a hundred under-age girls. And so what? Not even the wall-newspapers printed a syllable about this. Even when they kicked him out of the Party, it was only under the banal formula, 'because of moral degeneration'. Here in the West all the newspapers and periodicals would be trumpeting about him. They would have put him on television. They would have made a film about him. But in the Union . . ."

"Turn this rubbish [i.e., *Don Giovanni*] off," roars Enthusiast. "Perhaps there's something better on another channel."

On the other programme there is an American thriller. Everybody with one accord expresses delight at this and at the same time indignation that they have missed the beginning. Who switched on that stupid opera? Hanging is too good for him.

INTERROGATION

"The Soviet system is bound to contain vulnerable spots, so that an attack on them could make the whole system explode."

"Certainly it does."

"So we agree. For example, Soviet society is tremendously centralized. Everything is decided by a small group of top leaders. Destroy that group and . . ."

". . . within five minutes you will have another 'small group of top leaders' in its place."

"What can be done then?"

"There are a great many vulnerable spots in Soviet society. But no

79

single blow at any one of them will kill it. Only a simultaneous strike at all the vulnerable places can have the desired effect. And one has to approach them by stealth. This is a task for history and not for a bunch of diversionaries."

"You're evading the question."

"Do you really think that a huge country like that is ruled by 'a small group of top leaders'? All right, let's assume there *is* a small group. But where and when does it meet? Are you convinced that the Soviet authorities don't bear in mind the existence of such, er, thinkers as you? Soviet society possesses a mighty system of power and administration. It has an amazing ability to restore quickly any organs and links in the chain of power that have been destroyed. Even if you wipe out half the population, the first thing that will be restored in the remaining half will be the system of power and administration. There, power is not organized to serve the population: the population is organized as material required for the functioning of power.

WE

"When I started my work in the KGB," said Inspirer, "my boss never stopped beating one idea into our heads: 'anything you like, but not terrorism'. For a certain time we can even permit small political organizations to exist. But we mustn't allow even one terroristic act. If that sort of thing gets out of our control you can give the conquests of the revolution up for lost. That's why we must keep all individual terrorism firmly in our own hands."

"Well, you certainly slipped up over the attempt to assassinate Brezhnev,* didn't you?" I asked.

"We prepared everything in the best possible manner," he said, "but at the last moment . . . That operation was a trifle. But the fact that we almost let the Armenian group** through . . . That was rather more serious. And it was pure chance that saved the day."

---

*The Lieutenant Ilin case in 1969.
**The "Metro" explosion in January, 1977.

THE WEST

A woman comes on the television. She is seventy-five years old. When she was sixty-five she took up karate. She wanted to be able to defend herself against possible rapists (there had been many cases of rape in her district). After one year's training she could defend herself against one rapist, after five years against two; and now she can defend herself against three. In ten years' time she hopes to attain such mastery that even five rapists won't be able to get the better of her. We were all delighted with this. Nobody asked whether she had had a chance to apply her skills at karate in real life.

THE IDEA OF A CENTRE

They are talking about creating a centre to unite the whole emigration. "It's an old idea of the KGB," said Joker, "but everyone's mulling it over as if it were brand new. It would be much better to open a restaurant on the Soviet model. Let's call it 'Chez Lenin'. It would be nice to say 'Let's go to Lenin's place'; 'we were round at Lenin's'. And it wouldn't be clear which Lenin one had in mind. It would be nice for the Lenin of today.* The latest Lenin himself could order someone to help us to get it started. And service would be in the Soviet style, with slogans on the walls: 'Eat what you're given'; 'If you don't like it, don't eat it'; 'There's a lot of you; I'm single-handed'; 'You can't please everybody'; 'Well, you asked for it'; 'You're the fool, not me'; 'I'm listening to a lout'. But to be serious, the only way to unite the Soviet emigration is on a pro-Soviet basis."

"You think," I said, "that we are the only clever people around here? Do you think that those who put the idea of a centre into the heads of the masses don't understand that as well as we do? I'm ready to bet that this idea was thoroughly thrashed out in the Lubyanka and the Committee of Intellectual Advisers before they let it out into circulation."

"And what is this Committee of Intellectual Advisers?" he asked.

"The fruit of my imagination," I said.

* An allusion to a term used of every current top Soviet leader.

WOMEN

I badly need a woman. It's not a matter of physiology. I need a woman not so much for her body as for her soul. In order to be able to talk with full mutual understanding, to pour out my soul and to get the feeling of solidarity. Incidentally, we were very spoilt in this respect in the Soviet Union. Nowhere else can you find such a number of women who understand you and are capable of feeling what you're feeling. Here I'm not the only man in this state. Whiner is incessantly begging me to find him a woman. He says it's so miserable to be alone and that women understand you. I told him that there were many body-satisfying women around, but none who could satisfy our souls. We might as well give up all hope of that.

THE EDIFICE

From the window of my room I can see an impressive building going up. I cannot guess what they're building, so I call the building under construction simply "the Edifice". It consists of a multitude of grey concrete cylinders and whimsically placed equally grey concrete angular blocks. No signs of windows or doors. That means The Edifice is not for living in. It's the first time I've seen such absurd architecture. "So that's what they call development!" I said to myself, feeling rather superior to the bloated West. "Even in our country they couldn't think up such rubbishy things as that."

IN MY OWN TRAP

In Moscow I had to deal with problems affecting large numbers of people. Thousands of human destinies came to my attention, most of them distressing ones. But I am an easy-going man by nature, and other people's dramas disappeared behind columns of figures, diagrams and conventional signs. The percentage of people expelled from their collective for drunkenness who have resettled themselves in a normal collective is such and such. The percentage which has taken up full-time professional crime is such and such. The majority of marriages are dissolved . . . The number . . . The degree . . . And that's it. Now I feel to the marrow of my bones what it's like to be a totally insignificant little unit in other people's cold-blooded calculations.

It's all so simple. There *is* a mystery to it, but it's one for the experimenters from the special services. For the guinea-pigs there are no mysteries whatever. And so one is only a digit in a mass process, not an agent with a special task of his own. It's humiliating, but still, if that's how things are, I'll have to behave like an insignificant little digit.

To hell with your great aims! I shall live for myself and only for myself. Having come to this decision, I remembered the ABC of my own profession: once you are a mere digit in a mass phenomenon, anything you do that seems to you to be a manifestation of individuality has been allowed for in the calculations of the organizers of this mass phenomenon. In principle you cannot tell Them to go to hell because even this "to-helling" of yours has been taken into account beforehand and is part of your "individual" task. You can behave as you wish. But all the same your behaviour will be grist to Their mill, because there are thousands of people like you; and when you are all taken together you do what They intend you to do. And They need only what they get as the result of your activity in the mass. You've fallen into your own trap. Remember how you put a plan before Inspirer for sending to the West a few tens of thousands of people, chosen at random, who would play all the logically conceivable roles for us? Then it was "for *us*". You were naïve. They turned out to be capable of handling several *hundreds* of thousands of such people.

A TALK WITH CHIEF

"Of course you've read the appeal of the leaders of your emigration that you should all unite?"

"Of course I haven't read it."

"But what do you think about it?"

"Nothing worthwhile will come of it."

"But how can you judge this in advance?"

"The purpose of science is to judge in advance. I know the human material and the general principles of organization."

"That's clear. Couldn't you define a Soviet man in a few words?"

"I can. He's an educated man. Any educated man is, as a type, at least a potential Homosos."

"You talk in riddles."

"On the contrary. I provide solutions to what may be riddles. The most perfect examples of the Homosos come from the most educated part of Soviet society. The broad masses of the people haven't yet grown to the stature of the real Homosos. It's possible that they will never attain such heights. There's no need. All that's needed is that the kernel of Soviet society should become homososized. But then the educated strata of Western society are hardly inferior to the Soviet Homosos."

THE COLLECTIVE

The Homosos's biggest loss is his separation from the collective. I hardly feel the loss of my relations and friends, my Moscow flat or the privileges of my professional position. But the fact that I've lost my collective torments me day and night. Not necessarily my last laboratory or my last institute but one, but any of our (my) very own collectives. Our involvement in the life of a collective in almost all the important and unimportant areas of our life: *that* is the foundation of our psychology. The soul of the Homosos lies in his participation in collective life.

Even the ideological processing which we protest about so often looks different from over here. It looks like a means of involving the individual in collective life. Ideology unifies the individual consciousness and unites millions of little "I"'s into one huge "We".

Even rebellion against Soviet society takes place within a collective framework. It is usually a rebellion within the collective and not one aiming at separation from the collective. The most powerful weapon against rebels in our society is exclusion from the collective. When rebels are thrown out of normal collectives they are unable to create stable and coherent collectives in their place, not so much because of the authorities' vetoes and repressions as because of the rebels' isolation from the conditions of normal collective life. You get no wages in an illegal collective; you can't make a career in one; you won't get higher qualifications; you won't improve your living conditions. In a word, you won't get any of the positive things that you get in a normal Soviet collective. At the same time you will get a bellyful of all the negative ones that any collective is bound to provide.

That is the viewpoint from which I myself took part in devising methods to be used against oppositionists, rebels, dissidents, critics and other phenomena of that kind. Some of my brain-work too found its way into the instruction manual that regulates the work of the Central Committee and KGB officials as well as that of the leaders of healthy

Soviet collectives. In general, the best minds in Soviet society don't go into the opposition but into the struggle against the opposition.

Here abroad there are organizations that are very like Soviet collectives, but only in their worst features, not their best ones. They don't give the individual that sense of being protected and the human warmth which he finds in Soviet collectives. Here mercenary interests are stronger and keener. People are colder and more merciless. It may sound comic to say so, but here, alas, there is no Party organization: the highest form of democracy within a collective. I want to attend a Party meeting. I want to volunteer for work on my Saturday off. I'm even ready to do a spot of physical labour in a vegetable depot and go out to a collective farm to lift the potatoes . . ."

THE ABSTRACT, AND THE REAL, COLLECTIVE

Seen in the abstract, the primary, basic collective of Communist society is something that is rational to the highest degree; it is the very apogee of the dreams of the best representatives of the human race. But in its concrete incarnation this abstract ideal looks somewhat different. For example, the head of a group of ten colleagues is a perfectly natural phenomenon. But equally natural is the fact that he uses his position for mercenary ends. The man who took me on to work in his group when I left the university was a total nonentity in the field of science and a pretty base operator in his day-to-day activities. For three years I did his donkey-work in return just for a promise to help me to get a little article of mine into print under my own name. In order to become a senior research officer I had to publish a monograph, quite short, perhaps, but all the same it had to be a separate brochure or a book. What it cost me to get some twenty articles into print before this I do not care to remember. For this reason alone one could come to hate Soviet society in spite of all its advantages. When it got to the monograph stage, real hell began. Twice my work was rejected by the academic councils. Moreover, the people who rejected it were people who were considered to be my good friends and acquaintances. Finally I decided to play a trick: I had the booklet printed in a provincial town, giving my whole fee away as a bribe to the people who fixed the publication.

In the end I broke through the barriers and became a senior research officer. What didn't it cost me to do this? If God offered me a re-run of my life I would say "No" just to avoid a repeat performance of this period of hacking my way through to promotion. And what did my tiny cooperative flat cost me? Even people who knew me well, who had fixed themselves up with splendid flats, regarded me as a scoundrel over that. Perhaps I did behave like a scoundrel over the flat. But after all, one has to live somewhere.

I feel simultaneously offended, saddened and amused when my interrogators here in the West class me among the Soviet *priviligentsia*. All right, I'm a member of the Party. I'm a senior research officer. I had personal friends in the official apparatus of the Central Committee and the KGB. Some of them were people in high positions. What more does a man need than that? When I look at these well-fed idiots of interrogators here, all so pleased with themselves, I want to bury them under the rubble of the three-storeyed Russian swearing-system. But then I see that it is quite useless trying to explain anything to them at all. You want to class me as a *priviligent*, I think. All right, go ahead! I have no objection. I shan't bother to try to get justice here. I know what justice on earth is like. The justest institution in the world is the good old Soviet working collective. I have felt its merciless vulpine justice on my own skin. So is it likely that I shall look for justice here in your hypocritical West?!

When I agreed to emigrate I hoped in the depths of my soul to be able to break away from the deadly, friendly embraces of the Soviet collective. But here in the West I experienced the embraces of other collectives which differed from the Soviet ones only in that they lacked the latters' merits. Having wrenched myself from my own odious family in my native land, I am forced here to join a family which is similarly odious, but completely alien. I am doing my utmost to avoid this new family and stay on my own like a wolf under nobody's control. How will it all end? I am afraid that having got away from the pack I shall be easy prey for the hunters. I can already see the small red flags of the beaters and hear the cries of my pursuers.

PULLING OFF THE MASK

Official opinion has it that a socially healthy Homosos is incapable of behaviour of the type that creates an extreme situation. And if he did act in that way that means he was unhealthy and merely pretending to be healthy. And then the collective has to unmask him. It must pull the mask off his face, put him against the wall and show him up for what he is.

I have been through this process of being "unmasked". All my innocent little transgressions of the past were brought into play. Before, I was considered a man who knew how to drink and have a fling with the girls. So now it's obvious: I'm a drunkard and a debauchee. Before, I was considered badly off as regards living conditions; a loser who could only get himself a miserable little flat, and that only with the greatest difficulty. Now it's as clear as daylight: I'm a string-puller and a swindler.

The Homosos who commits actions that are potentially blameworthy but hasn't yet landed up in an "unmasking" situation doesn't feel himself to be morally deficient. But when he does find himself in one, he begins to feel a bit of a cad, even if he's convinced of his innocence. I knew that my own unmasking process was only a bit of theatre. But all the same I felt it to be genuine. And it *was* genuine, because all the actors played their roles correctly and naturally. Once he has felt himself morally vulnerable in such a situation, the Homosos can no longer get rid of the feeling. So I was mortally wounded. And I doubt whether I will ever recover from this wound.

CYNIC

Cynic came to the West intending to set himself up comfortably, take a look at the world and become a millionaire. In the Soviet Union he was a brilliant "organizer" and had everything that his heart desired. But he longed for more. Even when he was living in Moscow he transferred his valuables to the West. While doing this he fell into the clutches of an even more brilliant "organizer" who took his shirt off him. From that moment he came to hate Soviet émigrés, especially if they were dissidents, since he considered them to be responsible for the emigration epidemic.

"Here everybody bids up his own value," he says, "and turns himself into something higher than he was in the USSR. A KGB lieutenant pretends he was a major; a hopelessly uninspired employee of the journal *The Godless* passes himself off as an important academic; a tenth-rate scribbler claims to be a leading writer; and a technical assistant of an official of the Central Committee makes himself out to be a member of the Central Committee. And the West itself helps to blow up the importance of all this émigré small fry. Why?"

"It's flattering for Westerners to have dealings with high Soviet officials. And the West wants to believe that the Soviet regime is being destroyed from within."

87

"Why did you leave? In Moscow you were living in clover! In your place I would ask to go back."

"Don't be in too much of a hurry to bury me. Who knows, maybe I'll still get a house, a couple of cars, a harem of black- and yellow-skinned mistresses and my own yacht in a warm ocean . . ."

"I understand. Of course a man like you wouldn't have left without good reason. You're doing the right thing. No point in selling oneself on the cheap."

ENTHUSIAST

They threw Enthusiast out to the West with one idea in mind: the West would see with its own eyes what these human-rights merchants are really like. But for the time being it's not so much the West that is looking at Enthusiast, it's me. The West looks at him only when it wants to look at this emanation of Soviet society; that is to say, when Enthusiast has washed, shaved and changed his linen; when he has got the "theses" of his latest declaration all ready—theses that the West wants to hear; and when Enthusiast himself wishes, as they say, to display himself and his wares before the public. I see him as a rule when I don't want to see him, when he makes his spontaneous and quite uncontrollable appearances. There's not a hope of hiding from him; he'll chase you up the stairs and follow you into the lavatory. And he roars for all in the entire *Pension* to hear that he can't agree with me, that I am mistaken (although as a matter of fact I don't make any assertions at all), and that my position is the position of the KGB.

But this is evidently divine retribution. Once upon a time I had occasion to take part in consultations on the dissident movement. I offered some thoughts of my own. I wanted to show off and so I expressed an idea that could have got me into a good deal of trouble. In every stable society, I said, the opposition's psychological, moral and intellectual qualities are on a par with those of the ruling circles of that society. Consequently, although I don't know any dissidents personally, I can say in advance what they're like (at this point titters and hissing began to be heard). Feeling that I had gone a bit too far, I tried to wriggle out of it as best I could. Therefore, I continued, a very effective means of struggling against our dissident movement would be to select some typical specimens and pack them off to the West. The West would see them in the flesh, realize what frightful dung they were (more laughter in the hall), and interest in Soviet dissidents would decline.

Sometimes Enthusiast seems an unfortunate and defenceless being, cast by cruel forces into an unknown world. But having actually watched closely how he does the round of all the institutes, extracting from them what he "deserves", how he travels all over Europe inveigling young people into his crazy designs, I see him as a real Soviet creature who gets his way by demagogy, lying, flattery, anger, tears and pestering. Soviet people go through such a strenuous training in go-getting, extortion, brow-beating, artful dodgery, and so on that for them the West isn't a battlefield at all, simply a walk-over.

In Moscow Enthusiast had his own narrow speciality among the dissidents: he portrayed himself as a genuine Socialist. When the Euro-communists came on the scene he attached himself to them. Then he was chucked out to the West as a specimen of Soviet Eurocommunism. Let the West have a glimpse of this Eurocommunism in monstrous carica-ture, that is, let them see what it's really like! When he got to the West, Enthusiast counted on being the darling of the leaders of the Western Communist parties. They ignored him; they had plenty of Eurocommu-nists of their own and didn't need an extra one in the shape of a Soviet paranoiac. He took offence and began to abuse the Eurocommunists for misinterpreting their own Eurocommunism.

But in the West it's simply impossible to think up any nonsense that doesn't pick up *some* supporters. Enthusiast soon found some. They pay for his journeys throughout Europe, they arrange contacts for him and they lobby for him to get him his own periodical. He needs a periodical urgently. He has something to tell the world. "A periodical," he cries indefatigably, "if only I had a periodical. I'd give half my life for a periodical. It's the basic link. When we've seized it we can pull out the whole chain. Lenin too began like this."

One morning Enthusiast went out to negotiate with Mrs Anti. "Very clever woman," he burbled joyously, so that the whole *Pension* could hear. "And her periodical isn't bad at all. It's too anti-Communist, but this can be put right. We'll break her in."

Late that evening Enthusiast came back to the *Pension*, deflated and gloomy. "She's a fool," he muttered limply. "She's categorically opposed to any kind of Communism. I asked her why we should reject a just and good Communism. And the bitch kept sounding off: 'The juster and better Communism is, the worse it is.' Where's the logic in that?"

I've got quite used to Enthusiast and can no longer imagine existence without him. When he goes off to his conferences and meetings I pine for him and await his return. And when he comes back he almost throws himself on my neck for joy.

"It's a shameful thing to have to confess, but we don't really know the basic mechanisms of the Soviet system, although we've lived in it for decades. For example, how is the district committee of the Party made up and how does it work? I don't dare mention the Central Committee."

"Would you like me to describe it?"

"I'm afraid that wouldn't help me. To describe it in a work of literature it's not enough to know about it from hearsay. One must feel it and live it oneself."

"Why don't you write about the emigration? It's all there before you. And you're living in the thick of it."

"But what's the point of that? If one shows that the emigration is bad that'll all be grist to the Soviet propaganda-mill. But if one says it's good, one will be lying. And it's not so easy to get published. Do you know who's the main enemy of the Soviet émigré in the West? Another Soviet émigré who got here earlier. The West has to share out the same amount of attention and goods among an ever greater number of claimants.

"And our position is especially bad. A mass of mediocrities has poured out of the Soviet Union, all pretending to be geniuses. And the first thing they do is try to extinguish the sparks of real talent among their own people. In general, this emigration is a dictatorship of duds. I came here thinking that Russian writers would welcome me. 'Well, our numbers have grown,' they would say, 'and we'll now surely beat our common enemy even harder.' Not a bit of it. There is no common enemy. There are only personal enemies. The enemy is always the one who is closest to you and the immediate threat or hindrance to your well-being. When I left Moscow, I counted on success and well-being here. But what from Moscow looked like success turned out in reality to be like a tarted-up harridan. All the chances of being published or getting some kind of publicity had already been cornered by scoundrels like me who had arrived here earlier."

KNOWING HOW AND UNDERSTANDING

Writer had lived his life in Soviet society without understanding anything about its mechanics. He isn't an exception. It is one thing to be able to live in a society and to know something about it for the purpose of living. It's another matter to understand that society's mechanics. It is an interesting fact that it's the current critics of Soviet society who have the stupidest conceptions of it. They regard everything that official Soviet science says as lies and by that very fact condemn themselves to utter even bigger lies. Homososes don't need to understand the mechanics of their society, because to understand that doesn't help them to live better in it. What they need is *not* to understand it, for that justifies their behaviour, which is already conditioned by their circumstances.

INTERROGATION

"How is it possible to get some terrorism going in the Soviet Union?"

"It's very simple. You slip some arms into the country, and especially explosives. You teach people how to use the arms and make bombs. Then you provide transport, flats, private houses, documents, stocks of food and all sorts of other things. You abolish the pass-system throughout the country and the obligation to have an official job. Naturally you abolish the death penalty, introduce Western legal practice and improve the conditions for prisoners. When you have done all that there will be no lack of people volunteering to take part in terrorism."

"But if you were to give a serious answer?"

"I'm perfectly serious. Do you know what the basic difference between the Soviet Union and the West is, in regard to terrorism? Here they are struggling against terrorism; there they are struggling against the possibility of its beginning. Here they are curing the disease, there they are practising prophylaxis. And do you know what enrages Soviet émigrés most about the West? Terrorism."

HOMO SOVIETICUS

There is a conference at the university on the subject: Homo Sovieticus. They invited all us Pensionnaires to go along. Why? Whiner was surprised. "As a visual aid," said Joker. He was dead right. The speakers vied with each other in telling us what Soviet man was. They produced quotations, they showered us with figures, facts and names. They showed in every possible way how clever and high-minded they were in comparison with that stupid and disgusting creature called Soviet man. Then they asked us to give our opinions. They pushed me forward as the only Pensionnaire who could speak German.

"I," I said, "am a characteristic example of the miserable and disgusting species which you are pleased to call Soviet man. I am flattered by the characterization you have given us. In reality, gentlemen, we are much worse. We were clever enough in our time to destroy a mighty state created by representatives of the highest race, *homo sapiens*, and to create our own mighty state from fear of which you here, if you will excuse the expression, have long since dirtied your trousers. We, gentlemen, are altogether more dangerous than you think. And do you know why? We are not such idiots as you would have us be. And the main point is that we are capable of losing things not only at others' expense but at our own expense too."

I didn't get any applause. I went "home" all alone. "Idiot," I said to myself, "it's high time you realized that these people want to promote a false picture of Soviet man because it keeps them in business. And truth doesn't provide anyone with a good job. It only causes suffering to those who strive to attain it and arouses malice in those to whom the truth-seeker appeals. Join the Orthodox Church or get yourself circumcised while there's still time. And agree with everything that the Western smart Alecs say about us."

INTERROGATION

"What are the motives which induce Soviet émigrés in the West to become KGB agents? What per cent of émigrés are KGB agents? What kind of tasks are they given?"

"For professional KGB operatives a job in the West is a comparatively good job. People compete for Western assignments. As for ordinary citizens, they agree to be KGB agents for a variety of reasons. A strict generalization isn't possible. Some do it simply because they are Soviet people to the marrow of their bones. Others, in order to get out to the West. A third group does it 'just in case'.

"I know one émigré who offered to become a KGB agent because he was afraid that the Soviet armies would soon arrive in Western Europe. It's impossible to assess the number of KGB agents among the Soviet emigration. The majority don't regard themselves formally as agents because they haven't signed any undertaking. They gave their agreement orally, and in many cases indirectly, by hints. Besides, the KGB is in principle able to make use of *any* émigré for its own purposes. Even enemies of the Soviet regime. For example, the KGB gets important information by permitting correspondence and telephone conversations between émigrés and their friends and relations in the USSR. And the very fact that correspondence and conversations are allowed plays its role, as it sows suspicion of co-operation with the KGB."

"What do you know about the assignments given to KGB agents who come to the West as émigrés?"

"The chief task of all of them is to penetrate Western society and find some means of subsistence in it. Some agents have specific tasks. For example, N was told to present the current Soviet leadership as the most liberal and peace-loving one possible and to spread the legend that it contains certain 'hawks' who supposedly want to restore Stalinism. M was sent on a much more serious personal mission. He had to arrange a system for the regular supply of foreign goodies to middle-rank KGB and Central Committee officials: leather jackets, jeans, sheepskin coats and contraceptives. He has been quite good at getting this operation going."

"What specifically is your own concrete task?"

"I was sort of allowed full freedom of action. But, to be frank, so far I myself am not quite clear about what I'm meant to be doing here. When there are only a few agents, their activities are strictly prescribed. But when there are many that isn't necessary. Then there's no need to hold an agent to a strictly defined line of behaviour. Then you get a mass of agents who are behaving in all sorts of different ways and you simply choose suitable individuals for particular tasks; and any kind of behaviour by any agent can be regarded as being of some potential use."

"What have you decided to do yourself?"

"I've decided to tell you who I am and to ask you to help me to get a job here and make use of my professional abilities."

"And what guarantee can you give us that you won't be working for the KGB?"

"How *can* I give you a guarantee? Tell me how!"

A TALK WITH WRITER

"You have too low an opinion of people. Are we all such nonentities? Are we all just digits in other people's calculations? Surely we each have our individual destiny? And surely we can contribute to our destiny just a little bit by our own efforts?"

"Mass processes are unconcerned *a priori* with individuality. Actors of real worth cannot take part in a nauseating spectacle. Whoever these actors are, they are bound to play a pathetic role."

"I can't agree. For instance, I have been fighting a battle tooth and nail now for many years. And I've won it."

"That's all part of the game. To compel strong people to fight tooth and nail over trifles and against trifles—that's one of the principles of the system."

"It's humiliating. And I could be of the greatest use to Russia, you know, if the authorities would make some use of me."

"They're already using you."

"What d'you mean?"

"Inasmuch as they've made it plain that they don't want to use you."

"I don't understand. Explain what you mean."

"I'm sorry, I can't. I don't understand it myself."

"We've all gone mad. I've got a friend here, also an émigré. He's been here for six years. He doesn't speak a word of German, but he's begun to speak Russian with a German accent. Isn't that funny?"

"Very. But mine host at our *Pension* now has a perfect knowledge of Russian swear-words. He swears all day long, especially in the company of women. Now is *that* funny?"

"Very."

THE EDIFICE

The mysterious building grows higher every day. But one can't see any people working on it. And one doesn't see any building materials arrive. The building just seems to be growing from within, out of the earth, like a living being. Mighty and terrible. Mysterious cylinders reminiscent of the towers of mediaeval castles have already risen higher than all the other buildings in our district. Every day now I go to the window to see how much my Edifice has grown. As yet I cannot guess its purpose, although I've gone through all the possible alternatives, from prisons to palaces of culture and churches.

INTERROGATION

"What do you know about the Institute of Social Prognosis?"

"Some of my friends work there. From what they said I could get only a very general idea of the ISP. I had a chance to get a job there, but I turned it down."

"Why?"

"The people who work in ISP have access to the most secret matters and automatically become 'people who don't go abroad'. In those days they occasionally let me out. And I wanted to travel. Besides, ISP officials are forbidden to publish their work, while I hoped to make a name for myself in science."

"And did you succeed?"

"No. I did my research elsewhere, but even so the results were immediately classified. I could only publish material that fitted into the framework of our ideology. You don't make a name for yourself in science by doing that."

"Right, but all the same you did manage to learn something about the ISP. What was it?"

"Initially this institute was planned as a research centre within the Academy of Social Sciences attached to the Central Committee of the CPSU. It was given the job of investigating the general trends of mankind's development in our times and of predicting them in the next century. But the CC Ideology Secretary said that Marxism had solved this problem definitively long ago and there was no reason to waste resources by setting up an institute which couldn't say anything new on the subject anyway. It was then that the KGB became interested in the institute."

"In what sense?"

"During the next war the most complicated problems will be social ones—the problems of organizing life in the West European countries we have conquered (conquest being taken for granted). So somebody has to work out now all the possible ways in which we could act after our victory in Western Europe. We have to bear in mind the lessons of the Germans and be ready to work with clock-work precision, but keeping all the possible variants in view."

"What variants did they have in mind?"

"Different variants for different countries and their diverse conditions after defeat or devastation. They introduced the concept of a 'sociological' type of situation to be subjected to organization. Several abstract behaviour-models were hammered out. As regards specific parts of Europe, a system of criteria was elaborated to assess their condition and immediately bring into action the appropriate organizational variant. Moreover, both the evaluative criteria and the organizational variants had to be fairly simple. Simple enough, for example, to allow a commanding general or the representative of the High Command to take and implement decisions. The success of the operation could depend literally on a margin of hours."

95

"How far could these ISP investigations have got at the present time?"

"No distance at all, I would imagine."

"What do you mean?"

"It's very simple. Any hopes that one can make scientific discoveries in the sphere of predicting the future are without foundation. First of all, in the Soviet Union predictions about the future are the prerogative of the highest Party authorities, and so scientific small fry are simply not allowed to make any discoveries in this area. Secondly, the Party authorities don't predict the future, they plan it. It is in principle impossible to predict the future, but it can be planned. After all, in some measure and in some form, history is the attempt to correspond to a plan. Here it's like the five-year plans: they are always fulfilled as a guide to action, but never as predictions.

"The problem is not what is going to happen but what should be done to force history to follow the course we want."

"Well, what sort of results can there be when it comes to planning the future?"

"In the Soviet Union there are lots of brilliant boys who are ready to work miracles for minimal remuneration. But in practice these miracles will hardly enter the equation."

"Why not?"

"Because they are carried out for infinitesimal remuneration. And the people who get the big money are all worthless hacks."

MEMORY

Suddenly it seemed to me that I was walking down a street in Moscow. Moscow . . . The greyest and most boring city in the world. The most cruel and the most hopeless. And the nearest and dearest. The future of mankind. A disgusting future, but the future all the same: the one that is going to replace the West's brilliant and dynamic past. But am I not passing off my personal discomfiture in the West as the future fate of the West itself? It would be good if that were so. But I fear that it isn't. The present state of the West is, in all respects, the acme of everything that humanity can attain; it is the living exception to dead historical monotony. Now the road can only go downhill, only get worse, only revert to the usual old monotony. To preserve the West's present condition for as long as one can, that is problem number one for . . . for whom? However strange this may be, it is the number one problem for us, the Homososes.

In Moscow I had a flat that was perfectly all right by Moscow tandards. When I got it I was at the peak of human happiness, and I topped dreaming of any improvement in my living conditions. It was the ltimate in what I could possibly expect of life. For two years I revelled in ny happiness. Two whole years. How much alcohol we drank in that flat, ow many words were spoken, how many ideas were rethought! Only wo years in all. And now it's all over, for ever.

In Moscow I had many friends who were ready at any time to keep me ompany and drink and talk with me. In Moscow there were people who umped ideas out of me, used them and knew what they were worth. Maybe they used them for themselves and not for me. But to give omething to people, that too is life. Whereas here I have only chance nd transient companions. And nobody here wants to exploit my intellect. As soon as people who could do that lay bare the muscles of my mind, they somehow take fright and disappear. And yet it's now that I have matured to such a degree that I could cram a whole academy of ciences with my ideas.

My cigarettes are finished. I must cadge one. But the city has metaphorically died on me. Well, why not break open a vending machine? I remember the words of one of my mentors from the KGB: no criminal activity. It would be a disgrace if you came a cropper over a packet of cigarettes. I made a solemn pact: I would sell my soul to the first person who offered me a cigarette. A single cigarette. But nobody came along anxious to take possession of the soul of a Soviet man.

In my dreams I saw a completely empty town. I was looking for a human being, anyone. It seemed to me that there were people over there in that building. I went in. Nobody. Perhaps there will be someone around that corner. No one . . .

MEDITATIONS ON THE BRIDGE

I stand on the bridge and watch. Far away the soldiers of the Special Amphibious Battalion in their bright orange life-jackets are blowing up their rubber dinghies. To judge by their gestures they are uttering sounds. But these sounds are drowned in the wails of the gulls and the Mephistophelian quacking guffaws of the ducks. Feeding the latter are former Nazi criminals and future victims of Communist criminals.

The soldiers embark and drift down to the bridge. They know me already. They shout something, laugh and wave their arms. "Greetings, soldiers of the Special Amphibious Battalion," I shout in reply, and greet them with something like a "Heil", raising my arm. "Have a good time,

my dears. Soon our soldiers will arrive and puncture your rubbe:
dinghies. Although your little river is knee-high to a grasshopper the
will drown you in your life-jackets like kittens. Let me join your regimen
and I will teach you what you need to have in order to give those Sovie
soldiers a drubbing."

"Well, tell me what it is, if it isn't a secret," says a mocking voice
behind my back.

"You need to have only one thing; and that's to have nothing."

"Oh, so we're a philosopher, are we?"

"No, just a Soviet émigré."

The man muttered something and vanished into thin air. Judging from
his age, he had already got it in the neck once from some Soviet soldiers.

However, my warlike mood soon changed into sober pessimism. Even
though the West seems chaotic, frivolous and defenceless, all the same
Moscow will never achieve worldwide supremacy. Moscow can defend
itself against any opponent. Moscow can deliver a knock-out blow on the
West. Moscow has the wherewithal to mess up the whole planet. But it
has no chance of becoming the ruler of the world. To rule the world one
must have at one's disposal a sufficiently great nation. That nation must
feel itself to be a nation of rulers. And when it comes to it, one that can
rule in reality. In the Soviet Union the Russians are the only people who
might be suited to that role. They are the foundation and the bulwark of
the empire. But they don't possess the qualities of a ruling nation. And in
the Soviet empire their situation is more like that of being a colony for all
the other peoples in it.

Until the Russian people become the best educated, the most cultured, the most prosperous and the most privileged within the country,
there can be no thought of world hegemony. More than that, once the
Russian people have really become the most privileged and dominant
nation in the country, they will still have to outclass the other peoples in
all the most important non-military spheres of life. And for this decades
will be needed, if not centuries. Whereas the actual position of the
Russians in the Soviet Union is that they are not even allowed equality
with the other peoples, let alone pre-eminence. Incidentally, those
Russians who have somehow raised themselves above their fellow-
nationals will not permit the regeneration of Russia as a nation. In short,
so I summed up my reflections, one can construct supremely felicitous
plans, but one can't implement them because of a trifle that seemed
hardly worthy of attention. Even before the war, my father told me this
story. In some institution a routine meeting was in progress. There were
two points on the agenda: 1) the construction of a barn; 2) the creation of
an abundance of consumer goods under Communism. As they didn't

have enough planks to build the barn, they moved on at once to the second question. Moscow would be able to build a grandiose world-empire. But alas, it doesn't have the planks to do it with.

IN THE *PENSION*

In the *Pension* there was a holiday mood. Enthusiast had been laid off by his beloved charlady. The reason he was sacked was that the charlady had increased the charges for her services because of inflation. But Enthusiast had refused to satisfy his charlady's legitimate demands. Cynic said that Enthusiast had committed an unpardonable error, because now he would have to spend even more on prostitutes. *They* had doubled their charges, whereas the charlady had only put hers up by 50 per cent. Enthusiast realized that he had been a fool and rushed out to try to put the matter right. But it was too late, the charlady had already given the vacancy to an émigré from Poland. Cynic said that that was her way of expressing solidarity with Solidarity. After all, the West was struggling against the Soviet threat. Enthusiast, in a state of fury, swore at the American President, the West German Chancellor and the Pope of Rome.

WE AND THE WEST

I saw in the newspapers a portrait of one of the most disgusting of the Soviet leaders. I couldn't overcome my curiosity and broke my vow never to have anything to do with the Western Press. It turned out that this devil incarnate had died. He died simply from old age, but in the papers there were suggestions that he had perhaps been helped on his way. They called him a "genius of behind-the-scenes manipulations in the Kremlin". In fact, he was an outstanding nonentity and mediocrity. I had dealings with him myself more than once and did some work for him. The newspapers were naming as possible successors certain senile characters for whom it was also high time to leave this world. They are all getting on for eighty. The papers attributed outstanding executive qualities to these sclerotic personages as well, albeit in the service of evil. They made guesses about imminent changes in the leadership and in "the policies of the Kremlin".

What is the reason for such monstrous mistakes that Westerners make when they evaluate the phenomena of our life? The reason is that they measure our life too according to their own yardstick. And in addition they don't want to recognize the fact that the leaders in Moscow, the most primitive people in history, are systematically making a fool of them. If a man of genius, however evil, wraps you around his little finger, that is understandable. It is excusable. One can even be proud of the fact, saying, well our type of morality simply doesn't allow us to sink to that level. But that one should be duped not even by a man but only by a primitive social function dressed in anthropomorphic guise, that just cannot be. And the result is that Party officials of the most primitive type intellectually—Stalin, Khrushchev, Brezhnev, Suslov, Gromyko and so forth—are transformed in the eyes of the West into geniuses of evil. They may well be evil; but they certainly aren't geniuses.

MEMORY

"For a time you will be in a state of helplessness and despair," my friends in Moscow told me. "But that will quickly pass." I believed my mentors. For them I wasn't the first or the last. They know their business with all the confidence of arithmetic textbooks for beginners. If only the KGB's arithmetic had worked out right for me! If only the despair and help-lessness would pass! If only clarity would come! Any kind of clarity. The speculative kind, the adventurous, the philistine, the amoral, the criminal, the decent, the double-faced. I am tired of waiting for it.

"I am glad for you," Inspirer said. "Live as you please. Seize the moment. We haven't got so long left to live."

"Then why don't you yourself set off for this Western paradise?" I asked.

"It's out of the question," he sighed. "I'm doomed to stay here. Incidentally, I can't even go on a tourist trip to Siberia or the Urals. Only to strictly specified sanatoria. Only special dachas. I am shadowed even in public lavatories."

ABOUT THE NEXT WAR

"After the First World War it looked as though the next one would be chemical and that all humanity would perish from poison gases," said Inspirer. "But it wasn't a chemical war. And humanity didn't perish: it almost doubled itself. Now it seems that the Third World War will be nuclear and that all humanity will perish from nuclear bombs and radiation. But it won't be a nuclear war. And humanity will remain intact. And most likely it will multiply even more. Why won't the war be nuclear? Because it isn't to our advantage that it should be nuclear. And so we won't allow it to be nuclear. We will unleash on the world the type of war that will be advantageous to us. And our opponent will fall for it. These aren't hypotheses or the ravings of a madman. We have applied all our resources to this problem. In principle we have already solved it. We just need a few more years to be completely certain. That is why we are struggling so fiercely for peace."

"Nevertheless," continued Inspirer, "the next war will be a war of masses of people against other masses of people, and not simply technology against technology. In war the human being will always remain the main weapon, because it is he who bears the weapons. The main theatre of operations will still be Western Europe. That's how we want it. And we shall impose our will on the world. That's why at all costs we need to de-couple Western Europe from the United States, to neutralize it, to demoralize it, to divide it and to soften it up. That is why our presence there in any form is part of our strategic aim."

INTERROGATION

"Is the present Soviet emigration a concession on the part of the authorities or is it a deliberate operation?"

"It results from the confluence of many circumstances, among which are the ones you mentioned."

"Is emigration damaging the USSR or bringing it advantages?"

"If you don't count a few outstanding cultural figures who have left, the losses from the emigration are minimal and the advantages obvious."

"But what about the brain-drain? For example, many mathematicians have left the country. And the decline of whole branches of culture? The Press compares this with German losses from emigration under the Nazis."

"The comparison is a stupid one. The émigrés make out that their departure from the Soviet Union has caused a complete collapse. This is either a lie or self-deception. The mathematicians you mentioned are insignificant figures. Their emigration meant absolutely no lowering of the level of mathematics in the USSR. Even the losses in music and ballet are quite replaceable. Do you really think that a country with inexhaustible resources of human talent is going to curl up and die from losses such as these? But the emigration has already fulfilled the role which the Soviet leadership counted on. Now they will cut it down sharply."

"But what about world public opinion? And what about the people wanting to leave the country?"

"Don't exaggerate the force of the one or the other phenomenon. And don't imagine that the Soviet leadership is easily frightened. The emigration was permitted not from fear of the West, but out of cold calculation. And if it were to follow from a new calculation that the emigration was not in their overall interests, they would cut it down whatever the row that that created in the West. But it looks as though the West isn't inclined to kick up a fuss about such things any longer."

"You talk as if you were a Soviet official giving an interview to the Press."

"Soviet officials don't tell lies all the time."

"If the emigration helps the Soviet Union, why will the Soviet leadership curtail it?"

"The leadership has many other things to worry about. With all the dense complexity of its agenda, it will be forced to cut the emigration down in order to decide other more important problems."

"But if it reduces the emigration it will strengthen the dissident movement within the country."

"The basic cadres of the dissident movement have already been chucked out of the country. All in all, the movement has exhausted itself. People in the USSR have already realized that emigration is far from being paradise. And in the West it has been recognized that far from all dissidents are the incarnation of virtue. In brief, the Soviet leadership has already let the surplus steam out of the Soviet kettle, and there won't be an explosion. Many long years will be needed, and exceptional circumstances too, before conditions will be ripe again for a new, potential explosion."

"What sort of conditions?"

"A new world war, for example."

RUMOUR

There's a rumour that I am intended to join the leadership of the future Centre. It looks as though Professor will be the director. Lady is to be his deputy for general questions and staff, while I am to be the deputy director in charge of research. This has completely changed Enthusiast.

When he sees me in the far distance, he lets out whoops of joy and comes out all smiles. In discussions in the evenings he supports everything I say, even if I make fun of his correct Socialism. All the same, I don't believe all that much in the reality of the rumour. But even so it's nice to think that somebody somewhere is taking note of my existence.

REALITY

My state of bliss lasted only a few days. Enthusiast returned to the *Pension* happier than usual and immediately fell on me without any reason. This means that there's nothing in the rumour. "Just you wait," I said to Enthusiast in my iciest tone, wanting to spoil his good humour. "They'll make me the director of the Centre; not a deputy, but the director himself. Then I'll show you what real socialism is like." Enthusiast turned pale and began to babble something about a conflict of opinions between people who were basically of the same mind. With the money he saved on the charlady he bought himself some jeans at a clearance-sale *and* a sheepskin coat: the dream of every Homosos.

INTERROGATION

"What do you know about research into parapsychology in the USSR?"

"There were conversations about it in the Committee of Intellectual Advisers, but only in very general terms. Roughly on these lines: the most powerful source of all evils and the most powerful of all weapons is the human mind. At the same time it is the cheapest and the most vulnerable. Why spend huge sums on bacteriological and nuclear weapons, which in the case of a mass application would almost certainly get out of control and whose consequences could very likely end in a world catastrophe? Much better value to concentrate our attention on the human brain and discover the means of influencing it. What they call parapsychology over here, and serves as the object of enthusiastic devotion for Soviet people who've failed in everything else, is only a cover for this programme."

"But it's a fact that there is this famous woman who heals people by sheer will-power and suggestion.* And there's a mass of evidence of

---

* A reference to Dzhuna, a lady from the Caucasus, who enjoyed great popularity in Moscow in the 1970s.

psychic impact from a distance . . . the transmission of information, for example."

"This faith-healer is ninety-nine per cent a swindler and a Soviet mystification. It is custom-made for Western sensation-mongers. And for every kind of Soviet cripple. There used to be a colossal number of such 'healers' in Russia. And as for psychic influence at a distance by means that cannot be explained by science—these are old wives' tales. Such rumours are specially put into circulation in order to distract attention from the main thing, which is the discovery of instruments that affect the human brain in ways that *can* be scientifically controlled. As for acting on people's will-power and consciousness at a distance, powerful 'ideal' methods of doing this have existed and operated for a long time: ideology, propaganda, the manipulation of the mass-consciousness. And this influence has long been exerted in daily life."

DISCOVERY

The *Pension* is a fairly old building. There is no rubbish-disposal unit. We carry the rubbish ourselves in plastic bags down to the cellar where the rubbish bins stand. One day when I had shoved my bag into the bin, I noticed some strips of paper with Russian words on them. "Well, well," I thought to myself, "so you chuck out waggon-loads of rubbish too." And I went back upstairs. But something compelled me to go back again and collect the scraps of paper. I locked myself in my room and pieced them together. Some bits were missing, but it was possible to make everything out. In all probability this was a fragment of a rough copy of notes for a Report on the behaviour of Soviet émigrés in the city. I was convinced earlier that more than one person had been writing denunciations regularly. But my conviction had had an abstract charac-ter. I experienced it as a well-nourished man experiences the fact that hunger is a lack of food and that many people on the planet are starving. Now that I was privy to the reality of denunciation I felt like a man who was himself actually caught up in a famine. Who was the author of this denunciation? For whom was it intended? Of course, it would be simpler to admit that everyone writes denunciations about everyone else and let the matter drop. But could one simply drop it? Suppose these denuncia-tions had something about oneself? Suppose they could affect one's prospects? No, the thing couldn't be ignored. One would have to keep watch on the Soviet émigrés as they carried out their rubbish, and on their little bits of paper. Sooner or later something about yourself would come into your hands. The main thing was to do all this in accordance with the methods of empirical sociology and show patience. If my former colleagues in Moscow knew how I was using my professional training and abilities, they would burst their bellies with laughter. A new branch of science: the sociology of the rubbish-bin. And I, I must own up to it, I counted on being offered a really good job in a university or research institute of standing.

THE EDIFICE

The more I look at my Edifice the less ugly it seems and the greater the hold it takes on my imagination. It is very like the ruins of a gigantic mediaeval castle. If I were the builders I would leave it in its unfinished state. Like that it reminds one of the transience of all things.

WE AND THE WEST

From time to time the local authorities uncover some Soviet spies. But the way they do it! Nobody would be surprised here if TASS issued a communiqué: at such and such a time and in such and such a place a group of Soviet spies will cross the frontier in a westerly direction. Would the frontier guards and Western authorities kindly refrain from hindering their transit and co-operate with them fully, because their trip abroad has a strictly scientific purpose: to steal secret scientific discoveries and technical inventions.

SHADES OF THE PAST

My relations with Lady are improving. I was even one of those who were invited to her home. The cream of émigré society was gathered together. It was quite jolly. According to Soviet custom we all ate and drank a lot. We sang Russian songs, including "Katyusha". A scion of the old Russian nobility was convinced that it was an old Russian romance. I corrected him: it was a gypsy romance.* And he agreed with me eagerly,

* *Katyusha* was written by the Soviet poet Mikhail Isakovsky in 1938 and awarded a Stalin prize in 1943. The music is by Vladimir Zakharov.

and began to address me in the second person singular, just as though we were in a sleazy Moscow snack-bar. I liked it very much. And the two of us got through bottles galore.

A reverend gentleman who had never been in the Soviet Union spoke about the powerful religious revival in Russia. He was supported from all sides. I too added my voice to his. "Things had got to the point," I said, "when even old Bolsheviks sang 'Our Father' instead of the 'Internationale' at Party meetings. And they had given the Soviet Patriarch the Order of the October Revolution as a way of thanking him for the religious revival." The clergyman said that the main thing was that the Church had stood its ground in its struggle against the regime. "When the Soviet regime collapses, the Church . . ." "will collapse together with the regime," I added. The clergyman didn't quite get what I had said and agreed automatically. Then he spent the rest of the evening trying to explain it away, saying that he had agreed with my barbed comment out of sheer inertia.

A comparatively young woman, whom everyone for some reason called "princess", consoled this man of God, whom by then everyone was fed up to the back teeth with, by saying that there was no reason to worry: the Soviet regime wouldn't collapse all that quickly. A man who spoke Russian with an American accent said that he also thought that this "notorious Russian religious renaissance" was an invention of the KGB. He asked me to tell him something about it. I told him a pack of tales and anecdotes. One of them was the story about some Soviet cleric who threatened to report a believer to his Party bureau for bad behaviour because he had refused to kiss the Cross. The man with the accent laughed so much that he just about fell off his chair. But in all this tomfoolery I delivered some home truths all right. "The Russian Orthodox Church," I said, "is wholly and entirely under the control of the authorities. If one were to reveal this control in all its details, people here simply wouldn't believe it possible. They would think that it was all an invention by the KGB. Why is religion allowed in the Soviet Union? Because it absorbs a certain amount of discontent and helps the authorities to manipulate the mass of the population. It is useful. And incidentally, it helps the State economically. I knew some first-rate specialists in Moscow who have at their disposal the richest material on this subject and who could write some sensational books that would debunk all those stories about the religious "renaissance". But the materials are hush-hush, and such books are banned from publication. So documents exposing the essence of the contemporary Russian Church are kept in the strictest secrecy. Why? Well, because the powers-that-be have an interest in keeping things exactly as they are."

The man with the accent asked me to tell him the names of the specialists I had referred to and also of the KGB agents working on the "religious renaissance" project, if they were known to me. I produced a long list for him, including all the employees of the Institute of Atheism whom I knew, as well as all the members of the Moscow intelligentsia who were flirting with Russian Orthodoxy. I got particular pleasure from adding the name of a popular Moscow chatterbox and schizophrenic who is considered there to be the leader and theorist of neo-Orthodoxy. "What makes you think that he works for the KGB?" asked Man-with-Accent. "I don't *think* he is," I said, "I know it. I was at school with him. He was already an informer then."

"But perhaps he's repented," said Man-with-Accent.

"Informers never repent," I said. "They can stop being informers by design or because they aren't needed. But I repeat, they don't repent, because they've nothing to repent of."

Then we all discussed a programme for the transformation of Russia after the fall of the Soviet regime. The idea of a monarchy naturally took first place, but with a multi-party system and free trade-unions. I enquired what they intended to do with the factories and the land: privatize them or keep them as State property. What, for instance, would they do with the railways, the airlines, television and other gigantic organizations and branches of the economy and culture? How would they organize the government of the country? Would they keep the Soviet Empire? As to the Empire, opinion was unanimous: the Empire must be retained; the task that Peter the Great had begun must be continued. As for the other problems, it was enough to drive out the Bolsheviks; then everything would settle itself. I said they were right. But unfortunately there had been no Bolsheviks in Russia for a long time; and our hostess would support what I was saying, for she had been a member of the Party and had even been elected to sit on the bureau of a Party province committee; but she was an ardent Christian and had never been a Bolshevik or a Communist. My words had an unexpected effect. All those present looked at their hostess with respect: a member of the bureau of an *obkom*! My word, that was like being a Countess! The scion of the gentry rose, stood dashingly to attention and clicked his heels.

THE FORMULA OF THE JACKALS

The man who gave me a lift to the *Pension* had been on a tourist trip to the West ten years earlier and didn't return home. The non-returner spoke about émigré circles with open contempt. Here is a part of what he said.

"When we come to the West we feel that we've suffered a lot and deserve a bit of happiness and that the West is obliged to provide us with it. We've suffered all right, at least a few of us have. But why do we deserve anything? Who is obliged to pay for other people's sufferings, even if they existed? And for whose sufferings? The West doesn't owe us anything. The West is doing something very stupid when it lets us in and gives us the chance to live here. The mere fact that the West takes the claims of us Soviet jackals seriously is itself a reason for despising the West. The West should defend itself against us in every possible way and let down an iron curtain in front of us. I remember an occasion after the war. I was demobilized from the army and went to the university. At that time they arranged 'leisure evenings' every week in the university building. One day I brought back with me my former commanding officer who had also been demobilized and was on his way home via Moscow. He was a good-looking fellow covered with decorations. But he was ill. He had caught syphilis in Germany and hadn't yet managed to cure it. During the evening he began to go after a first-year student. Naturally, she rose to the bait straight away. I reminded him of his illness. He said to hell with that: he had suffered, he deserved something and he had a right to it. 'If somebody owes you something,' I replied, 'take it from the debtor. What does this girl owe *you*? She didn't cause the war, she didn't give you your wounds and she didn't give you syphilis.' But he wouldn't listen to my arguments. Then I said straight out, 'Either you leave this girl alone or I'll tell her that you are ill.' The girl didn't believe me. He told her I was jealous and wanted to get hold of her myself. And he took her off. From that day onwards I've hated all people who demand what doesn't belong to them on any reckoning from people who owe them nothing."

The non-returner wished me all success. He didn't say a word about our perhaps meeting again. He didn't give me his name or address. And I didn't try to get them out of him.

RAYS OF THE FUTURE

They hadn't gone to bed yet at the *Pension*. They greeted me as they greet a man in Moscow after he has returned from abroad. How are things over there? Is the Eiffel Tower still where it was? I said that *we* needn't worry about the future of Russia because the best sons and daughters of our people were thinking about it. The Pensionnaires then decided to join the cohorts of the best sons and daughters of our people on the spot. Artist and his wife insisted on a constitutional monarchy, but one without any political parties. They assured us that the standards of life and democracy in pre-revolutionary Russia were even higher than in the West. Enthusiast insisted that the Jugoslav way was the right one, but with due regard to the Polish experiment; moreover, it needed a genuinely Marxist party at the top. Joker suggested that an Egyptian pharaoh should be made Russian head of State. Whiner said that whatever happened, nothing good would come out of it, so the best thing to do after the fall of the Soviet regime would be to leave the present regime as it is; it's not as bad as all that. There are even worse ones. I said that I didn't care what there was after the fall of the Soviet regime because then there would no longer be anything except rats, bugs and cockroaches. And, perhaps, genuine Socialists. But as a theorist I considered that we ought to restore private property. Inasmuch as the people don't want to return to pre-revolutionary private ownership, the factories, plants and other enterprises should be given to the present Party leaders, directors, managers, ministers, generals and other big shots as their private property. The Pensionnaires were all up in arms against me: they wouldn't hear of the possibility of private property. The most they would do would be to rent out land to the peasants so that they could provide the towns with vegetables. I said that unless there was private property in Russia, what it now had would simply come back again. It can't be excluded that Enthusiast will become the General Secretary of a "correct" Communist Party of the Soviet Union, but I doubt whether he will behave any better than Brezhnev.

Personally, I prefer Brezhnev. Even though he's not as clever as Enthusiast, at least he doesn't burst into my room without knocking; he doesn't flirt with anti-Communists, and he despises Eurocommunists just as they deserve to be despised. Enthusiast declared that he wouldn't shake my hand in future. But no more than half an hour later he was suggesting that I take part in a competition for the best title for his future publication. "If it's a periodical," I said, "call it *The Bell*. If it's a newspaper, call it *The Spark*."*

The Bell was published by Alexander Herzen from 1857 to 1867, *The Spark* by the Bolsheviks from 1900 to 1905.

THE HAPPIEST DAY

Today is the happiest day of all my life in the West. So many nice things have happened together. I received a document which allows me to go to Paris for a conference. Some organization has given me a sum of money as an outright gift. I went to a restaurant and had a good meal. I made the acquaintance of a beautiful woman and fixed a rendezvous with her for this evening.

Now I'm walking past the windows of luxury shops, filled to the brim with Great Happiness. "Dear God," I whisper, "thank you for such a generous gift." I turned into the park and . . . came to in the bushes. My head was splitting with pain. No money. No papers. I stagger to the police station. They quickly establish my identity, but they keep me there until late at night. I don't go to my rendezvous. It is too late, and I have no money.

At home I racked my brains until morning over the questions, "Who?" and "Why?" It's clear that somebody needs me to go to Paris and somebody needs me not to go. Or perhaps they just want to give me a fright once again? What for? Am I really such an important personage that I deserve an individual assassination attempt? If I had access to the mass media I would have made a declaration to the whole world. "Please," I would have said, "don't exaggerate the importance of my presence in the West. Regard me as a run-of-the-mill Soviet nonentity, which is indeed what I really am!"

ENEMIES

The attack on me has become known to the *Pension*. They all think it was the work of the KGB and insist that I should give publicity to what has happened. But why? The police will hardly back up my story. And my words alone won't be enough to create a sensation. Everyone advises me to be more careful, not to go for walks after dark, to avoid out-of-the-way places and never to go out alone. The last piece of advice touched me especially. Where was I to find people to go out with me? And I decided to do the exact opposite: to walk about until late at night, by myself and in out-of-the-way places. This would actually be safer, because my enemy is like the youth of today which prefers to make love in sight of everyone. My enemy is himself afraid of out-of-the-way places and darkness. And even more, of being alone. He is most likely to get away with it if he does his deed in the sight of everybody. In a crowd and in daylight he wouldn't be seen. And who is he, this enemy of mine? The most reasonable thing to do in such a predicament is to assume that everyone is your enemy.

FRIENDS

Enthusiast is certain that the blow I received was intended for him. The KGB men had simply mixed us up. "What do you mean?" I said in annoyance. "Look, I'm twice as tall as you are." "Very simple," he said. "They looked down from above. From above I'm even a little bigger than you. But the main point is that you're not in the least bit dangerous to the Soviet Union. Why should they try to kill you? Whereas now I'm their Enemy Number One."

"You're right," I said. "And so as to avoid any more confusion, I'm going to crawl on all fours from now on so that even from above, the KGB men will see that it's me and not you. But all the same I doubt whether they will kill you. The KGB hit-squads will think up a more terrible revenge."

"What will that be?" Enthusiast proudly raised his shaggy mane. "They will ignore you," I said.

"That trick of theirs won't work," he shouted. "I'll force them to take notice of me."

Professional Revolutionary replaced Enthusiast. Would you believe it, there are even people like that around in the West. He thinks a new revolution is needed in Russia to bring about in reality the ideals of the previous revolution. Somebody gives him money for his little periodical. He spends most of it on trips to resorts. On behalf of his journal he quite brazenly exploits newly-arrived simpletons from the Soviet Union. He justifies this in terms of "our common interests in the struggle against Soviet pseudo-socialism". On this he makes common cause with Enthusiast. But in the positive part of their programmes for change they part company in principle. Enthusiast wants to create genuine Socialism, Soviet style, while Revolutionary wants genuine Socialism, Western style.

Revolutionary quizzed me about all the details of the assassination attempt. He too was certain it was the KGB up to their tricks. And he also advised me to make a statement to the Press. I said I hadn't yet learned how to deduce which particular organization had inflicted a blow on the back of the neck from the particular type of blow. When I'd had a

111

few more clips on the back of the head I would make a scientific generalization and a public statement. Perhaps it was the Red Brigades?

Having exhausted the theme of my attempted assassination, Revolutionary turned to his programme for the Soviet opposition. I said it would be very simple to work out a programme for it. He immediately got out his note-book. He asked whether I would mind if he wrote down some of the things I said. "Write away," I said. "It doesn't trouble me. The Soviet regime is rubbish. Soviet power is rubbish. The Soviet Communist Party is rubbish. The KGB is rubbish. Soviet life is rubbish. One should consign the whole lot to the devil . . . And instead do nothing, because everything that you could do would be even worse rubbish."

He said he agreed with me about everything except for the last point. After all, something positive must be offered. "All right," I said, "here are a few positive ideas for you. There are general rules for drawing up programmes which are intended to win mass support. For example, it is essential to dress up what people want as something historically pre-ordained (for history moves exactly where we want it to go) and in accord with certain inalienable qualities of human nature. What is it that we want? ('We' of course means 'we Soviet people'.) We want to preserve all the advantages of the Soviet way of life, eliminate all its defects and, instead of them, get all the advantages of the Western way of life. Of course, we have our own understanding of what the Western way of life is—an abundance of food, clothing and other blessings with all possible freedoms thrown in. So there it is, this hybrid of the imagined blessings of Communism and Capitalism; and we must formulate it as the ideal for which the best representatives of the Soviet people will fight. Really, it's so simple."

"But that's what we were struggling for over there in Moscow!" cried Revolutionary.

"True," I said. "A good programme should always fix on paper what is already being fought for. And even better, what has already been achieved. In the Institute in Moscow we usually planned for the future what we had already done in the previous year. And we regularly received the Red Challenge Banner of the Party's district committee; and last time we even got the 'Enterprise of Communist Labour' award."

Revolutionary left, and Enthusiast popped up again. He turned the conversation to events in Bolivia, or was it Chile? It was all the same to me what events and what country he was bumbling on about: I have no idea of any of them. But Enthusiast identifies with them all passionately. I got sick of it and told him he didn't know what was really happening there. He retorted that I didn't know either. I agreed, but added that I didn't know better than he didn't know. He demanded an explanation.

112

"You intend to transform the whole world," I said, "but you can't even cope with an elementary little problem like that. Here's another elementary little logical problem for you. You tell me that when you were living in Moscow you were nearer to death than you are here. Let's suppose you will die tomorrow. The interval of time between your life in Moscow and tomorrow is greater than the interval of time between your arrival in the West and tomorrow. So why were you nearer to death in Moscow? I give you my word of honour that if you solve that problem I'll allow you to transform the world at your own discretion. I will even let you build correct Socialism in the Soviet Union." Enthusiast called me a scholastic and a sophist. But then Joker appeared and turned the conversation to another theme.

"There are many foreigners here," said Joker. "We should turn them into a party and begin a struggle for power. When we've seized power we can drive all the Germans out of Germany."

"An excellent idea," I said, "and completely realistic. I can assure you that the Germans themselves will rush to join your Party. They've got a very strong guilt complex and feeling of shame about being Germans. Moreover, only the Germans themselves are capable of properly organizing the expulsion of Germans from Germany."

"Rubbish!" exclaimed Enthusiast. "How can you expel a people from its own country?"

"Very simple. We've already had some practice in this. Remember East Prussia."

"And whom will you settle in Germany instead of the Germans?"

"The Jews, of course. Well, and Arabs too."

"They'll cut each other to pieces."

"No harm in that! Well, perhaps the Germans from the Soviet Union and East Germany."

"And where will you send the West Germans?"

"Siberia; there's room enough there."

"But if you send all the Germans out of Germany everything here will go to ruin and then the foreigners will leave Germany."

"That's all right. Then we'll put the Germans back again in all the vacant places. And after that we can all live here in peace and plenty."

DREAM

Inspirer was drunk and gloomy. "What's happened?" I asked.

"I've had a frank conversation with top management. I said I wanted to get our work running in the West in the best possible way."

"What did management say?"

"It said the present situation was the best possible situation because it suited everyone except 'geniuses' like me. Besides, there's another good reason why the leadership doesn't want to improve our work in the West."

"What's that?"

"The correlation of forces. For the time being it's in our favour, but our enemies don't seem to realize this. If our work got noticeably better it would compel our adversary to improve his own operations. And then the balance of forces would begin to tilt over to our disadvantage. Is that good logic?"

"The logic of idiots is generally irrefutable."

A VALUABLE DOCUMENT

It was hardly light when they sent a car for me—the first time in all my screening process. That meant that something quite out of the ordinary had happened. It transpired that a new personage had come over to the West and "chosen freedom"—a KGB officer travelling as a member of some delegation. He had brought with him a "most valuable document": the transcript of a conversation between the head of the KGB and the general responsible for "Operation Emigration". My interrogators wanted me to give my opinion on the genuineness of the "document".

I said: "Would you like me to tell you the contents of the 'document' without even reading it? Of course the 'document' is genuine. But it was written specially for you."

"Disinformation?"

"Quite the contrary," I answered. "The most accurate information."

"What sort of information?"

"It's been decided to round off the emigration."

My interrogators exchanged glances and took the "document" back without my having read it. They didn't utter a word about the attempt on my life. And I behaved as if nothing special had happened.

PENSIONERS

In the park there were only old-age pensioners. As likely as not they were all conservatives and reactionaries. And what's wrong with that?

There's a glut of progressiveness and revolutionariness in the world. That means pensioners are a good thing. Only pensioners can still save the West. Pensioners are former young people who have lost youth's illusions and acquired some common sense. They've got time to think things out. They've got some experience of life. They've nothing to be frightened of: they can express themselves directly and openly. Their life is nearing its end and therefore they have an interest in human life continuing in the same form. Old men, the future of humanity is in your hands! Unite in the struggle against progress in the world to come!

One old man guessed from my face and clothes that I was a foreigner and said something nasty about me to his neighbour on the bench. His dog started up at me malevolently. Of course there and then I changed my view of pensioners into its opposite. All evil lies in old men. Down with old men!

PENSIONNAIRES

In the *Pension* Joker and Cynic were solving some problems connected with the new world war.

"Here too they're not such slouches. They're getting ready for war here too, secretly and on the quiet."

"You can't get ready for a big war secretly. You need to prepare the whole people for war, especially the young people. If something happens the USSR will turn itself into a single armed camp in a couple of days. But here they need a couple of months just to get to grips with their young people and the pacifists."

"In the new war the mass of the population won't play a big role. Nuclear weapons . . ."

"Let us suppose for a minute that a way is found of changing the flight-path of the enemy's rockets and even sending them back to him. What then? War will once again become a war of masses of people in the first instance."

Enthusiast came back from the rubbish bins. He'd carried out an absolute mound of muck and now began some demagogy about Western garbage.

"People here chuck out things that people in the Soviet Union are ready to pay large sums of money and stand in queues for."

"Do you think they don't know the value of things here? They know it better than we do. That's why they throw them away. It's cheaper to throw them away than to keep them."

"And if they do keep their garbage the world situation won't change to any noticeable extent."

"In the world at the present time there are hundreds of millions of poor, hungry people," (this was my contribution to the discussion) "but it doesn't follow from that that this rich, well-fed nation has an obligation to be poor and hungry too. It's not these people's fault that millions and millions of other people have come into the world. Why did they do it? By the end of the century the population will grow by further hundreds of millions. What for? Why should this nation take care of them? Every people has the right to struggle for its own existence and well-being. In your excrement one might discover nourishing elements for which people in other parts of the planet would fight over. But what follows from that? It's easy to be humane at other people's expense. You've got three jackets already. Give one of them to the beggars in India and Cambodia."

Enthusiast said that I had gone too far and ran off to the lavatory. Nowadays he goes to all sorts of receptions and gets fed five times a day for nothing.

"If you talk like that in public," said Cynic, "the local Croesuses themselves will call you a 'reactionary' and a 'racist'. Here they're all for democracy, equality, justice and humanity."

"In words. It doesn't stop them from using foreign workers and looking on them as a lower race."

"There are five million foreign workers here and two million of their own unemployed. But you just try and make those unemployed work in the conditions in which the foreigners work!"

"Contemporary society needs a large number of people in a position like that of the slaves in Rome. And at the same time it generates a large number of people who can be compared with the Roman *plebs*. This is a general law. It operates in the USSR too, but in a hidden manner. Whatever the humanists may say, society can't exist for long without a hierarchy and without inequality. Our Soviet experience is a brilliant confirmation of that."

OTHER PEOPLE'S LIVES

Artist lives with his wife in the room next to mine. The walls are thin. I often hear their intimate conversations. They are certain that in the West the partitions between rooms are sound-proof, and so they don't keep their language in check.

116

"We need money," he is saying.

"I can get work as a model."

"For that you need to be a different shape. You're getting on a bit, you know."

"Don't be a cad."

"Here they have a different idea of youthfulness."

"Well, what about being a nude in an art school? Or with a private artist?"

"They're all private artists here. And all the nudes are prostitutes."

"It's in Moscow that all the nudes are prostitutes. Here there are enough prostitutes even without the nudes."

"It's just not on. Perhaps you could go out cleaning flats?"

"Here the Turks do all that."

"That man who arrived yesterday is definitely a KGB agent."

"Everybody here is a KGB agent."

"It's odd, I never got a summons from the KGB. They never even suggested that I should be an informer. Why do you think they never did that?"

"I never got a summons either and they didn't try to recruit me. All this talk about Soviet spies is complete baloney. Hey, wait a bit before you start snoring. I'm not seventy yet."

"Incidentally, the best-known womanizer in history, Casanova, wrote that he spent the most delightful night of his life in bed with a seventy-year-old countess."

"Rubbish!"

"It's not rubbish at all. It was simply the only time in his whole adult life when he got a really good night's sleep. Ha, ha, ha!"

"Idiot."

I crossed Artist and his wife off my list of Soviet agents.

INSOMNIA

I couldn't sleep. I flipped through a book by a critic of the Soviet regime which they're boosting here as an outstanding event. I hit on the following statement: "People make revolutions so that man shouldn't rule over man." I threw the book under the bed. Then I leafed through the programme of some "Democratic Union". The programme had 50 points. Point One was about the collection of donations in aid of the "Union". The drafters of the programme could, as a matter of fact, have stopped at Point One, having formulated it more clearly as "Give us Money".

The programme said that power in the country should belong to "the whole people; that is, to all citizens of the country as a whole and only to them". But a little further on it said that power should belong to "a majority of the population"; and that it should be implemented by "the elected representatives". But all this is what has long since come about in the USSR. The programme's authors insist on action "within the framework of the law"; but further on they talk about some "independent groups", ignoring the fact that these groups could be forbidden within the framework of the law. When I had skipped through this masterpiece of political thought, I threw it under the bed too.

DREAM

Even so, I fell asleep towards morning. I dreamed that I was present at a special conclave of the KGB. A new secret factory had just got under way in the West, and at this conclave the question was how to get hold of the secrets of this new venture. Various proposals were put forward: to organize a protest demonstration against it; to force the opposition in Parliament to table a question about it; to compel some hacks to do some investigative journalism on it; to send in terrorists; to infiltrate some of our own people; to provoke a government crisis; to invite some of the specialists involved to come and have a symposium with us; to arrange an international congress . . . in short, all possible lines of action were given an airing. Then the gaze of all those present was fixed on me. "We needn't do anything," I said. "Just wait a little and they'll show us all their secrets themselves. They will even ask us to accept them. And they'll pay us for doing so."

All those taking part in the conclave came down on me like a ton of bricks. "You mean there's no need for people like us?" they shouted. "You mean there's nothing for us to do? Give the scoundrel a sock in the jaw. He's working for the Central Intelligence Agency from inside our Committee of Intellectual Advisers!"

A ZIG-ZAG OF HISTORY

The story of the assassination attempt has suddenly subsided. Everybody is acting as if there hadn't been any attempt at all. It's just as if someone has given the order to stop talking about it. I myself have begun to think that my "happy day" was one of history's accidental zig-zags.

THE IDEA OF A CENTRE

Writer said that the idea of forming a Centre to unite the forces of the emigration in their critique of the Soviet Union was being discussed "at the highest level". That's where I will be able to apply my professional skills. He is ready to put in a word on my behalf.

INTERROGATION

"In the Soviet Union you occupied a privileged position."

"I was only a PhD and a senior research officer."

"But you were a member of the Communist Party."

"Most members of the Communist Party have pretty low living standards."

"You were close to responsible officials in the apparatus of the Central Committee and the KGB."

"That didn't give me anything except personal contacts. The most influential figure among them was Inspirer. He lived in a small flat, earned only a bit more than I did and had no special material privileges. And his rank was ludicrously low. Such people never make a big career."

"Are you a Communist?"

"The term 'Communism' has many meanings. For example, if I have one pair of trousers, I don't feel poor. If I have two pairs, I don't feel rich. I don't feel hungry if I eat a rotten potato. And I don't feel I've eaten my fill if I have a fresh beefsteak. I will be happy if I get a good flat. But I can live in a tiny little room. I could have inscribed my name in the history of science. But I can give away my ideas, free and for nothing, to all and sundry, as I've done hitherto. In that sense I'm a real Communist. But I don't believe in the Communist Utopia and I can laugh at Marxism and the Soviet way of life more bitterly than any Western anti-Communists and Soviet 'critics of the regime'. In that sense I'm not a Communist."

TRUTH

"We have a duty to tell Westerners the naked truth about our society," said Writer.

"Naked, that's good," I said. "They'll like that. Here they don't look at or read anything unless it's naked."

"I'm not joking."

"Nor am I. This is what happened to me. They invited me to some research institute to tell them about the basic features of Soviet society. They showed me over the institute and told me how its work was organized. I've been at research centres in the Soviet Union. Compared with the general situation in our country the living standards and working conditions for people there seemed to me to be fabulous. But what I saw here in the West stupefied me. Now the Soviet centres seemed poverty-stricken. For instance, the professor who received me has only one laboratory assistant. But the project the two of them are working on is equal in scope to the work done by a whole Soviet laboratory staffed by fifty people.

"I gave my lecture after I had seen round the institute. 'It is easy,' I said, 'to compare different countries which have the same type of social system. But to compare countries with different social systems and produce a verdict on which is better and which is worse is the task of history. Let's compare, for example, your position (I pointed to the professor) and the position of an academic of the same calibre in the Soviet Union. In our country such a person would have his own laboratory and a minimum of fifty subordinates.' (At this point the whole gathering laughed.) 'But,' I said, 'let's look at the matter from this angle. You are the boss of only one person, whereas your Soviet colleague is the boss of fifty. With respect to his place in the Soviet system as a whole, your Soviet colleague feels himself psychologically like a general in command of a powerful body of men. And this is how others regard him. Do you sense the difference? Which is better: to live in order to produce and increase the productivity of labour; or to produce (and not necessarily very productively) in order to have a certain status in society?' Then a discussion began in which the locals literally thundered against their comfortable and sterile conditions. I learned that many of the workers were going round the bend from boredom. Psychic depression was an everyday occurrence. Some of them had to go to psychiatric clinics. It sounds ridiculous, but they regarded our meetings, collective work-trips to collective farms, voluntary compulsory labour and other loathsome features of Soviet life as blessings. I warned them that real-life Communism is basically tempting, but on that very basis it transforms itself into a new kind of serfdom. But they only saw the first part of my formula: the temptation. So there you are, try and tell them the naked truth. There's no such thing."

"Your example sounds as if it could be turned into literature. You won't mind if I write it up?"

"Write it up. After all, that's what you're a writer for."

OBJECTIVITY

The West is tossing about between two extremes: between an extreme exaggeration of the military might of the Soviet Union and an extreme exaggeration of its difficulties in satisfying consumer demand. Here's a magazine with some photographs which give the impression that the Soviet Union is backward in consumer goods and in its economic, cultural and industrial life. But gentlemen, where then have its achievements in space, its military power, its outstanding musicians and its sporting triumphs come from? The Soviet way of life does not lie between the two extremes we've mentioned, but on a quite different plane. But on which plane nobody wants to know. The fear of objectivity in the investigation of social life is one of the most striking phenomena of our super-scientific age.

But is it possible anyway to be really objective? Well, here on television they're showing a film of the Party Congress in Moscow. It gives an awful impression. Especially the appearance of the Soviet leaders. The Party officials with their stupid flabby faces stand up and start to sing the Internationale, with bits of paper in their hands that provide the text of the Party anthem, which everybody has forgotten. Now they're bawling out the words of the anthem, "Arise ye branded with damnation, thou world of hungry men and slaves". Look at their mugs right now! That's not a face you've got there, it's the snout, the jowl, the ugly mug of Communist society in its most expressive incarnation. Well, what about the locals here? They look at the film with complete equanimity and even with a certain amount of respect for the snout of Communism.

THE EDIFICE

At sunset the Edifice looks like a sorcerer's castle or a temple. No, more like a spaceship. But then darkness dissolves the outward contours and in place of the fabulous vision there is a terrible black void.

KNOWING AND UNDERSTANDING

"Your task," said Inspirer, "is not to know but to understand. We've got more than enough knowledge, but no understanding at all to speak of.

121

My Chief, for example, knows all the important leaders of Western Europe by name and all there is to know about them. But what's the good of that? Western Kremlinologists know the details of the lives of our leaders better than we do. And what does that give them? We don't need keys to Georges, Hermann and John. We need keys to countries, to the masses, to processes, to epochs. For that, it isn't enough to know. What counts is understanding. With all the knowledge in the world you can still understand nothing. But one can understand even with only a modicum of knowledge. Don't stuff your head with trivia. Just live, think and wait. Sooner or later, understanding will come.''

PLANS AND ACHIEVEMENTS

I left Moscow with the secret intention of studying Western Europe and working out a plan for the speediest and least painful conquest of it by the USSR. I supposed that two years would be enough for that. Then I intended to send my plan to the KGB. Although I'm not altogether a fool, I still imagined that my plan would make quite an impact on Moscow and that I would receive a good position in the system which would bring my plan to fruition. I didn't count on being Number One in the system; I counted only on becoming the privy counsellor to some exceptionally high-up official, on playing the role of a latent genius to a patent idiot.

My plans were Utopian for two reasons. The first was the time-span. I've been living here for almost a year now, but I still know next to nothing about the town I live in. If I'm to make myself familiar with the whole of Western Europe at this tempo, it's going to take me a thousand years. The second reason is the degree of confidence I have in my own proposals. The better I understand the West, the nearer that degree will sink to nothing.

Then I even tired of making plans of that kind. With all the means at my disposal I tried to extract some miserable little hand-out from the West; I, who had just previously been working out plans for its conquest. I tried in vain. But if the West knew about my plans it would certainly dish me out a bigger deal, perhaps even a good fat sop, because then I would no longer be a reject from a collapsing Soviet society, but a representative of a mighty power.

As I'd tired of my vain attempts to get my hands on a nice little sinecure but had a good rest after my Utopian plans for conquering the West, I dived head-first into new plans. Only this time I began to work out plans for weakening the Soviet Union and for reducing its influence on the West. Why only weakening and reducing? Because this time I decided to be a realist, not a Utopian. As a realist I understood that to destroy the Soviet Union and stop its incursion into the West altogether was impossible. And so I decided to send my plans to the CIA (the American one). This time I wasn't counting on getting any sort of a job out of it. I only expected to receive a slightly larger pay-off than the one they're doling out to me at the moment.

When I was drawing up my plans for the subjugation of the West I made a very large assumption: I assumed that the West was clever and would resist a Soviet invasion. When I began to draw up plans for the defence of the West I made another very large assumption: I assumed that the Soviet Union was clever and would press on unswervingly to implement its intentions towards the West. But just recently I have begun to doubt the validity of both assumptions. The strength of the West doesn't lie in its brains and in its determination to defend itself; it lies in its stupidity and in its readiness to capitulate. On the other side, the strength of the Soviet Union also lies in its stupidity and in its inability to keep up a high level of determination for a long enough time. Consequently, I decided, in the interests of scientific accuracy I must change my assumptions into the opposite ones. But then . . . Then no plans are needed at all because everything happening in the world is happening in complete correspondence with these new assumptions. That is to say, the idiocy of current developments suggests that what we have is the perfect incarnation of plans of genius. That's the essence of the matter.

And so I threw away my plans for the defence of the West. "Let everything happen as it is happening anyway, independently of you," I said to myself. "The point isn't that the course of history is incorrect. It's all perfectly correct. It's your presence in history that's wrong. In a battle between two almighty idiots there's no room for a clever dwarf. One or other of the combatants will do him in—or both of them together. Best to get out of the way. But to get out inconspicuously so that nobody pays any attention to your exit. But get out as quickly as you can. Society isn't interested in the great discoveries that might have written your name in the history of science. On the contrary, it's interested in their not happening. Your position is that of a visitor from space, quite in-different, i.e., hostile, to everything on earth. So get back to your own Cosmos—i.e., to your miserable little personal shell, and pipe down!"

"Have you noticed how sharply the attitude of the public in the West towards our emigration is changing for the worse? What's happening?"

"Earlier we came here as heralds of the weakness of the Soviet system; and we strengthened hopes of its imminent collapse from internal causes. Now we come as heralds of the strength of the Soviet system, as the vanguard of an attacking army. Now we provoke anxiety in the West about its values and very existence. We're destroying the hope that Moscow will crack because of its internal non-viability."

"Well, that's a good thing."

"Of course it's a good thing. But in such cases there comes into operation the law of reaction-transfer: transfer from the real, strong enemy to the weak, pseudo-enemy. The West has begun to defend itself not against the Soviet threat itself but against those who try to explain the essence and strength of that threat."

"Unfortunately you're right. From what I've observed it seems that the West is up to its eyes in lies, hypocrisy and self-deception. Here everyone lies about everything. They lie about racial and national problems, about dissidents, about pacifists . . . As for what's happening in literature, or in connection with literature . . . and the cinema! Do you know the frightful conclusion I've come to? That this is what a real, highly developed civilization is! In principle civilization *is* lies, because civilization is artificial. Truth is something natural. And so it's usually unpleasant and terrible. The lie of civilization consists in its concealment of the truth. For example, the representatives of different races usually hate each other according to the natural laws of human existence. What does civilization come along and do? It brings a lie into race relations. Everybody pretends that all races are of equal value and that there's a great urge towards inter-racial love and friendship. Everyone unanimously condemns as racists all those who draw attention to natural occurrences in relations between the races. Or take another example. The population of the planet has exceeded its natural norms. Why? Can one really say that an increase in the number of people increases the volume of earthly happiness? Or that the degree of progress depends directly on how many people there are? In the Russia of Peter the Great the population was only twelve million. Then, in spite of everything, the population began to grow. Why? Thanks to serfdom. Human beings acquired material and prestige value for their owners, who began to breed people. But why breed them now? Now it's time to cut back the stock. What do you say about that?"

"It's a good job that nobody can hear us."

"I've already looked around and read enough of everything in the West. The art which predominates here is superior to official Soviet art only in its sophisticated technical refinement, in its originality, its volume and its wrappings. But its essence is the same: to put a mask over the real, behind-the-scenes life of the West and romanticize it. Western man is *also* up to his eyes in a system of mass cretinization, only in a rather different manner from ours. I am beginning to notice that the Soviet system of cretinization leaves more freedom for people like us to preserve ourselves spiritually as personalities: in the Soviet Union, at least, a protest against mass cretinization does result in its direct opposite, a greater realization of one's own individuality. Whereas in the West, protests about cretinization are an integral part of the cretinization system itself."

HISTORICAL MANIA

Artist has got some paints which are like oils but dry at lightning speed. He complains that these paints will last for only 50 years. But he needs paints that will last for centuries. He needs everlasting materials. An artist totally devoid of talent who hasn't yet sold a single picture lays claim to eternity. Writer talks out aloud about himself very contemptuously. But in reality he too writes not for the needs of the day but for all eternity. What is the nature of this mania about eternity? A confused feeling that one won't even be remembered for decades. The manic quality at the heart of our social system. We must strive towards the absolutely complete abundance of everything in order to satisfy people's most elementary needs. We must dream of a grandiose turning-point in culture in order to make even the most miserable contribution to it. For this reason our dissidents and critical writers who have become more or less known in the West fall ill with God-mania and begin to regard themselves as the creators of world history. There's no need even to mention our leaders. But in what respect are *we* better, I and my double in Moscow, Inspirer? His speeches, all delivered in the spirit of Greek tragedy, pursue me even now, and still find their echo in my soul.

"In war the conqueror is he who reunifies his country the more quickly after purely military operations and prevents his opponent from doing the same," said Inspirer. "Preparation for war is first and foremost preparation for what there will be after the war. In the Soviet Union we have a whole institute that deals with the problem of organizing, and disorganizing, populations after the next world war: such as how to restore the unity and governability of our own surviving population and how to destroy the remnants of unity among the enemy's surviving population and establish our control over it. These problems are investigated in relation to all conceivable variants of the future war. And the most interesting thing is that they are preparing specialists who will deal with these matters in practice; who will be supplied with the relevant information and invested with full power. In the first place, of course, these are specialists in the enemy countries. Gradually they will be infiltrated into Western countries and take up their position in what are presumed to be the least vulnerable locations. It is possible that they will receive information about such places in advance and thus their precise posting won't be so important. If we can train a large enough number of such specialists and ship them into the West, the problem of their deployment will have been settled. Possibly these specialists will even remain in the USSR right up to the outbreak of war and be parachuted into the West in large numbers only when the results of the first strike have become clear.

"On the table here there's a speck of dust," continued Inspirer. "You can't see it with the naked eye. At the same time there are bacteriological and psychological bombs of just that size which exceed the old one-ton aero-bombs in destructive power. Half a glass of these mini-bombs is enough to paralyse the USA entirely. But for the time being every little microscopic bomb costs the country much more than the old one-ton aero-bomb. Even more expensive is the storage of these bombs. There are difficulties about their delivery and sensible use. Plus unexpected consequences. In a word, in order to solve this whole complex of problems connected with our mini-bombs, we need huge resources and the development of whole branches of science and technology, the finest equipment and electronics. The most brilliant and fundamental discoveries in this area have already been made. But in order to use them we need Western technology and electronics. In a word, in order to destroy the West we need the help of the West.

"Everyone regards the outbreak of the next war largely as a technical and only partly as a political problem," Inspirer went on. "But the beginning of a big war depends not only on the state of military technology, weapon stockpiles and the vanity of politicians and generals: it depends on the psychological and ideological condition of the peoples involved. A people as a whole has to be psychologically ready for war so that its leaders can unleash it apparently arbitrarily and apparently unexpectedly. As yet there isn't such a nation anywhere in the world. But our people is nearest of all to that condition.

"In brief, the problem of a new world war is a problem for thinkers like you and me and not for officials and special services."

THE EDIFICE

My Edifice takes on ever more unearthly, cosmic forms. It looks as if it will house institutions connected with the opening up of the Cosmos. It was for this reason, one must suppose, that its builders thought up such a fantastic and at the same time frightening architecture. It evokes a sense of the hugeness of the Cosmos and of mystical awe before the Infinite and the Inevitable. The towers of the Edifice have already outgrown the highest buildings anywhere in the town.

NEWS FROM HOME

Enthusiast rushed into my room with eyes round with horror. "You sleep your head off in here," he roared, "while God knows what's happening in the world outside."

"What's happened?" I asked, jumping up from my bed. "War?"

"No, something worse," bellowed Enthusiast. "They're putting a tax on dogs in the Soviet Union. Just imagine, a tax on dogs!"

When I heard what it was I was rather relieved. "If I had been in the position of the Soviet authorities I would have put a tax on bed-bugs," I said amicably.

"You turn everything into a farce," he said reproachfully. "And people used to think you were a dissident!"

And indeed in the KGB they really did want to pass me off as a dissident. I think that was a big mistake. And they made it out of purely formal considerations. In this respect the Soviet system possesses all the faults of any large system.

127

Writer was carried away by his own chatter and committed an unforgivable mistake: he went to Lady's flat, taking me with him. Lady was extremely surprised to see me. Writer took her into the kitchen and they whispered together about my unexpected visit. Some of Lady's words just reached my ears: "business consultation"; "important problems"; "serious people". Then came Writer's words: "take him on board"; "use him"; "help to us". In the end they evidently came to an agreement. Lady came out all brilliant smiles. She said: "We almost thought that you had forgotten us, that you didn't want to know us. But why are you not taking off your coat? No, no, we can't let you go just like that." And so I was admitted to the drawing-room. There, besides Husband and Professor, whom I already knew, plus two employees of an anti-Soviet radio station, the director of a local émigré society and the leader of the local branch of a well-known émigré union, were also a number of elderly men and women. I was introduced "in general terms". They nodded, didn't extend their hands and didn't give me their names. My hostess threw a last troubled look in my direction. She turned her eyes towards a grey-haired, gloomy man. He nodded slightly. I interpreted his nod as "don't be afraid, he's also one of us; just let him take more of a hand".

"Comrades, ha, ha, ha, I'm sorry. Gentlemen," began Lady, "on the agenda of our conference . . . ha, ha, ha, . . . is the question of the unity and co-ordination of our actions in the ranks of the Soviet emigration in the West. We are going to hear a discussion paper given by . . ." (But what I seemed to hear was this: "The closed session of Party members from the Soviet Intelligence group in the city of M is hereby declared open. We are going to hear a discussion paper given by a member of the Bavarian Province Committee of the Party . . .") The grey-haired, gloomy man took some time to get his papers out of his folder. He leafed through them. "We-e-e-e-ll, ladies and gentlemen," (he spoke in the well-trained voice of a Party official of not lower than district rank), "you will all fully realize the complexity of the time we are living through and the importance of the tasks that confront us . . ."

OUR CONCERNS

"Wise old bird," said Writer. He was referring to Greyhead, as we walked home. "The conversation was business-like on the whole. It's nice to realize that people are sincerely concerned. . . ."

"With what?" I asked. "Do you want me to decipher some of the ideas in Greyhead's paper? Well, for instance, he spoke about the fall in Soviet prestige in the West; about the strengthening of anti-Soviet propaganda and the new forms it is taking. In a way all this is true. You can't find any factual mistakes in it. But the fall in Soviet prestige in the West is perfectly compatible with the rise in actual Soviet influence. Prestige decreases in one sector, influence increases in another. People who, in one way or another, have a stake in Soviet interests in the West can do whatever they like—among other things, engage in anti-Soviet propaganda. But this activity must be organized and directed so that its end-product on balance favours the Soviet Union. So any action aimed at strengthening anti-Soviet activity may produce a result directly opposite to the one stated. The manipulation of people is a science. It is no less exact a science than physics. And there's experience; and highly trained staff. The task of the KGB is merely to know the situation and manipulate people. But it's the people themselves who do everything that's necessary; moreover, they do it without being official members of the KGB."

WRITER'S CONFESSION

"On the whole, you are right about many things," Writer acknowledged. "Straight after my arrival here I wrote a book. Something in it didn't please the publishers. They asked me to correct it and indicated how I should do it. I refused. They printed the book all the same: the contract had already been signed. They printed it; and it was as if the book had never existed. It simply disappeared as soon as it came out. So what is the difference between non-publication, as in our country, and murder by sheer indifference, as in the West? I would prefer the first system now: at least you're taken for a hero for a while.

"In the USSR we are used to a situation where if a book is well written, that is enough for it to find its way to the reader. A book can become a best-seller independently of the Press and the critics, even in the teeth of them. Here, you can create the most superb books. But without advertising and Press-puffs, nobody will read them. And they won't buy them. And as for the readers . . . In our country they swallow several books a day. People read themselves unconscious. But here? I've a friend in this city. A very intelligent man. He has made a plan, notice the expression 'made a plan', to read one widely advertised book during his holiday. And he's a typical Western reader.

129

"Freedoms. Do many people in our country really need them? If a man needs freedom, sooner or later he'll get it, even in the Soviet Union. Only for himself personally, of course. But why get it for anyone else? Nowadays you can publish just about everything you want in Moscow. For that you have to have lived all your life in literary circles and expended a good deal of energy in learning how to get what you want printed. Well, what of that? The overcoming of non-freedom and the achievement of what you want as the result of a struggle can give a man the highest satisfaction life can offer.

"Incidentally, if I had published in Moscow a little book just half as critical as the one that was such a flop over here, it would have had a resonance not only there but here too. And as things are now, I *could* have got it printed there.

"Up till now Westerners have seen us only as something exotic, something that departs from the usual norm. Therefore they have an image of the Soviet way of life consisting only of extremes and exceptional phenomena that don't exist in the West. Here they would all be very happy if the whole of the Soviet Union really was one big concentration camp. That's why our revelatory literature had such an unprecedented success in the West. When anyone begins to write about the ordinary phenomena of Soviet life, readers lose interest: they've got things like that at home. Whereas one might have thought that only after reading *that* sort of literature could a real interest in the USSR arise. After all, then they would find out a lot about themselves too. You have to have a long experience of life in our country in order to grasp the importance of the obvious. To have a fresh look at things that have been familiar for a long time, that too is worth something.

"And what lesson have I learned from all this? The same one as I learned in Moscow: to write in such a way that my scribblings are acceptable to those who decide the fate of our literature. However, Moscow literary standards are now beyond my reach.

"All my past life was an unspoken trade-off with the authorities, with my colleagues, and with my friends. I got out here thanks to the same silent collusion. My flat used to be boiling with informers. I pretended I noticed nothing and talked to all of them, convinced as I was that my words would be recorded somewhere and weighed in the balance. In particular, I swore I wouldn't have anything to do with politics or write any anti-Soviet books, and would be very glad to meet any visitors from Moscow. In other words, I gave them to understand that I was typical Soviet rubbish. When I got to the West I made an attempt to gain my independence. It was to do that that I scurried off here. But I hadn't had time to get my breath back before I found myself in the same sort of spider's web of deals, big and small, as before. The only difference was that it was an even more prehensile and humiliating one. And you can't extricate yourself from this one! There's nowhere to escape to. From bondage there is an escape: to freedom. But from freedom, there's no way out. And the most awful thing about it all is that the West isn't a subject for great literature any more. From the literary point of view the most interesting phenomenon of the century is the Soviet Union. It is in Moscow, not in Paris, New York or London, that the tree of life is growing. Russian literature has an unrepeatable chance of describing this phenomenon . . . Not to unmask it, but to depict it in all its vital potential and thereby become a great literature. I am not an apologist of the Soviet regime, but I've come to the conclusion that great Russian literature is possible at present only if it is apologetic, and certainly not if it is critical."

I crossed Writer off my list of Soviet agents. What I'd like to know is: will I be able to cross myself off?

AGENT

I don't feel myself to be a Soviet agent at all. Usually I just forget about it. In Moscow I had a friend in military intelligence. He said the same. They dumped him (I will call him "Agent") in the West by the marriage-method. Later, at a resort, the pair of them met a couple from the same town. I will call them Husband and Wife. Agent became Wife's lover. He learned by chance that Wife worked in a firm that fulfilled military contracts. He realized that success had come to him on a silver platter. On the whole he stuck to the principle that success either simply comes along or doesn't come, however hard you try. "It's on the cinema screen and in novels that events which in real life take many months and even years to happen are squeezed into an hour and a half or a hundred pages. It's there that the spy feels himself to be a spy and behaves as if he was risking his life every minute," said my friend. "But in real life it's all so long drawn out. I lived in the West for two years and for the most of the time I forgot I was a spy at all. Even when I found out that Wife had access to some military secrets I didn't seize my chance at once."

One day he suggested to her that they should go to a very expensive resort together. "But," he said, "I need a lot of money for that. I can easily earn it." Would she bring from her place of work every bit of waste-paper that she could lay her hands on, and then he would dispose of it for good money to "some idiot from some firm or other"? And she began to lug out "waste-paper" for him with such zeal and in such quantities that he could hardly manage to send it all to Moscow. He himself couldn't make head or tail of these documents. And he didn't want to. He had already got used to doing nothing. This went on for three years. In the end, thanks to the "waste-paper", Moscow got to know everything to do with a new, important invention concerned with guiding tanks.

Now just imagine that there are scores of agents like that. They lead a normal life. They don't feel themselves to be agents at all. They commit no criminal acts. They wait for favourable opportunities. Not all of them ever get them. But if there are heaps of agents, then one or other of them is going to hit on something. There is another point: agents of this type are not necessarily dispatched from Moscow. Western citizens themselves are ready, for quite small sums of money, to sell you everything your heart desires. The risk of disaster is small. Sentences in the West are too feeble to deter people from succumbing to the temptation.

MY SOURCES

I lived in Moscow all my life. I drank more than one tankerful of vodka with officials of the Central Committee, the KGB and other important services. And they too are human beings, and Homososes into the bargain, who are inclined to open their hearts and beat their breasts under the influence of drink. Is it possible then for Western agents in Moscow to use this opening? To do it systematically isn't possible. You would need too many agents for that. They would have to live as freely as the locals. And one must be a Homosos, too, to have real access to the hearts of one's fellow-drinkers. Can one buy information? Again, as a rule that can't be done. It's not all that easy to spend large sums of money in the Soviet Union. People who do have access to secrets value their social position and are under constant observation. The real secrets are far from the places where Western agents can operate, while the secrets that are available to them are either dummy secrets, or trifles, or disinformation. But why should Western agents need Soviet secrets of the sort that Soviet agents go after in the West? The things that should interest the West in the Soviet Union are different, things which no agents can understand and which can be understood without great effort even without agents: the mechanisms of society.

132

"What would you do if you were the Soviet No. 1?"

"Nothing. The Soviet No. 1 has only apparent and purely symbolic power."

"But let us suppose that you have real power."

"The first thing I would do would be to stop subsidizing Cuba. You can do what you like with it."

"Excellent."

"I would do the same thing with Africa and Asia. You can do what you like with all the Arabs too."

"Fine."

If I had stopped there, perhaps my interrogators would have ended the screening and given their okay to my getting a job. But my ambition carried me further. "If I acted like that, I should do no damage to my own country at all. In those parts of the world, events will go in the direction desired by Moscow just the same. Without interference from Moscow they will go even better. Besides, I would let you have our expensive involvements in Africa, Asia and Latin America not for free, but for bread, meat and electronics. And for non-interference in our Eastern Europe."

"Hm!"

"I would devote all the resources of the country to the improvement of the population's living conditions, to the education of young people, to crushing the opposition and to modernizing industry. And of course to strengthening the army."

"Well, yes."

"I would stimulate culture. I would expand contacts with the West. I would develop our peaceful penetration of the West."

"Wait a minute!"

"I would wait for the moment when the West got completely tangled up in its own contradictions and totally bogged down in its own little games in Asia, Africa and Latin America."

"And?"

"And then I would occupy Finland, Sweden, Norway, Austria, Holland, Denmark and Belgium."

"?!"

"France and Italy too."

"How dare you?!"

"Why not, if one can?"

"But that would be world war!"

"Well, what of that? Sooner or later war's coming anyway."

"But this is inhuman."

"But you asked me to be an imaginary all-powerful Soviet leader."

"But what do you yourself think about all this?"

"The Soviet leaders are not clever or determined enough to adopt a strategy like that, so you can sleep in peace. The Soviet Union will go on dragging behind it the burden of its present stupid foreign policy."

"What do you base your programme on as an imaginary leader?"

"When a boxer is getting himself ready for a decisive match, he takes off superfluous weight, tones up his muscles and concentrates psychologically on the battle ahead of him and the opponent he is to meet. It's obvious."

"Yes, it's obvious."

I DEFEND EUROPE

"Well, if you were a Western politician who had real power, how would you defend the West?"

"I would try to prevent the Soviet leadership from switching to the strategy I have just outlined. I would try to impose new expenditures on the USSR that it couldn't afford and inveigle it into activities it couldn't completely control all over the world. I would step up the arms race. I would prevent the Soviet Union from resolving its internal difficulties."

"That's obvious."

"Yes; but there's one thing here that isn't obvious."

"What's that?"

"That all this is obvious."

THE CONTINUITY OF THE GENERATIONS

"It's amazing," said Cynic, reading a Russian émigré newspaper. "A man of a hundred and ninety-five has just died; a lieutenant in the Life Guards of His Imperial Majesty's Semenovsky Regiment. It's ridiculous. One hundred and ninety-five and still only a lieutenant."

"He's not a hundred and ninety-five," corrected Whiner. "He's only ninety-five."

"All the same, it's absurd. Can these mummies still hope to bring back the past?"

134

"This wretched little paper is edited by young people. They don't hope for anything, but they're ready to express hope for anything you like, provided someone pays them for it."

"I would also agree to do that, for money."

DEMOCRACY

"Watch out! A programme about homosexuals is just beginning."

"They've gone quite idiotic."

"Homosexuals too have a right to exist."

"Homosexuality contributes to the destruction of the family and undermines the foundations of society, so society has the right to defend itself against them. Moreover, homosexuals make up only a tiny minority of the population."

"Under democracy even a minority has a right to exist."

"Depending on what kind of a minority! Gangsters and terrorists are also a minority. Democracy isn't freedom for everything. It's merely a certain form of political organization of society. It's a society which lives under the rule of law. Which minorities have the right to exist is for the majority to decide."

"The homos I have had occasion to see were all frightful trash. But if they want to exist, then let them exist."

"But they want more than that. They foist themselves on to society, draw attention to themselves and bring normal people into their sphere of interests. Society, I repeat, also has the right to defend itself against this plague. And on the whole, discussing the problem of homosexuality in terms of democracy is a degradation of democracy."

"But can we consider our Soviet homosexuals as champions of the rights of man?"

"But how are they worse than religious sectarians?"

"But all the same the Soviet regime is pure sh-t."

NEWS FROM THE MOTHERLAND

The programme about gays was followed by a programme about the Soviet Union. That means that they attach great importance here to relations with Moscow. All the inmates of the *Pension* came running in. We laugh, groan, curse, recognize familiar places. Now a Western journalist is conducting an interview with an "ordinar worker".

"Idiot," everybody cries with one voice. "It's a KGB officer. You ca▸ see it a mile off." "We all look like KGB officers," sighed Whiner "When they showed you [that meant Enthusiast] on television, everyon◖ here was sure that you were a KGB agent."

Then all the same they showed us some Moscow queues and talke◖ about food shortages and new arrests. And we calmed down again Everything was normal. It's an interesting fact that it's enough to ge▸ away from our country for a little while for it to seem that everything there has started to change, although you yourself know perfectly well that it will never be any different in any circumstances or at any time. A◖ tiny bit better or a good deal worse, but not different. Moreover, émigrés fear not so much that things will get worse as that they might get better. And one can understand this. If they get better, emigration loses its point. The Soviet authorities have only to improve conditions in the country (which happily for us is impossible) for spirits in émigré circles to fall dramatically. The only thing which gives the emigration spiritual support is the awareness that in the Soviet Union "there's nothing to eat and they're arresting more people than ever". The second part is now an obvious lie: there's nobody left to arrest. But if the USSR were to bring about a radical improvement in living conditions, a psychological and ideological panic would begin in the West.

Finally, the television told us about the price-rises of food products back home. What rejoicing there was then!

NEWS FOR THE MOTHERLAND

Artist came in, proud and unapproachable: he had managed to show a few of his works in a seedy art-gallery. I doubt whether anyone will buy any of them. They've got heaps of that sort of stuff of their own. But he will write to Moscow as though they had given him an exhibition in the Louvre itself. And the artists who knew him back at home will shrivel up with envy. Writer also describes his position here to friends and relatives in Moscow as though he were the centre of world literature. This is a lie. But try to live here without lying! If I had anyone to write to in Moscow I suppose I would also write the routine cliché to the effect that "freedom liberates one's creative forces and arouses extraordinary energies". I would present my sociology of the rubbish-bins as a contribution to world science.

136

THE SOCIOLOGY OF THE RUBBISH-BINS

The study of the Soviet emigration's dustbins has really got a hold on me as a scholar. By studying the Soviet emigration one can pass judgements on the society that has engendered the emigration. In exactly the same way and with a considerable degree of accuracy, one can judge people and their lives according to their waste-products. I have enriched the usual observational methodology with my own special techniques. From part of a sheet of paper I have learned how to re-establish the whole page of text; and from indirect hints I have learned how to dig down to the real hard facts. My method would be an inestimable boon to the KGB. It would enable it to reduce at least tenfold its expenditure on the collection and processing of waste information. Who knows, maybe it is in this very field that I am destined to write my name in the history of science. But then the image of Inspirer rose in my memory and shattered my rosy dreams.

OUR ENEMIES

"Your fundamental failing is that you're a born inventor," said Inspirer. "Incidentally, it's a good job that there aren't many people like you in the world."

"But what's wrong with being an inventor?"

"If there were a lot of people like you, there would have been nothing left of the world a long time ago."

"And what's wrong with that?"

"Point taken. Somehow I hadn't thought of that. But let's get back to earth. I think that you've already learned your lesson from experience here and that you won't display this failing of yours over there. Remember the axiom of our profession: an agent isn't a creator, he's a destroyer."

"I know that. I think about all this simply as a hobby."

"Don't try to be clever, you won't take me in. I myself am in a worse position still. I can see myself that our leadership only has to make a few very simple moves to win the game. To win quietly, soundlessly and without any sensations. But I know the reality of our system and its leaders. They aren't capable of making such moves. If I were now to present my own plan to the highest leadership, having proved its assertions in advance as theorems, they still wouldn't believe me. Worse than that, they simply wouldn't even give me the chance to have my say. Even if they were all sure I was right, they would still shut me up before I began to speak. That's why we have to resort to tricks. Before outwitting the enemy you first have to outwit your own side. Brother, there *is* no alternative.

"For the time being, the West isn't our enemy but our field of operation," Inspirer went on. "For the time being our enemies are our own leadership and our own agents in the West. The first lot are incapable of attaining a scientific understanding of reality or of making scientifically based political calculations. The second carry out our plans in the good old Soviet way: they botch, they cheat, they don't do what they ought to, they merely give the impression of working. Here's a typical example for you. Several scores of our people—embassy, consulate, trade and cultural representatives—were suddenly expelled as spies from one Western country. World sensation. Furious articles in the Press. Protests. Demonstrations in front of our embassies. An unprecedented anti-Soviet campaign. That's what lies on the surface and meets the eye. Our leaders panic. One secret meeting after another. A load of people lose their jobs. Resolutions. Orders. Instructions. In a word, total depression and black despair. Our services in the field flood Moscow with dispatches in the same spirit.

"But what was really happening at that time deep down at the centre of events? What was it that could be revealed and evaluated only by the methods of science? Well, this. We exercised a little patience and made a few insignificant gestures (for instance, a hint that the topmost leadership condemned the behaviour of certain very high officials, and was about to dismiss them), and many firms whose co-operation was very important to us were signing contracts with us again. Important people in the state and armed services of the country in question gave us to understand that they were ready to work for our intelligence.

"But the leadership shot down our evaluation of the actual situation; they rejected our plan to make good use of what was *outwardly* a wretched situation. Our agents in the field behaved so stupidly that they disrupted the recruitment of the people I mentioned. Net result: huge damage to our country, not only on the surface of the historical process, but in its depths as well.

"Then I could give you examples of what seemed outwardly a success being linked to very real hidden losses. There are hundreds of such cases. We have studied them and elaborated strict theories, backed up by facts and knowing hardly any exceptions. But how do the authorities react to all this, and what use do they make of our advice? It doesn't bear speaking of. Our operation to subjugate Western Europe should be

138

carried through on the plane of fine mathematical calculations. Like space-flights. In principle this can be done. But in practice . . ."

WE, OUR OWN ENEMIES

"But our position is tragic," said Inspirer. "You know as well as I do who the greatest danger of all to our system is: none other than the real Soviet man who could do his job better than the others. He becomes a danger to these others; and then they push him into the role of enemy of the whole social structure. The most dangerous person for the Soviet system isn't the person who takes advantage of a convenient situation and joins the opposition; he is the man who is compelled by society itself to become its enemy and is literally pushed into this role. At the moment it's fairly hard to separate these real enemies of the Soviet system from the dissident soap-bubbles. But when these bubbles burst, perhaps certain things will become clearer. We must use our ingenuity so as not to become the enemies of the cause to which we have dedicated our souls."

THE EDIFICE

They've begun to face my Edifice with some sort of stone slabs. Sometimes they sparkle like mirrors; sometimes they turn blue; sometimes golden. A random interweaving of blocks and cylinders is acquiring strict forms. Now I am amazed at the boldness of the architects who decided on such forms. Such a thing would never have been permitted in Moscow.

INTERROGATION

"How can the KGB make use of you?"
    "Most likely by not using me at all."
    "Why is that?"
    "Because of their internal relationships. They want the appearance of action, not real action. And there are too many people like me. It's physically impossible to make use of every individual."
    "But suppose they try to make use of you just the same?"

"If you think that this could really happen, seize the initiative from them. What prevents you?"

"Our own internal relationships. There are too many people like you. It's even more impossible for us to make use of every individual."

"Well said. That's one nil to you."

THE CENTRE

The Centre has been approved. By whom? (There is no Central Committee here!) Obviously by those who will provide the money. Professor will be the director, Lady will be his deputy. Enthusiast thinks they will need a professional sociologist and there's nobody here except him. He asks me to put in a word for him. He is prepared to take on his own shoulders the running of the section dealing with Soviet dissidents. He is prepared to edit a periodical: the Centre is bound to publish a journal.

I doubt whether they will have *me* in the Centre: a professional has no place in the company of charlatans. But I would like to get into it. It's some kind of job, when all's said and done. Once I had a foothold in the Centre I could look for a better job later. Whiner is also asking to be fixed up at the Centre. His demands are very modest: he's willing to work as a guard, cleaner or errand boy.

WRITER'S BIRTHDAY

Writer is sixty. All the thinking part of the emigration has gathered at his flat. They've been eating, drinking, shouting, just as in Moscow. And the blethering was quite like Moscow blethering; about everything in the world, chaotic, wise in parts and ridiculous as a whole.

"They've got a high standard of living, you can't take that away from them."

"That's exactly what you *can* take away from them."

"The future of the West depends on its youth."

"Very profound. I will go further and say that it depends on its babies."

"Don't joke about this! Look at Western youth. Debauchery. Hysteria. Ideological chaos. They revolt against the consumer society, but in the depths of their hearts they too want to have everything, but straightaway and without doing any work."

"A perfectly healthy desire. I wouldn't say 'No' to it myself."

"They've gorged themselves silly, the swine. If only we had even half of what they have . . ."

"We Russians see the ideal of the future located not in time but in space—in the West. Waiting for the right time would take too long, but we can go and get it all in space."

"When there's a couple of Soviet spies here for every Western citizen, they will give it to us themselves."

"Then the West will have to go to Moscow to do its shopping."

"I can't understand why they don't expose our spies over here. It's so simple. You can tell them by their mugs."

"Here they have democracy. If your passport says you're not a Chinaman and if it can't be proved in court that you are a Chinaman, then you're not Chinese, even if you're Mao Tse-tung. According to your mug you can be the head of the KGB himself. But if your documents say you are a dissident, then a dissident is what you are."

"I watched a demonstration today," said Writer. "A very curious spectacle. One ought to describe the typical demonstrator together with his psychology and his curriculum vitae."

"You can try it," I said. "But if you pick out an individual demonstrator and try to analyse him as an individual being, you'll be compelled to leave out of account the very fact that he took part in the demonstration, and the fact that he belongs to this varied and temporary aggregate of people. But if you regard the individual demonstrator as a representative of this agglomerate of human beings, the things that you will be forced to leave out of account will be his individual characteristics and circumstances."

"So you don't think that such phenomena deserve study?"

"They do deserve it, but in moderation. For such a demonstration it would be enough, for instance, to have a few lines in a description of something else, let us say in a description of the experiences of such a person as you yourself."

"I suppose you're right. My personal impressions of this demonstration are more important for literature than the psychology of the participants in the demonstration."

"To reflect the psychology of a participant in a demonstration through the psychology of a man who hasn't the faintest idea about the life or the psychology of the demonstrator—only members of the Union of Soviet Writers are capable of something like that."

I love all this sort of blethering. Nothing we say is in any way binding. There's no need to hurry anywhere. Time is at one's disposal. It certainly isn't money. It doesn't even exist. Begone dull Time, lose yourself

141

pointlessly. Pointlessly? Profitlessly, yes. But not pointlessly. This is our life. Life in general is only a waste of time.

It's already light when we disperse to our homes. The soldiers of the Special Amphibious Battalion are still tucked up in bed. Fat Germans are jogging earnestly in the park, losing surplus weight. The Germans are a people of genius. Once they take something on they do it well and seriously. Now they're taking off surplus weight. In less than six months they've already taken off the weight of the population of a whole Soviet Baltic republic.

WE AND THE WEST

Enthusiast tried to get a meeting with the President. For a long time they played him along, but finally they refused. He was mad with rage. He howled that even in Moscow there wasn't bureaucracy like that, and that if he had wanted a meeting with Brezhnev, sooner or later he would have got one. Listening to Enthusiast's wails I recalled one of the methods, devised by the psychologists in our institute, of receiving visitors to very important personages in the USSR. A man thirsting for an audience is given a day and a time. One of the assistants of Very Important Personage meets him and politely asks him to go into another room. In this room there are no portraits and no windows. Only a table and two chairs. Very Important Personage's assistant politely requests Visitor to take a seat and give him the gist of his request or complaint before going into the presence of Very Important Personage Himself. Visitor does this with enthusiasm. Having heard him out, Assistant proposes to Visitor that he should accompany him into another room. Exactly the same as the first. There an Assistant exactly like the first asks Visitor to summarize the essence of his request before going in to see V.I. Personage. Visitor repeats himself but already with less enthusiasm and fewer details. Then Assistant takes Visitor into the next room, where the same procedure awaits him. At the third stage, Visitor is usually gripped by terror and asks to be allowed to go home. They let him out. It is rare for anyone to get through to the fifth room. Incidentally, there are only two rooms altogether. And only two assistants. But as early as the third stage Visitor has lost the ability to identify people and things.

Not long ago in Moscow, some Soviet dissident was telling me with horror about this ploy. I acted as if I was hearing about it for the first time and advised Dissident to reveal the secrets of this "criminal system". He said that unfortunately there were no formal proofs of its existence. And he was right. Nobody who has been subjected to this method has ever let the cat out of the bag. Why? Because we recommended that this method should be applied only to members of the intelligentsia. You won't catch a worker or a peasant with "fine psychology" like that. They apply simpler methods to them, for example, the use of "look-alikes". One old alcoholic told me that in Stalin's time workers were especially keen to be received by Budyonny or Voroshilov. One day he too tried to get in to see Budyonny with a request to improve his accommodation. The official accompanying him was drunk and, instead of taking him to Budyonny's reception room, he took him into a room where about twenty Budyonnys were relaxing between sessions. They were drinking beer, playing draughts and dominoes, swearing like troopers and roaring with laughter. It was the most horrifying spectacle Alcoholic had ever seen in his life. For a start they gave him a good beating; then they put him in a lunatic asylum. When he came out a couple of years later, nobody would believe his story.

THE EDIFICE

They've done more than half the facing of my Edifice. It is becoming extraordinarily beautiful. It will be the most beautiful building I have ever seen, and I await its completion with impatience. Now I can guess its future appearance in detail, and my visions of it are coming true. I plan for instance that such and such a part should have such and such a facing and, lo and behold, on the very next day my wishes are carried out to the letter. I have guessed the intention of the builders. And I already foresee how the Edifice will look when it is completed. It will be a fairy-tale come true.

JOKER'S ADMISSION

"I've travelled all over the world," said Joker. "I have seen enough of the likes of us and our influence in the world. I must admit that we are the carriers of a terrible epidemic. A few more of us and we shall infect the world so thoroughly that it won't recover for a century. We are infecting it cynically, consistently, systematically, and with the consciousness of being the practitioners of great progress. We are carrying the disease as if it were the highest form of health. By the mere fact of our existence, we are transmitting to all the riff-raff of the West the certainty that they are a natural phenomenon, and that the future will be theirs. With every day that passes my hatred of ourselves grows greater."

We are crossing the bridge. The soldiers of the Special Amphibious Battalion have been jumping out of their little dinghies, letting out whoops as they climbed up the bank. This time they are armed. It is serious training for war.

"I've served in the army," said Joker. "Such things aren't done any better in our armed forces. Maybe even worse. But that's not the point. Here they do their hack-work seriously, whereas we do serious jobs like hack-work. Western armies, however much they put on airs and try to seem serious, always manage to look like something out of an operetta. The Soviet Army, despite its absurdities, sloppiness, stupidity, eyewash and other characteristics common to all Soviet phenomena, is a real army, an army for killing other people and for meeting its own ruin for the sake of killing others. The Soviet Union as a whole is a huge army which is being prepared by the entire system of our life to be ready for a non-joke war. And I don't want it to win."

I crossed Joker off my list of Soviet agents. If this goes on much longer, who will be left on the list?

OUR PROBLEMS

"We can send thousands of agents to the West," said Inspirer. "The value of each of them in isolation is next to nil. But in the system . . ."

"But you know very well that the Soviet type of system can't maintain a high level of organization for long."

"What's the solution? How can one make a reliable system out of unreliable elements?"

"One of the ways of doing that is via a hierarchy of systems with a gradual transition from the completely unorganized majority to the completely organized individual at the top of the pyramid."

"I know. That has been proved in theory. But we still have to try to accomplish it in practice. It will be the first experiment of its kind. And as such, of course, a contribution to science."

I never attributed any serious significance to my conversations with Inspirer. They were conversations which, from my point of view, were an end in themselves. We talked away and passed the time more or less pleasantly and that was the end of it. But thousands of people held, and hold, conversations of that type, and in the long run these conversations

144

result in certain human actions. The proof of this is that there are tens of thousands of our agents in the West. And I'm here too. And here, one must suppose, not for doubting and self-analysis, but for a genuine reason.

"Remember my words," said Inspirer. "We will create such a network of agents in the West that even a thousand years from now historians will be amazed that we were clever enough to build such a grandiose building out of such sh-t. If we win the next war—and we *must* win it—it will be thanks, first of all, not to our tanks and rockets, but to our agents. The next war will, above all, be a war of spies. And we are its genuine soldiers and generals."

TO HAVE AND NOT TO HAVE

The streets are full of beautiful young women ready to give themselves at any moment; for nothing, moreover. But not one of them belongs to me. One must have a certain minimum of money in order to have a woman who can be had even without money. If you haven't any money, it's noticeable in all your being. And the woman who is willing to give herself for nothing to anybody who has money will not give herself to you, simply because you haven't any monetary substance. In Moscow it is the social position of the individual which plays that role. Women feel this substance in a man and give themselves free of charge to this substance as such.

My intellect, which brought me victories over the women of Moscow and was a part of my substantial situation there, isn't worth a tinker's cuss here. Here in the West, you even have to pay extra for somebody to agree to notice that you have an intellect. Here intellect turns into capital only for those who have capital already, rather as in Moscow it was transmuted into something socially significant only when it had a social position to rest on. In the West a clever person without money is like a clever person without a good job in Moscow.

In Moscow I considered myself to be something of a debauchee. Here I feel utterly chaste. It turns out that our relationship to sex is determined not so much by our sexual practice as by the whole system of our relationships to the good things of life.

WAR AND PEACE

As they announced on television and in the papers, the manoeuvres went successfully despite difficult weather conditions: it had been drizzling. One soldier had drowned. He slipped on some wet stones. Thousands of people had demonstrated in protest against the victims of the manoeuvres (what on earth does *that* mean?) and against the militarization of the country. The demonstrators carried slogans. To look at them one might imagine that they had been vetted in Moscow by the Central Committee. The most popular one was "better red than dead".

Thousands of young men liable to be called up burned their registration papers (not their call-up papers, just their registration papers) in front of the Ministry of Defence. In the tussle with the police two policemen were killed and about twenty injured. It is worth noting that most of those who took part in the scuffle had no connection with the call-up of young men for military service. And there wasn't any call-up either. One thirty-year old "student" who arrived here from the north of the country specially to take part in the struggle against the "fascists", was run over by a bus while trying to get away from the police. It's very likely that it was he who killed the policemen, but he is regarded throughout the country as a victim of mindless police brutality. The funeral of the "victim" will be turned into a grandiose demonstration. Already tens of thousands of people have arrived in the city from every part of the country.

OUR OPPORTUNITIES

I met Lady with Greyhead. Lady and Husband (and Greyhead, of course) were absent from Writer's open evening. They occupy a loftier position in the émigré hierarchy. The position of Lady and Husband here corresponds to that of Party leaders of province level in the USSR. Greyhead evidently aims to reach the level of an important personage in the apparatus of the Central Committee or the KGB. Whereas Writer and even the most eminent of his guests could at best be regarded as equal to professors, colonels, district Party workers and shop-managers in the Soviet Union.

Lady and Greyhead gushed over me as people gush over an old friend whom they haven't seen for a long time (and whom, with luck, they will never see again). I don't attach any particular meaning to this because this too is in the nature of the Homosos—sometimes to display joy at meeting a person he doesn't like and doesn't want to see. We decided to "have a little sit-down in a nice little restaurant". They took a table in the very bowels of the restaurant, by the wall. From force of habit Greyhead took a seat with nobody behind him so that he could see the whole room and all who entered and left. He it was who did the ordering. He ordered the cheapest item on the menu—obviously the result of the pernicious influence of the West. He might have tried to show off Moscow-style, I thought. After all, he'll keep the bill and the "firm" will reimburse him for his "business-expenses". Joker often expatiates on the techniques of petty rascality in this area. For example, you can get a bill for twice the sum actually spent if you give the waiter a mark or two extra.

"What do you think of those long-haired fellows over there?" asked Greyhead, nodding towards a group of shaggy young people who had lunged into the restaurant. "What are the reasons for all this rioting by young people?"

"The recent manoeuvres. But they are only the pretext, and not the reason. It's pointless to look for reasons. A few days ago a group of young squatters took over an empty house not far from our *Pension*. What caused this phenomenon? A housing crisis? Well, if there's a 'crisis' here, it's a state of affairs we wouldn't dare to hope for in Moscow in our wildest dreams. I've spoken to the squatters. You know how much they like to give interviews and pose for television. One girl was squatting because her lover had brought her along. Another was the only daughter of well-to-do parents. They own a mansion. I didn't notice a single student among them who could have been studying seriously. They laughed out loud when I asked them about their studies. One student was past thirty, and he's very unlikely ever to get a degree. In short, one can find a number of reasons why this squatting business attracted this or that individual person. But one can't do this for the phenomenon as a whole. Incidentally, this time the police decided not to touch the squatters. And by the morning they had all vanished into thin air. With this kind of thing, media coverage is vital. Sometimes sheer indifference kills these movements. They wanted to provoke a clash with the police to attract attention to themselves. These affrays are dangerous only for the police, not for the 'rebels'. But there's another more interesting point here."

"What's that?"

"The fact that there's any amount of surplus human material to hand, and exceptionally favourable conditions for mass phenomena of this type. There's no Komsomol; there's no KGB. The police is liberal. The 'rebels' have transport, clothes, food, a nice climate, democracy and the attention of the Press. There's a huge number of people who have nothing to do, who don't want to work and who are bored and out for violent sensations. Any amount of them. Especially young people. There's an intense desire to create spontaneous associations of people. And for many people social disturbances are a way of spending their time, a business, or a means of self-assertion."

"And what follows from that?"

"That it's easy to manipulate this mass of people. If one could give them an aim and direct them skilfully enough one could get a move on and do something serious. For example, prevent the construction of an atomic power-station or a military aerodrome, disrupt the military call-up, and make it impossible to set up any new rocket installations. In principle, one can organize a mass movement for any purpose you choose in advance. It's enough to display initiative and expend a minimum of organizational effort. You need only a few hours to organize a 'spontaneous' demonstration or punch-up with a few hundred people taking part. In a week you can organize one with tens of thousands of participants. In a month you can arrange literally a hurricane of demonstrations and disturbances. You know about the riots in F? Only five per cent of the people involved in them were local inhabitants. The rest came from every corner of the country within three days. Of course, as you increase the scale of the disturbances you have to raise the social standing of the participants and also the level of Press coverage. For a bit of rabble-rousing involving tens of thousands of people you've got to have television cameras at the ready, as well as debates in Parliament and interviews with well-known personalities. Naturally, you must have some writers, professors, pop priests and other people who love publicity and enjoy playing at being spiritual leaders. That's no problem. Many of them are ready to contribute money themselves if only someone will pay attention to them."

"I see that you haven't got a very high opinion of these people."

"The intellectual level of any mass movement is very low. The level of the leaders of such movements is suited to the level of the mass: otherwise nobody could become a leader. A leader needs only enough intelligence to be able to turn himself into the sort of fool appropriate to the mass of fools he leads, and to master the art of talking nonsense while looking clever."

The waitress brought the bill. Greyhead studied it carefully. "You've got to check them carefully here," he said. "They respect you if you try to catch them out." Having made sure that everything was correct, Greyhead asked for a receipt with a rubber stamp and some indication that the expenses had been incurred in the course of "official duties".

148

When we were leaving the restaurant a crowd of young people was rushing along the street howling, breaking shop windows and overturning café tables. The young people from our restaurant jumped up and dashed out into the street without paying and began to tear along with the others. An unknown dog rushed at me and kissed me all over. Then the dog's owner appeared in a rage and swore at me.

DOGS

Fairly often the local dogs react to me in a completely different way from their owners. When they see me in the distance they rush towards me, straining at their leashes. If they manage to slip their leads or run up to me before their owners can stop them, they lick my hands and face, look into my eyes, yelp joyfully and smile. Their owners get very angry, call them back and drag them away from me. They resist, whine pitifully and keep looking back at me. And I love being with them. We understand each other. As soon as I get a job I'm going to get a dog. But a dog like me, without a lead.

PEOPLE

"Don't forget about this crucial factor of history: the invasion of the Whites by the Yellows and Blacks," said Inspirer. "Only *we* can defend the world of the Whites against this danger. So it is our role according to the law of history to subjugate the West: to subjugate it in order to save it. If the West doesn't subjugate itself to us it will perish. Having subjugated itself to us, the West will be reborn. Having subjugated the West, we will ourselves be subjugated by it. That is the general law of the continuity of civilization. My dear fellow, we must think in large historical blocks, not in days and years but in epochs."

"You are idealizing our role," I objected. "You are not taking into account the nature of our society and of Soviet man. I know what our society is really like. It's a disgusting society. I know what Soviet man is like. He's a disgusting creature. We haven't the strength to change the quagmire we're in or to change ourselves. We've got used to living in this mess. We've got the strength only to invent face-saving lies about our quagmire and about ourselves and to foist these lies on all and sundry. And to make the lie eternal we have to destroy anything it can be compared with—all the beautiful rivers, lakes and seas of real life. That's what the West is for us. Its existence irritates us and makes us suffer. We've only one way of asserting ourselves over it: to bring it down and destroy it. We can save the West from the Yellow Peril and the Black Peril by imposing our world upon it. But then our world isn't the White World, but a Grey World."

"A Red World, you mean."

"What's the difference? Red means Grey."

"That too is a general law of history supported by numerous facts and allowing no exceptions. Even the most mighty trees grow out of the ground; the brightest flowers have their roots in the earth. All right, we're mud, dung and so on. But we are the soil. You must realize that the West has imposed so many restrictions on itself that its hands are irrevocably tied: humanism, democracy, human rights, and so on . . . But we shan't stand on ceremony with anyone, Black, Yellow or Red. If it's necessary, we shall stop at nothing. And the West knows that."

THE CENTRE

The Press has announced the creation of the Centre. In the same announcement Professor has been promoted to be a member of the Academy of Sciences of the USSR (a former one, of course), although he wasn't even a full professor. Lady has been promoted to the rank of professor. Naturally, they don't deny these cock-and-bull stories. I haven't received any offers of work at the Centre. I haven't even received a personal invitation to the ceremonial opening. Enthusiast has received an invitation. He looks down on everyone else. He's glad they didn't give me a post at the Centre and doesn't hide it. He says it's true I'm a professional sociologist, but in Moscow "that business" is in such bad shape that he, Enthusiast, "in effect knows his way around in sociology better than all Soviet sociologists put together" (these were his very words).

In the *Pension* we are having a stormy discussion about the problem of the Centre.

"This Centre's a gift for the KGB."

"Exactly the opposite."

"The real truth is that it's a gift *from* the KGB."

"Don't be a sophist."

"It would have been better if they'd organized a Special Centre called

'The Soviet Way of Life'. Organize life there as it is in the Soviet Union. Sell cheap trips to it. It would be a howling success."

"I don't think it would. Westerners can go to the Soviet Union any time they like. Plenty of cheap trips there."

"Yes, but then they have to look at what they're shown. And live in special conditions. Whereas in the Special Centre they would live as Soviet people live."

"I also doubt whether a Centre like that would work. In order really to savour the Soviet way of life even a year isn't enough. Sometimes even a decade. And then visitors to the Centre would live in it knowing that it wasn't for long; whereas real Soviet people have no hope at all of ever escaping from the Soviet way of life. And in such a Centre how could you get across the problems of rearing children and giving them a good start in life, a decent education and a career?"

"Why have a Special Centre when it's so much simpler to give them a truthful description of life in the Soviet Union on paper?"

"It's never simpler to tell the truth. And you won't earn any money writing descriptions like that. But with a Special Centre one could make a fortune."

"In that case, according to the laws of business, you'd have to deceive people. For the Centre to make a good profit you'd have to find people who enjoyed living there in frightful conditions. That means that the frightfulness would have to be purely decorative."

"True. But that's what I'm talking about. My idea for a Special Centre was not that people should live in the real USSR but in a sort of imaginary one."

"For that matter this *real* Centre here won't study the *real* Soviet Union but a sort of imaginary one."

A CANDID CONVERSATION

A man we didn't know was listening in to our conversation. When we stopped talking he asked me whether I could spare him a few minutes. He said he wanted to talk to me alone. Not for publication but for background information only. I said I would prefer it to be for publication. He ignored my words and asked me to explain how my views differed from the views of other Soviet émigrés.

"Well, the first difference is that I have views and they don't," I said.

"And secondly?"

151

"In the main orientation of my consciousness. Western sovietologists and journalists, together with Soviet oppositionists and 'critics of the regime', have thought up a new lie about the Soviet Union in place of the official lie. And this new lie serves the Soviet authorities just as well as the official lie does."

"I don't understand. In what way can criticism of the Soviet regime serve the regime?"

"Because it too is a smoke-screen, only of a different colour. And it doesn't matter what the colour of the smoke-screen is so long as it hides an opponent who is on a genuine offensive."

"But where is the guarantee that *your* words are not a smoke-screen?"

"Your own common sense. Throw away your prejudices. Think for yourself. The truth is simple if you're prepared to put your mind to work. And besides, only individuals speak the truth. I'm an individual."

"You speak of an opponent on the offensive. What do you have in mind? A future war?"

"No, the attack of the Soviet Union on the West that has already begun. For the time being this is taking the form of peaceful penetration of the body of the West by masses of Soviet people. The latest emigration . . ."

"But that doesn't amount to much. There are data-banks on all these people. Their access to the vitally important points of society is either closed entirely or restricted."

"But they don't need any kind of access. They are already actively creating the smoke-screen. Their main function is simply to be present in the body of the enemy."

"But what can they do?"

"Just imagine how many people are needed to control and isolate one man in normal conditions of life. But when you have to keep an eye on ten men, a thousand or a hundred thousand? Ask the mathematicians who are concerned with social problems, and they will tot up for you how many people are needed to cope with a 'fifth column' which can totally demoralize a country when it's told to do so."

"Do you think that they've already worked that out in the Soviet Union?"

"Of course they have."

"And they've turned the calculation into reality?"

"They're close to it, at any rate."

"Forgive me, but this is a fantasy."

"Well, have a try at giving my 'fantasy' some publicity; or at least try to bring it to the attention of the circles which . . ."

"That's difficult. One needs chapter and verse in order to . . ."

"But you don't need chapters and verses in order to spread a smoke-screen."

"But we've got more than enough facts . . ."

"You can gather as many facts as you want to support any old lie."

"Tell me, how does the Soviet people react to the phenomenon of opposition within the country?"

"As a whole, negatively."

"But why? After all, the criticisms of the regime are just. The demands of the opposition are natural and sensible."

"That depends on the point of view. From yours, the Western one, they are. But from the viewpoint of the Soviet population the opposition's demands are demands for privileges which are far beyond the reach of the mass of the population."

"I don't understand at all. Please explain."

"The Soviet opposition is demanding things which are already available in the West; and so the demand for them seems natural to the West. But for the mass of the Soviet population all this is light years away and so the demands of the opposition merely provoke irritation. Only a small segment of the population can be allowed access to these blessings for the time being. Naturally, they are enjoyed now by those people who can use their position in Soviet society to get a decent slice of the national cake. But this is done according to the norms of society and not in the teeth of those norms. It is easy to become indignant at certain facts of Soviet life when you're sitting here in the West. But you go there and have a try at satisfying the opposition's demands in real Soviet conditions. It's easy enough to be a do-gooder and a humanist if somebody else is paying the bill. If you start doing these things at your own expense you may understand what it's all about."

"But hang it all, it's easy enough to satisfy the demands of the dissidents. For example, the right to emigrate."

"How many people would your country like to take from the Soviet Union? As far as I know, you've about two million of your own people unemployed."

"Those are our problems, not yours."

"And how we deal with dissidents is our problem and not yours. I'll tell you an instructive story. Every summer in the Soviet Union many millions of people are sent to the countryside to bring in the harvest. I've done it more than once myself. One day a dissident turned up in our brigade. He said that these trips out to the farms amounted to compulsory slave-labour and that the conditions of work were ghastly. And he refused to work as a sign of protest. What do you think of his conduct?"

153

"He was a brave man. If everybody had followed his example, then . . ."

"Then the food situation in the country would have been even worse. For you this man is a freedom-fighter with guts, a defender of human rights and other beautiful things. But for us he was just a parasite and a demagogue. We put up with him for a while and then we threw him out of the brigade."

"How could you do such a thing?"

"The brigade had been given a certain amount of work to do. And he was cutting a figure as a brave and high-minded champion of democracy at our expense.

"And here's another example for you. Last night a Soviet émigré appeared on television. He waxed all eloquent about his struggle with the regime to get a car. Tell me, do you think it's natural for a former Soviet citizen to want to have a car?"

"Of course I do."

"And do you know what that man's pay was over there? To save enough to buy a car on his pay, you would have had to wait a century. I'm not joking, this is the literal truth. Where would a man like that get the money from? Soviet people knew where. For them this man is a common or garden scoundrel. The Westerner doesn't know this; and he doesn't want to know it. It doesn't matter to you where this man got the money from. The important thing for you is that he has the money and he wants to buy a car. And, incidentally, they don't make many cars in the USSR. Why should this dentist with his illegal income be able to get a car when professors, artists, writers and people like that can't? You have a car yourself? Well, go and give it to a dissident in Moscow who is dying to get a car, in accordance with the norms of Western society, not Soviet society. When you defend this man's right to have a car in Moscow, you are not fighting for the rights of man and democracy; you are trying to make Soviet society give this man a share of the good things of life to which he is not entitled according to the norms of Soviet society. Over there he didn't deserve a car. By doing what you're doing you are fighting for privileges for this man and against justice. And it's the same with all the rest, including freedom of speech, freedom of publication and freedom of conscience."

"But shouldn't we somehow try to influence Soviet people?"

"When it pressurizes the Soviet Union the West is pursuing its own aims: to weaken the enemy. Its *modus operandi* is to tempt an insignificant part of the Soviet population with Western goodies and to urge it to struggle against 'the regime'. The calculation is not so much that Soviet society will evolve in the direction of Western society (that's just demagogy to hide the real intention), as that Soviet society will be weakened from within and that the West will acquire a sort of fifth column inside it. This calculation was at the heart of the Western operation in the Soviet Union known as the 'dissident movement'. The Soviet authorities replied to it with a series of operations of their own, of which the most important was 'Operation Emigration'. Now we can add up the profit and loss . . ."

"I look at this rather differently. You don't understand Soviet society correctly, either the Soviet leadership or the Soviet opposition. If you will allow me, I will explain . . ."

WE AND THE WEST

All the same that politician whom Inspirer was talking about has been murdered. The West is in a panic. My interrogators have forgotten, or so they pretend, that I warned them about this, and I don't want to remind them myself. My thoughts are working in a different direction. There's panic here. But if such a thing happened in the Soviet Union, the reaction there would have been the opposite; we would have closed our ranks even more tightly, strengthened, reinforced, increased . . . And it's a strange thing too, that they should elevate this run-of-the-mill politician to the ranks of the great. Here in the West great politicians are impossible in principle because their influence on the real course of events is tiny and their power insignificant. They are subjected to public criticism. The Press debunks them and tries to drop them in it; they are selected in such a way that they themselves think more about their own personal position than about the position of their countries.

Chief asked me what I thought about this murder.

"An outstandingly successful experiment," I said, calmly.

"What do you mean, experiment?" Chief's eyes nearly popped out.

"Just imagine what would happen here if about ten 'great politicians' like that were rubbed out all at once," I said, without any emotion. Chief didn't reply.

"Incidentally, the Soviet Union will begin the war against the West," I said, "after there has been a fall of snow. The West will be paralysed, and . . ."

Chief went out without saying goodbye.

THE OPENING OF THE CENTRE

The opening of the Centre took place, as Professor remarked in his inaugural address, in a ceremonial atmosphere. This was the only passage in Professor's speech which deserved attention; the event bore a strong resemblance to a ceremonial celebration in a Soviet institution on the occasion of an official holiday, a jubilee, an inauguration, a launching ceremony, an investiture or the award of the Red Challenge Banner. It only needed the portraits of the classics of Marxism and the Party and Government leaders, a bust of Lenin, and some red flags and slogans . . . But we who have been trained for years to behold with our own eyes these attributes of our triumphs can easily supply them in our imagination. And our imagination was given a boost when the congregation greeted the missive to the Centre from Writer-of-the-Russian-Soil with "tempestuous applause" and a "standing ovation". The missive gave precise instructions to the Centre and to the entire Soviet emigration (and, for good measure, to the Presidents of all Western countries, cultural figures and ordinary citizens) what to do and whither to lead humanity. The directives boiled down to the two cornerstones of the programme for saving Russia, and thereby of course all humanity: (1) don't live by lies, (2) write the word "God" with a capital letter.

Then they read out a missive from Great-Dissident-of-the-Soviet Union, which was also greeted with tumultuous applause and a standing ovation. In this missive it said that the situation was pregnant with consequences. Then they began reading out other missives. These were applauded too, but sitting down.

Joker, who was sitting beside me, said that all that was missing was a missive from the Central Committee and the KGB. "Give them time," I said. "It might still get here in time." And I wasn't entirely wrong. Professor began reading out extracts from Soviet newspapers with this kind of headline: "How our enemies evaluate our noble activity for the good of . . ." While Professor was doing this, a murmuring started in the hall so that he had to call the congregation to order. Lady, who was fulfilling the function of Madam Chairman at that point, remarked reprovingly that after all they were not at a Party meeting in a Soviet institution, and would they kindly behave more quietly.

In the audience one could see representatives of the Western intelligence agencies and anti-Soviet organizations. I noticed at least a dozen people of whom I could be a hundred per cent certain that they belonged to the KGB, and more than a score about whom I was well over 50 per cent certain.

Then came Lady with a wide-ranging paper on the tasks of the Centre. Every word had been typed out in advance. She read it out in involuntary imitation of the present General Secretary of the Central Committee of the Communist Party of the Soviet Union. I wasn't the only person to notice the resemblance. But the thing had ceased to be a joke. "Where are we?" Joker asked. "At a Party meeting?" "Pitch it a bit higher," I said. "We're at the Province Party Conference level at the least."

"Ladies and gentlemen," Lady began, and, relieved that she had safely negotiated an accident black-spot, smiled. "It is with a feeling of great responsibility for the fate of humanity, progress and democracy that our Centre commences its activity in the field of . . ." Lady gave us a sketch of the international situation and of the state of play inside the Soviet Union, and then presented a sort of Report on the activities of the Soviet emigration over the last few years ("during the latest five-year plan", as Joker put it). She noted that with every passing year the Soviet emigration was gaining in strength, that a collective of many thousands had been formed, all of them warriors against the Soviet regime, that the volume of anti-Soviet published material had been trebled, and the number of meetings devoted to anti-Soviet problems had been increased tenfold, that co-ordination between the work of different groups had been developed, and that co-operation between all three waves of the Soviet emigration had been strengthened . . . There had been particular successes in the field of . . . etc., etc. But having given the successes achieved in the struggle against the Soviet regime their due (here Lady moved on to the critical part of her Report) "and as we carefully nurture the positive experience we have gained, we must at the same time admit our omissions and shortcomings, frankly and in a business-like manner . . ." It was essential to raise in every way . . . decisively terminate . . . exploit the reserves at our disposal . . . overcome departmental barriers . . . listen sympathetically to proposals for rationalizing . . . to apply in practice . . . to back the initiative . . . combining a variety of approaches . . . life itself dictates new methods to us . . . "Moved by a common enthusiasm," shouted Lady in conclusion, "we Soviet émigrés, victims of the Soviet regime and fighters for human rights, we will struggle consistently and tenaciously for . . ."

". . . the title of 'Enterprise of Anti-Communist Labour'"—Joker completed Lady's sentence in a fairly loud voice. People shushed at us.

After the meeting the important personages made off to a restaurant to celebrate the event. At the expense of the Centre of course; i.e. at the expense of the local tax-payer. They didn't invite Writer. He was deeply hurt and behaved like a Moscow Party "champion of truth" who has not been elected to the Party bureau; that is, like someone who has been offended and knows he is superior precisely because his colleagues have offended him. "Why didn't they give you a job?" he said, spotting me in the crowd of those who had not been invited.

"It's very strange. I tried so hard to get you on board. Although they don't pay much attention here to my opinion either. Why not come back to our place? My wife will give us a better meal than that restaurant."

The soldiers of the Special Amphibious Battalion in their inflatable dinghies and, as always, wearing their bright orange life-jackets, were returning to their comfortable barracks.

"Look," cried Writer. "What's that?"

"Warriors."

"What's that on them?"

"Life-jackets."

"What for? The water only goes up to their knees."

"In order to be closer to a war footing."

"Why haven't they got any weapons then?"

"Because they're Western soldiers. They don't need arms. They're only interested in how to survive."

"But why are their life-jackets so bright?"

"So that the enemy can recognize them from far off and stop firing."

"You're joking?"

"No, not at all. There's only one problem which troubles everybody here: where to run to when the Soviet army arrives, and how to surrender to it in the most advantageous way possible."

"That's odd. We never had to face the problem of how to live under the Germans. We fought against them. And the first thing we did was to chuck away all the superfluous means of defending ourselves: gas-masks, helmets and bayonets. As our political officer liked to say, a soldier should have with him only what enables him to run *towards* his death as quickly as possible."

"Very well said."

"He was killed, that fellow. I was wounded three times, fighting for the

Soviet Union. But if the Soviet army marched in here, I'd volunteer to fight against it."

Writer's wife gave us a meal in true Moscow style. Writer said what a good thing that we didn't go to the restaurant: restaurant food gave him heartburn. Then we looked at the television and saw an absolutely meaningless but technically superb film. Writer said that what was characteristic of Western art was the non-correspondence between form and content. Grandiosity about nothing, that was the essence of it. With us in Moscow it was the reverse: wretched treatment of the grandiose.

When I went home nobody at all was to be seen on the streets. In Moscow at this hour of night the streets would be full of people. Not far from the *Pension* a police-car drew up beside me. For a time it moved slowly alongside and then suddenly went off at high speed. Evidently the custodians of law and order had decided that I presented no danger to their democratic society.

THE ESSENCE OF THE MATTER

Night passes for me without sleep. In order to make the time go by I recall my conversations with Inspirer.

"There's no need to exaggerate the strength of our network of agents in the West," said Inspirer. "We shouldn't exaggerate the impact we make on the West, or imagine that the West is all that gullible, vulnerable and defenceless. There, too, there are intelligent and realistic people occupied with 'Soviet affairs'. In short, let's forget about the detective-story nonsense and the ideological rubbish and consider the situation sanely and soberly. The West is like one of these enormous juggernauts. If it moves off in a certain direction, then no type of Soviet policy towards the West and no amount of agents in the West are going to push it off its chosen course. For us the problem is as follows: will this Western juggernaut go trundling off in the general direction we want it to, or not? And if so, what can we do to make it coast along further in the same direction, and more rapidly into the bargain, so that it can brush aside from its path all those who want to prevent it moving in that direction? Our own activities can succeed only if they correspond with the objective tendencies of history—that's the essence of the matter. We need to clarify with absolute precision whether they do or not. We have more than enough information of all kinds about what is actually happening in the world. There's no let-up from all sorts of experts and specialists. But the more information there is and the more experts there are, the less confidence we have that we understand deeply and correctly enough what is taking place. Right now we desperately need just a few people who are capable of such a task and who would deserve our trust. We need real geniuses in this field.

"The greatest battle in history is approaching," continued Inspirer. "On its outcome will depend whether we stay in power for centuries or whether we have to step down from the pages of history as a temporary zig-zag and curiosity. We are staking everything on the outcome. Our forces are not limitless. There is still time for us to choose our path: either we can shut ourselves up and turn our country into a well-defended fortress, or we can spread over the whole planet and penetrate all its pores. Our choice of path depends on whether we truly understand the course of history or not and whether we believe in our view of history or not. For the moment we are still using a matrix of long-familiar guidelines and acting from inertia, that is, in the dark. But perhaps this path will lead to catastrophe. We are beginning to lose confidence and experience fear. Already we find we cannot carry out our brilliantly conceived and well-thought-out plans right through to the end any more. We begin to implement them reluctantly and then gladly drop them half-way through. Take Operation Afghanistan, for instance, and for that matter Operation Emigration, which we will hardly push through to the end. Perhaps we shall have enough guts to do Operation Poland. But that's a very simple one. And even over that there are voices at the top calling out: stop that mess, enough of it! At the moment we need something like what Marx, Lenin and Stalin did together in their time. The irony of history lies in the fact that now we can only do such things secretly. Now it's only a secret agent like you, and a middle-rank pen-pusher from the Organs like me, who can fulfil the intellectual functions of a historical genius. But in many years' time . . ."

"In many years' time," I thought, "the man recognized as a genius of that kind will be he who, at a suitable moment, will express only a hundredth part of what a genuine genius can say today. Besides, we haven't got the problem of choosing our path any more; we are doomed to what's happening independently, and at times regardless, of our will. In this situation genius is necessary only to satisfy one's own idle curiosity. I have satisfied mine fully. Everything is clear to me; moreover, it's clear for many centuries ahead. Finally, in our time a genius is the agglomeration of numerous mediocrities fulfilling primitive functions. Today's computers are the materialization of the genius of our time. But, as always, it is the degenerates and scoundrels who make use of the products of genius. Schoolchildren here in the West don't even know the multiplication table, but all of them can use computers which

160

are hardly bigger than a matchbox. The leaders of the Soviet Union can hardly manage to spell out their speech-writers' texts, let alone learn to master school computers. But it is they who decide the problems of the epoch."

THE EDIFICE

There is only one bright spot on the dark horizon of my life (I am beginning to express myself really beautifully; this is symptomatic): it's my Edifice. It is especially beautiful early in the morning when the sun comes up. It becomes so radiantly joyful that I want to weep from ecstasy. It will, of course, be the Temple of a new and clean Religion. Within its portals a young and triumphant God will dwell.

HOPES

Lady rang this morning. "The Centre's leadership," she said solemnly (it was as though she was saying "The Party Leadership") "intends to take you on board." Her voice made it sound like the Party bureau. "For the time being, of course, without pay: voluntary service to the community, so to speak" (at which she gave a Muscovite giggle). I would deliver an introductory course of lectures on sociology to the staff of the Centre. "In addition, we are preparing a collection of articles. Couldn't you contribute one? For the time being we can't pay a fee."

Having spent my last copper on writing equipment I sat down to write the article. I got quite carried away—I was ravenous for work. Next day the article was ready.

THE ARTICLE

To understand the nature of real-life Communist society (and that is what society in the Soviet Union actually is), one must be a sophisticated dialectician. But the dialectical method of thought is either clean forgotten or, in its caricatured form, serves as an Aunt Sally for every kind of "educated" nincompoop and snob, or, in its stultified and vulgarized form, it has become part of the State ideology. Contempt for the

161

dialectical method of thought is itself the first major hindrance on the road towards an understanding of Communism as it really is.

Nowadays an enormous number of people think, talk and write about Soviet (and in general about Communist or socialist) society. But they are all bogged down in a swamp of worldly, everyday passions, vanity and cupidity. Some defend this society at the expense of the truth; others criticize it at the same expense. Some look at it through the eyes of the sufferer, others through the eyes of the profiteer. Some are after a topic which will make them look clever and noble; others want to make a fast buck by pointing to the ulcers of Soviet society; a third lot propose programmes for the transformation of that society and suggest that what they want is actually possible. Nobody wants to look at this society simply out of intellectual curiosity, giving no preference to any *a priori* doctrine and without assuming the stance of any particular (not even the "progressive") social category of people or advancing any particular programme for the liberation of the people from the evils of this society or for the construction of some "genuine Socialism (Communism) with a human face". This inability to entertain a disinterested intellectual curiosity is the second serious obstacle on the road to an understanding of real Communism.

In this short article, I shall try to outline the views held by a dialectically thinking man about real Communist society. For him this society is neither good nor evil; he does not want to prescribe what it ought to be like according to its own political demagogy or megalomania. Rather he accepts it as an objectively existing fact that is at least worthy of the idle curiosity of the intellectual bystander.

THE CONSEQUENCES

My article created a real rumpus at the Centre. Professor declared that it was a provocation by the KGB. Lady said that she had not expected such despicable behaviour. The article was doomed. But in order to give the Centre the appearance of democracy they gave it to Enthusiast for his comments.

Enthusiast came in to see me looking important, without his usual tittering and with the mien of one who is the arbiter of destiny. He said they had given him my article to look at and express an opinion on. He, Enthusiast, was in categorical disagreement with my basic concept, and if I did not re-work the article from top to bottom he would be forced to turn it down. I asked him what had happened to freedom of opinion. How was he intending to construct true socialism with all the civic freedoms, among them freedom of opinion, when he himself showed such intolerance of someone else's opinion and when, into the bargain, he was already living in a society which had all these civic freedoms?

"We," he said (notice that it is already "we"), "are not preventing you from publishing your opinion in any other place. And we shan't subject you to repression as in the Soviet Union. But our [already 'our'] periodical [already 'periodical'] has its own political complexion [it has it already, although the first issue still hasn't come out]. We cannot . . ."

FREEDOM OF SPEECH

I translated the article into German and sent it to a magazine famous for its "objectivity". A fortnight later I received a refusal. I wanted to know what was up. It turns out that the famous periodical had contacted the Centre to ask its opinion of the article. Lady sent them the pogrom-like comments of Enthusiast. I reminded the latter of his phrase about how "they" were not going to prevent me from publishing my free opinion elsewhere. To start with Enthusiast was at a loss and began to titter and babble some disconnected words. Then, remembering the importance of his new position, he adopted the pose of an all-powerful giant. "Struggle is struggle," he pontificated. "We won't stop at anything; we'll open the eyes of the world to . . ."

I didn't bother to listen to what these pygmies intended to open the eyes of the world to: I was late for my regular interrogation session. "You are a loner," I thought on the way, "and that's why you're doomed to a miserable existence here. In the Soviet Union you could allow yourself to be an independent loner because you belonged to an official collective, an official Party, an official society, all of which had legally and openly assumed the functions of a mafia. Personally this was not humiliating. Inasmuch as the Soviet mafia is all-powerful, it can sometimes be magnanimous towards persons such as me. But because the local mafias here in the West are limited and powerless, they are both merciless and humiliating."

And I crossed Lady and Professor off my list of Soviet agents.

WEEKDAYS

Enthusiast's alliance with the Centre wasn't a success. He overwhelmed them with his reams of bumph. They made heroic efforts to beat him off.

He abuses Professor, Lady and "all that riff-raff". He assures me that they forced him to demolish my article and offers to place it in Mrs Anti's periodical. He rather imagines that he can come to a compromise with her. "Of course there will be differences between me and her. After all, we're in the West and not Moscow. Freedom of speech!" I said that an anti-Communist periodical which developed the theory of true Communism would indeed be a world sensation. There was only one difficulty: how is one to define true and untrue anti-Communism? And won't true Communism turn out to be untrue anti-Communism? Enthusiast gave a contemptuous neigh and rushed off to plan the first combined programmatic issue of the periodical. But which of them is going to out-paranoia the other? Can Soviet paranoiacs have taken the lead over Western ones already?

THE BATTLE AGAINST THE REGIME

"Great Dissident has declared a hunger-strike," Enthusiast announced proudly.

"At the moment the food situation in the Soviet Union is so bad," said Cynic, "that Great Dissident's noble example will be followed by the whole people."

"I'm not joking." Enthusiast was offended. "He declared a hunger-strike as a sign of protest."

"Against Soviet intervention in Afghanistan?"

"Against the authorities' refusal to allow his daughter-in-law to go to the United States."

"Well, he's a fool. The generals of Soviet dissidence have transformed the opposition into petty trouble-makers. Great Dissident is like a giant fighting with a sewing needle. And he himself doesn't really know what he's fighting against."

Cynic had hit the nail on the head. Many years ago in the Committee of Intellectual Advisers they were thinking up ways and means of forcing big-name dissidents to make a fuss about trivialities and waste their energies on trifles. If one measures Great Dissident's personal concerns against the historic problems of the country, then Cynic's remark about the giant with a sewing needle instead of a sword is very pertinent. The tragedy of the Soviet opposition movement lies in the fact that it always remains inadequate to the scale and scope of our history. And the West, by inflating the insignificant doings of the dissidents to unbelievable dimensions, increases this disproportion even further.

164

At the *Pension* some journalists turned up to find out about Great Dissident's hunger-strike. With the exception of Cynic all the inmates put on a show of exultation. I declined to give an interview. The next day the interviews with the Pensionnaires came out in the newspapers, but without Cynic's contributions. "So this is freedom of speech, is it?" raged Cynic. "A couple more things like this and I'll be the keenest defender of the Soviet system."

THE SOUL AND BRAINS OF HISTORY

"In the West," said Inspirer, "people think that the highest leaders of our Party and State are the soul and brains of our historic aspirations. This is a bad mistake. The soul and brains of our history are you, me and millions of other representatives of the intellectual élite. We are dispersed throughout society and hidden in the wings of the visible theatre of history. There are many of us. But we lack organizational unity and the solidarity of an élite. And you can't resolve great historical problems without a monolithic ruling élite. There is only one force in this country that can create such an élite: ourselves, the Organs. But we've too little time and too bad a reputation. We need to go on a crash course to change our moral standing by force. To do what we'll have to return to Stalinist methods. The cretins in the West are afraid of our 'hawks', of our unreconstructed Stalinists, of our 'old men'; and they place their hopes on the 'doves', 'liberals' and 'Young Turks'. But they ought to be frightened of the exact opposite—they ought to fear *us*. It was young people, incidentally, who were the heart and soul of Stalinism in its heyday."

But where are they, these young geniuses, I thought. They've vanished without a trace. Their names will never appear on the pages of history. We make titanic efforts to persuade society to use even a tiny part of our genius (on the whole, genius *is* service to the people). Society uses us unwillingly, but it's always glad to punish us because of our talents.

"Don't think I'm a Stalinist," said Inspirer. "I only mean that until now Stalinism has been seen either from outside (under Western eyes) or from the viewpoint of Stalin's personal power apparatus and his system of repression. The time has come to take a look at Stalinism from below, that is, as a mass phenomenon, as a great historical process in which millions of people were lifted up from the very dregs of society into education, culture, creativity and active participation in life. It's true that

165

many perished. But a great many more survived, changed their way of life at its roots, got on their feet and lived out a life that, compared with the past, was an interesting life. What happened was unprecedented in history: a cultural, spiritual and occupational take-off by the great mass of the population. It was a creative process in all of life's fundamental sectors. Its value still hasn't been properly appreciated. I think centuries will pass before this process is given its due with all objectivity. What we have now is wretched, grey and miserable in comparison with the Stalin period. However, you and I are not historians, but executives and thinkers," said Inspirer. "This is why I've been talking my head off about Stalinism: if a new Stalin came along and promised me full power in my sphere of activity just for two or three years, but warned me that after these two or three years I would be shot, I would accept his proposal. I would like just once in my life, if only for a short time, to pour my thought and will-power into one of the little streams that run into the great river of history. In Stalin's time one could do this. Now you can't. I know that it wasn't a matter of Stalin's personality but a matter of the character of the very epoch which, among other things, generated Stalin himself. But we have got used to personifying epochs and pinning impossible hopes on particular personalities."

A CREATIVE LABORATORY

Today Writer was talking to me as if he had been made secretary of the Party bureau or chairman of the local Party Committee. And he had quite good reasons for doing so. A magazine had interviewed him. Moreover, the interview was not about the burdens of censorship in Moscow, and not about creative freedom in the West, but about his, Writer's, creative laboratory.

"I've finally had enough of politics," said Writer proudly, gazing at the ceiling. "Damn it all, I'm an artist; I'm a master of words. It's more important for me to talk about my creative techniques. Do you know which question of theirs came as a complete surprise to me?"

Writer's wife, who had been listening in to our conversation from the kitchen, also burst out laughing. "You won't guess in a month of Sundays," she said.

"They asked me," Writer got it in before her, "they asked me: do I use dope?" "And," said Wife, forcing a word in edgeways, "he asked them 'What is dope?'"

"You can imagine how they laughed," Writer had seized the initiative again. "They said that we Russians were all very witty and that my answer would cause a sensation among their readers."

"They said they would put it on the cover of the periodical together with his portrait," cut in Wife. "Then they said," interrupted Writer, "that like all Russians I must drink vodka. And I asked them . . ." "And he asked them," broke in Wife, " 'Is vodka dope? It's just the Russian national drink, like your coca-cola.' "

SUCCESS

"They've published it, the swine!" cried Enthusiast, waving a little émigré journal with his article in. "The first serious scientific work in the world about the Soviet dissident movement. Read it."

"I'm sorry, I can't. I've made a decision."

"I know you have, but I don't approve of it. It isn't comradely."

"All right, I give in."

I quickly ran through Enthusiast's opus. From the very first lines the picture was clear. It was typical Soviet eyewash. All Soviet Reports are constructed on the same principle. And although everything in the article was sort of true, taken as a whole the thing was a typical Soviet fabrication: Made in the USSR.

"That's marvellous. The Soviet system has only a few minutes left to live."

"You never stop joking."

"I'm not joking," I said. "I'm sad. I'm sorry that Communist society has had such a brief life-span and that soon it will disappear for ever."

CYNIC'S OPINION

Enthusiast is convinced that at least a thousand copies of the issue in which his article appeared will be smuggled into the Soviet Union and that his influence on the "liberation movement" there will grow even further. Cynic said he agreed with Enthusiast's declaration, as he was familiar with the system of sending anti-Soviet literature into the Union. More than that, he's even certain that the KGB will not make any special difficulties, because it knows full well the value of such rubbish and just how much influence it will really have on the "liberation movement": for the dissidents it will mean disillusionment, depression, contempt and irritation. ("Over there they've gone quite crazy.") And Enthusiast's influence on this "movement" will indeed change, but not in the direction he thinks. Cynic said that if he were the KGB he would issue a special digest in Moscow containing all the works of sages like Enthusiast without any commentaries. The digest would be called "Paranoiacs in the service of Communism". Besides, this kind of idiocy is absolutely in the Western spirit. At the moment everyone's going mad here about the predictions of some Nostradamus or other. A thousand books and articles have been printed about him. It amounts to a complete epidemic of roguery and charlatanism. But you won't get the West to read a single book with a serious prognosis or a serious analysis of mankind's real perspectives, try as you may.

DESPAIR

Cynic's mention of Nostradamus touched the wound in my soul. How much time and money the world spends on charlatans and swindlers! Only a thousandth part of it would suffice to work out a scientific theory that would enable one to make reliable prognoses about the future. Not idiotic predictions about the date on which this or that Soviet bureaucrat will kick the bucket, and of what disease, and who will take their place; but predictions about vitally important trends in real life; about the conditions of large groups of the population, of whole countries and groups of countries. For a bet, and purely out of intellectual curiosity, I would be ready to work with a small group of good assistants and construct a theory with which one could predict the important moves of the Soviet leadership and the evolution of Soviet society as a whole over the next decade or two; and to construct a computerized model of the USSR which would enable us to make use of a general theory in conjunction with empirical facts. But . . .

"But," I hear the mocking voice of Inspirer, "God doesn't give horns to a cow that butts. It's a good job that nothing is working out for you in the West. We counted on that in advance."

"But if you knew in advance what I would think about all this, why did you let me come here?" I asked.

"Because we are not all idiots," he said. "Because we know that human psychic phenomena are not something that is permanently fixed, immovable, unchangeable. It's a pity I didn't have time to show you one of our agents whom we consider to be a model of courage, devotion, unswerving faith in our ideals, and other virtues. He would have told you in detail what these qualities involve in real life, that is, spread over many years in time. He got caught, but stood firm and didn't betray us. But he had periods of spiritual collapse and readiness to betray no less often than he had periods of uplift and of wishing to remain faithful. He would have told you that qualities like courage and devotion were just one of the sides and tendencies of his psychic life; and also the result of a confluence of circumstances.

"One day he took the firm decision to 'split' and sell himself to the enemy. But the enemy himself prevented this. And so, in the last analysis, this agent became a hero merely because of chance circumstances. There are opposite examples when agents with, as it seemed, even greater moral qualities than this agent, have become traitors and lost their powers of resistance. In brief, the consciousness of the intellectually developed, cultured and educated person, that it to say, of a member of the intelligentsia, will over the course of time contain every logically conceivable piece of filth. The important thing is that the number of different types of situation in which the intellectual will find himself and the number of possible external manifestations of his internal condition are not very large. It is easy to calculate this in advance and make predictions. Well, you know this business inside out yourself."

THE BATTLE AGAINST THE REGIME

Western heads of State have asked Brezhnev to allow Daughter-in-Law to go to the West. The Pensionnaires are rubbing their hands with glee: look how they are needling the Soviet authorities! Cynic said that if the Soviet authorities agreed to this request he would cease to respect them. Enthusiast declared that if Cynic continued to respect the Soviet authorities *he* would cease to respect Cynic or shake hands with him.

THE VIEW FROM ABOVE

What follows happened long before I found myself involved with Operation Emigration. Inspirer and I were sitting in the National Hotel drinking and chatting about this and that. I was cursing our topmost leaders for their inability to solve what seemed to be simple problems. "Everything will seem different if you look at it not from below but from above," said Inspirer. "If you like, I will give you a chance of looking at

169

the world from above. The best part of our intellectual élite is going to meet at one of the Central Committee villas. They will show films of all aspects of life in the most important parts of the planet. [The films were mostly commissioned by the Western special services, and our intelligence agencies then got hold of them. But our own services made some of them too.] They will give a series of briefings without any ideological adjustments or censorship. Then the participants in the symposium will discuss problems of epoch-making significance on the basis of the information they have received. If this experiment is successful, similar symposia will be laid on regularly."

I naturally agreed. In three days we picked up more information than we had accumulated in all our past lives. After all, many of the participants travelled abroad regularly. We were confused and literally overwhelmed by what we had seen and heard. It took me a week to recover my former calm and capacity for sober thought. At the end of the symposium I arrived at the following conclusions. When one looks at the world from above one can see that enormous masses of people are struggling quite simply for physical survival. From this viewpoint, the Communist system of organizing people, as it is implemented in the USSR, seems to be the best one. Best not for people's lives within the system, but for the survival of a given collectivity struggling against other collectivities. Compared with the West, it is an integral and centralized system, and compared with Japan (and to some extent China), it is a natural system supported by natural qualities found in human nature. Our system doesn't require such cruel training of body and spirit as the Japanese system does. It can exist without a cruel work discipline, without accuracy and precision in everything done. A system of the Japanese type presupposes the reliability of all the constituent elements and the ability to control all the conditions necessary for its functioning. Our system consists of unreliable elements which function, moreover, in uncontrollable conditions. We have our own methods of control, organization and reliability. Nevertheless, they are freer and more human than the methods of the Japanese type of system and nearer to the spiritual achievements of Western civilization. Say what you will, we are still focused in a Westerly direction . . .

Despite everything, our leadership acts in the only correct way. It promotes a type of production and culture suited to the people's abilities. It tries to take from the West everything we can't produce ourselves. We don't imitate the West, like Japan; we just take from the West whatever is lying around and ready-made for us. Japan competes with the West. We don't. We simply use it.

Finally, our leadership is attempting above all else to develop the country's military might, and subordinates everything else to this aim. To prepare the country for the next war, and do everything around the world that can contribute to victory in the war—that is the epoch-making task of our leadership. As to economic and cultural competition with the West, that's for later, after we have knocked it out.

"Well, you've had a look at the world from above," said Inspirer. "What could we usefully do, taking into account everything you've just learned?"

"Just one thing," I said. "We should do everything we've been doing until now, only more persistently, and more consistently. But if only we could raise the quality of what we do just a little."

"You've hit the nail on the head," he said. "You and I are the only people around here with a common-sense outlook. You know, even our highest leaders lose their heads when you bring them in touch with reality, however slightly. And then they begin spouting nonsense just as bad as the nonsense talked by the best minds of our society gathered together here. Our leaders need to be taught the science of epoch-making leadership right from the beginning; moreover, you'd have to do it cynically, without any ideological flimflam. And we need a new Stalin. Otherwise we might still lose the battle for the world because of our inability to see our brilliant plans right through to the end."

"If your new Stalin suddenly looms up on the horizon, let me know," I said. "I will serve him selflessly to the end. I won't save even a grain of my abilities for my own personal use. I'm also prepared to be shot for doing this."

"Unfortunately," he said, "this is impossible for the time being. We can't even manage to compose false Reports for middle-rank officials."

TRUTH AND LIES

Writer has a whole library of anti-Soviet, revelatory, sovietological, kremlinological and other such literature. He extracts evidence and judgements about Soviet society mainly from this literature and not from his own experience. The latter proved to have been extremely scanty, as is the case (with rare exceptions) with all the other critics and unmaskers of the regime. I never cease to wonder at the blindness of people who have bathed in the ocean of facts of Soviet life but understand almost nothing about it. For instance, I have in my hand the book of a well-known critic of the Soviet system and Stalinism. He's very popular in Moscow's dissident circles. "The Red Army," writes this former

Soviet Party bureaucrat, "didn't want to fight (during the war with Germany), the people was longing for the defeat of its own government". And further on: "the decrepitude of Stalin coincided with the decrepitude of the regime". And there are stupidities and absurdities of this type on almost every page.

"What do you think of this?" I asked Writer. "Rubbish, of course," he said. "I was at the front from the first days of the war. We were dying to fight. But such slips of the pen are minor matters. What counts is the description of the structure of power and of the system . . ."

"But that's even greater nonsense," I said. "I'm telling you this as a specialist. These wretched books are aimed at ignoramuses with a particular mind-set. Their intellectual level is no higher than that of a run-of-the-mill Party *apparatchik*. And objectively the role of such ignoramuses is to fuddle the brains of the Western man-in-the-street about Soviet society."

"But what can one do?" asked Writer.

"Reveal the facts," I said, "but cleverly and justly. You spent sixty years in Russia. You took part in the collectivization of agriculture, the war and the struggle against Stalinism after the war. Write about all that, but write the truth."

"They won't print it," he said. "And if they do print it, they will destroy me as a 'Soviet agent'."

"Well, all right then, tell lies," I said.

"They won't come," he sighed.

DECISION OF THE FATES

Whiner hanged himself. We didn't know about this for three days until a nasty smell emanated from his room. We were asked to keep quiet about Whiner's death so as not to spoil the general harmonious image of the emigration. But there was no need to persuade us. We forgot about Whiner on the day he died. It was as if he had never existed. I crossed him off my list of Soviet agents; and erased him from my memory.

THE BATTLE AGAINST THE REGIME

The Soviet authorities have allowed Daughter-in-Law to leave the Soviet Union. Cynic declared that he was disenchanted. He had believed that the Soviet authorities were real tyrants; and now they had turned out to be simple weaklings. Enthusiast shook Cynic's hand. And I crossed Cynic off my list of Soviet agents.

MEANWHILE . . .

The West is gloating over the great victory of the forces of democracy. And why not gloat?! Daughter-in-Law has got permission to leave behind her the frontiers of her unloved country. What a grandiose event! But what is going on meanwhile in the depths of Soviet life? The West couldn't care less about that. From its viewpoint there aren't any depths and cannot be. What could be deeper than the desire of Daughter-in-Law to leave the torture chambers of Bolshevism? And if at the same time, "on the quiet", the authorities have liquidated several real but, save to the KGB, unknown fighters against the "regime", that wouldn't matter. Inasmuch as the West doesn't know about them (or even want to know), then that is a non-event, and that's the end of it.

There was a similar case a few years ago. Then another Great Dissident waged a heroic battle to be able to telephone to France. Three hours after the resolute protest of world public opinion, Great Dissident was allowed his call to Paris. During the conversation he confirmed that they really had forbidden him to have the conversation. Then the West gloated over that victory too. But meanwhile in a provincial Soviet town they were rounding up a dangerous group of "terrorists" . . . A friend who was a KGB investigator blabbed to me about this in his cups. He also told me that members of the group had been trying to establish contact with Western journalists and the dissident leaders in the capital. But the latter thought the provincials were KGB provocateurs. Very convenient! Our leading dissidents couldn't even imagine that there might be people in Russia capable of fighting against the "regime" apart from themselves; and to fight against it selflessly and, moreover, without counting on recognition in the West.

DECISION OF THE FATES

Cynic has found work in a small town in the north of West Germany. All day we drank with him uproariously. "As soon as I've settled in I'll let you know," he said as he bade us farewell. "Come and stay with me.

Now I'll have plenty of money. We'll drink properly, in the Moscow style. We'll talk. Don't be downhearted. Your future will soon be settled too."

THE BATTLE AGAINST THE REGIME

On the front pages of the newspapers there were details of Great Dissident's hunger-strike. Somewhere on page ten in the News in Brief there was a mention of an increase in Soviet arms deliveries to all the African countries that are building Socialism, and of another 20,000 Soviet troops being sent to Afghanistan.

Joker says that Great Dissident has now learned how to fast. "So now he can use his experience and declare a new hunger-strike demanding . . ."

"Demanding that all Soviet soldiers be withdrawn from Afghanistan," shouted Enthusiast.

"Why should he worry about trifles like that?" said Joker. "He's got something much more important to strike about. The light bulb in his corridor has just burned out."

INTERROGATION

"How can we weaken and destroy the Soviet system from within?"

"If you'll allow me, I'll begin by telling you a parable, and then a general idea. Like Christ, I could confine myself to the parable. But, as the experience of history has shown, even Christ's closest disciples didn't understand the meaning of his parables, and later generations interpreted them in every conceivable manner. With us Russians, right from the time of the fable-writer Krylov, we've had an excellent custom—to give a popular explanation of even the most primitive parables. True, this doesn't help much either: people understand nothing all the same. But on the other hand, it clears one's conscience.

"Once upon a time there lived a good, intellectual Soviet family. Husband and wife were scholars. The flatlet, of course, was far too small. Their parents died, and everything in the flat became freer, lighter and happier. But for this almost happy pair there was one big fly in the ointment: an aged grandmother. Grandmother was nearly ninety, but she hadn't even thought of dying. She was a tough old bird, may she suffer for it in the world to come. She even had some of her own teeth left. Strong teeth, like a horse's. Life was impossible with her there.

"And so this intellectual couple decided to starve the grandmother, whom they now thoroughly loathed, to death. Not all at once, but gradually. They devised a food ration that would do the trick. The husband had a job in an important institute; he worked the rations out on a computer. And they began to put their plan into action. Even in a horror film you will never see anything like what happened to the old woman. Gaunt, yellow, with chattering horse's teeth, she wandered about the flat right round the clock looking for something to eat. But . . . But the desired effect didn't come to pass. Three months went by, then another three; then three more. And all the time the old hag was even growing stronger. They called a doctor. He examined the grandmother. He said to her adoring grandchildren that she was in the best of health; she was like an Egyptian mummy and would live for a thousand years.

"Horror seized the spouses. What could they do? They had heard of a certain Wise Man who cured incurable diseases and helped to solve insoluble problems.

"'Well, my good people,' said Wise Man, 'you know that the strongest force in the world is Virtue. Love your old granny, surround her with attention, buy her a chicken, or better still a duckling. Let her have the run of her teeth. And live in peace.' And the couple cursed Wise Man, using the most dreadful language. But what were they to do? They decided to give his plan a try; after all, there was nothing to lose. And so they did. And three days later, beloved grandmother was dead and buried.''

"Does that mean that the West is doing right when it sends food products and technical equipment to the USSR?"

"Verily, Christ was right: they that have ears to hear do not hear. Western help doesn't make things better for the Soviet population; it only helps the authorities in their efforts to increase the country's military might. Soviet society is a bit more complicated than the poor old woman. How much good and evil, and what combination of the two should be applied to the USSR in order to satisfy your cherished dreams: that is something that should be quantifiable and, moreover, quantifiable through studying the nature and state of health of this 'old woman'. But that task is beyond the powers of Western sovietologists, kremlinologists, intelligence officers, journalists, critics of the regime and the dilettantes of the emigration."

"Well, who *is* up to the job?"

"If almost anyone does offer to do it, it's bound to be a put-up job. Take that as a play on words."

175

"Could the people at the Centre do it?"

"Never in a thousand years."

"And could you see to it yourself?"

"I could, but I wouldn't be allowed to."

"Who wouldn't allow it?"

"All the people who have anything to do with the matter. And they are legion."

"But surely in our times you need a large number of people to work together to get any serious results?"

"That's true. However, in this case you also need an intellectual dictatorship exercised by a few people, but by a few who are really competent and tenacious in their efforts to achieve scientific success."

"That's a purely Soviet idea. Here we're living in a democracy."

"There's any amount of that kind of democracy even in the Soviet Union. But there too, alas, there's a great shortage of real dictatorship."

AGAIN ABOUT THE FUTURE

In the Centre there's now a symposium going on about the social and political system in Russia after the fall of Soviet power. Specialists are gathered there from all over the world. Out of boredom I made my way there too. I happened to catch a lecture by a leading theorist of the emigration. The basic thesis of his paper was that Russia must (really must) return to its "post-February" but "pre-October" state of affairs. Storms of applause inspired the lecturer to yet greater stupidities. "Private property has indisputable advantages over public property." He cast irrefragable argument after irrefragable argument into the hall:-

"For example, only one per cent of workable land in the Soviet Union is in private hands; but on that one per cent more vegetables are grown than in all the collective and state farms put together. What could be more convincing than that? Centralized economic management hampers the development of industry and technological progress. The planning system has collapsed. Plans are not being fulfilled. Chaos reigns in the country. Marxist ideology is bankrupt. Nobody believes in Marxism any more. Ideational disorder is shattering the monolithism of society. Total corruption has become the driving force of people's behaviour. Committed fighters for Communism have disappeared. The degradation of culture . . ."

I began to feel sick. I slipped quietly out of the auditorium. Some Individual latched himself on to me. "To think that I emigrated just to

176

near idiots like that," he said. "They think that if a given plot produces so many vegetables then two, three and four times more will be produced on a plot two, three and four times the size. But a man's energies are limited. On a plot that's twice as big he will perhaps produce only one and a half times as much. And at a certain point the increase in the area of worked land will have no positive effect, or will have an inverse effect, on the return. And as the plots grow, so do the numbers of people involved in the whole business. And that means problems of storage, marketing, deliveries, competition.

"And what sort of crack-up in the ideology of the Soviet system are they talking about?" Individual continued. "Here there are millions of people who are ready at the drop of a hat to betray all the values of Western civilization. It's my tenth year here. And I've yet to find a single committed defender of these values. It's only among us Soviet people that defenders of the West's ideals can be found."

NO WAY OUT

We went out into the street. "That's where the West's future is," said Individual, pointing at some groups of students. "Will the West be able to get them under control? However, that's their task, not ours. We've got our own problems. Here there are swarms of people making a living out of Russian topics, but hardly a Russian among them. Western society doesn't accept real Russians. Here they can accept God knows whom, but not a real Russian. There is some sort of hidden fear of Russians here. In their heart of hearts Westerners want us to remain on the level of our 'matryoshka'-dolls, balalaikas, samovars, funny sayings and folk-dancing. And they get very annoyed when we reveal our superiority in anything. Then they try to hush it up, denigrate it or smear it. And back at home, to be sure, we ourselves do everything we can to prevent our neighbours from achieving anything worthwhile.

"They chatter about Russia," Individual continued, "but what do they know about the real Russia? If you call a Russian a bast-shoemaker, he'll ask you what a bast-shoe is. Once we did a survey of people in the most out-of-the-way corners of Russia. The majority of those questioned said they had never seen a bast-shoe. Not so long ago all Russians were convinced that potatoes had been grown in Russia from time immemorial. It even seemed that Russians had appeared in the world as a result of our animal ancestors switching from meat-eating to potato-eating. Wait a few years and most people in Russia will believe that potatoes grow only in America, and on trees at that; while Russia produces tanks, rockets and sputniks.

"The Russian people has already had its future. And that's why it's so indifferent about the future. It has already decided its long-term historic orientation. Only a catastrophe can change it. And on the whole, the fate of the Russian people isn't a Russian problem. It's a problem for those who fear that the Russian people will display its hidden reserves of strength and fight for the position in the history of mankind that its scale deserves.

"These chatterboxes think they're Russians. But to be a Russian it's not enough to be able to speak Russian, to grow up in a Russian milieu and to read Russian writers. You must have something more: the destiny of a Russian. But that is exactly what they don't want to have. They prefer the destiny of Western-type people who merely specialize in Russian subjects.

"People think that we Russians are given to nostalgia. It isn't a question of nostalgia, though, but of something else. What it's a question of I still haven't been able to make out. Only when I got here did I sense what Russia had been for me, and what I had lost. I had lost it irrevocably. If a miracle occurred and I went back, my former bond with Russia still wouldn't be re-established. Once broken off it can never be mended. I'm sure that the original pain of parting would be even worse if I went back. Here in the West there is still some kind of hope that one can bring back the past.

"But if one returned to Russia one would have to abandon even this final hope. Now I can fully understand those émigrés who in their time returned to Russia to certain ruin, dismissing all the terrible facts and warnings with contempt. With my mind I know that the Russia that I yearn for here has long ago ceased to exist in reality. But that doesn't weaken the yearning at all. On the contrary, it strengthens it even further: the yearning is for my own past joined to the yearning for a Russian past that has gone for ever. I know that our Russian life was a nightmare in the past as well. And the awareness of that makes my yearning even greater than before. And not a single ray of light illuminates the future."

We were walking along the narrow little streets of the city, chock-full of motor cars. A special police vehicle was towing away a luxurious Mercedes which had been parked in the wrong place. "It's laughable, isn't it?" said Individual. "The West is full of cars but there's nowhere to park them. We have hardly any, but there's any amount of room for parking. Which is worse?"

I listened to Individual and felt a sense of relief that I wasn't alone in my fate. We exchanged telephone numbers. Next day I rang him on the number he had given me. A voice answered that nobody of that name lived there.

MY MISTAKE

In Moscow I tried to construct a scientific theory of Communist society. One, moreover, not for the broad masses of the population, but for official use only within a limited circle of the intellectual élite. They took away my manuscript. Then they made a careful search of my flat for rough copies. They made me sign an undertaking that I would not work on the subject again, or circulate my ideas. They did this because documents marked "For official use only" quickly become public property, and my theory could be used for anti-Soviet propaganda. My idea that the shortcomings of our society were the inevitable consequences and manifestations of its advantages was deemed scientifically invalid and ideologically pernicious. If society's foundations are good, as they are, then all the phenomena of life which grow out of them must be good too. In other words, our shortcomings are transient and have no bearing on the essence of our social system. I admitted my mistakes, and for a number of years I kept my thought processes to myself.

When I agreed to Inspirer's proposal and got permission to act as I myself saw fit, I decided to avail myself of what seemed to be an unrepeatable opportunity to serve my own personal interests. I immediately let it be known to everyone I was in contact with here that I had my own objective theory of Soviet society and I, better than others, could organize the scientific investigation of it. This was a mistake that couldn't be undone. In the West as well it is lies that people can rally round that are needed, not the sort of truth that arouses pessimism. When I state my view that within Communism there is a unity of shortcomings and advantages my Western critics leave out of consideration my stress on the shortcomings and notice only my assertion of the advantages. From their viewpoint, bad effects stem from bad causes and so Communism cannot have any real advantages. This means that my scientifically objective theory is pro-Soviet propaganda.

179

Enthusiast has got a *Sozialwohnung*. That means a two-roomed flat at a dirt-cheap rent. Now he is threatening to send for a bunch of relatives and friends from Moscow. The KGB will certainly chuck a few more parasites, schizophrenics and old-age pensioners out of the Soviet Union with the greatest pleasure; along with a few of their own agents too, of course. But the Germans, with their "uneasy consciences", have gone so far down this road already that they can't stop it.

All the Pensionnaires who were at hand helped Enthusiast to pack up his goods and chattels. During his time at the *Pension* he had well and truly loaded himself up with junk from nearby clearance-sales. And he had been clever enough to bring a whole library of books with him from Moscow, including the complete works of Marx, Engels and Lenin. After Enthusiast had left, the *Pension* became quieter and even emptier.

JOKER

Out of our "intake" at the *Pension* there remain only the married couples. Artist and Dissident, plus wives, whom I hardly ever see, and Joker. Joker is waiting for his visa to the USA. He and I go on the bummel around the town and drink everything that comes our way. He tells me some amusing Moscow stories, in spirit all like this one:

"I lived in the most dissident district of Moscow," he said. "Our house was almost entirely dissident, with a few exceptions. The KGB, naturally, played all sorts of tricks with us, mostly idiotic ones. Can you tell me why they are all such idiots over there? If I had been given the job I could have made a Brigade of Communist Labour out of those dissidents within six months. In our house, on the same staircase, there lived a bloke who was one of the non-dissident exceptions I mentioned. He was Secretary of the Party bureau in his institute. 'N' lived on the floor below. The KGB decided to organize a provocation against Dissident 'N', plant some dollars on him, carry out a search and accuse him of illegal dealings in foreign currency. The KGB agents mixed up the storeys (nothing surprising about that) and planted the dollars on the Party Secretary. Secretary's wife was spring-cleaning and found the dollars. Like good Communists, they stashed them away, and next morning rushed off to the foreign currency shop. There they were arrested. The KGB was most annoyed with them. Secretary failed to be re-elected at the next Party bureau poll. And Dissident 'N' demanded an equivalent sum of money from Secretary by way of compensation, as the dollars were intended for his flat. If he had discovered them in his home (and he certainly would have done), he wouldn't, he said, have bungled the job as Secretary had. Life's a nightmare, isn't it?''

THE EDIFICE

The building work is complete. Now I can see with my own eyes what Absolute Perfection is. But whatever will be housed in this Enchanter's Castle, this Temple, this Dwelling of God, this Space-Ship, this Palace of Beauty and Happiness?

MARIA

Writer complains of a creative crisis.

"If only I had an important theme and a gripping plot," he said, "I would write a novel in a couple of months that . . ."

"I can tell you a Moscow anecdote. You can blow it up into a novel that will bite harder than Kafka.

"There was a scholar living in Moscow. In his youth he fell in love with a woman who didn't want to marry him. She was called Maria. He tried to hang himself, but they saved him. As he was hanging, he experienced sexual satisfaction. Before this he hadn't had any women, nor did he after. Then he invented a machine. A special love-machine. He called it 'Maria'. When he felt the need for sex he would go to his 'Maria', hang himself, satisfy his passion, and 'Maria' would save him. And he lived with her like that for thirty years. He was totally devoted to her. He called her tender names. He gave her flowers. He made declarations of love to her. Sometimes he quarrelled with her. He would accuse her of coldness. He would become jealous. He would suspect her of infidelity.''

"How do you know all this?"

"From his diary. One day his favourite Pupil and closest assistant happened to read some pages of the diary and guessed at the existence of 'Maria'. Pupil chose his moment and started a relationship with 'Maria'

181

himself. After that the complaints of 'Maria's' coldness in Teacher's diary became ever more frequent. And she in turn began to feel disinclined to have a connection with him. She preferred young Pupil to old Teacher. Then came the day when 'Maria' decided not to save her now repugnant old lover."

"This is in the spirit of CF, cybernetic fiction, of course."

"You are right. I specially thought up an explanation like that to make better literature out of it."

"But what had really happened?"

"Pupil envied Teacher and wanted to take his place. Having discovered 'Maria', he broke a small part of her mechanism."

"This is just a mystery story. It's second-grade literature. You can't squeeze even a page of decent literature out of a story like that."

"If you don't like that plot, I can offer you another, a social one with real bite: let's say, how to defend the West or, which is just the same, how to subjugate it."

HOW TO DEFEND THE WEST

What can the West put up against the Soviet army if it comes charging in? First, against every tank it can put up ten platforms from which the defenders of the West would freely criticize—not Moscow of course, heaven save us from that, but their own social system and their own governments. Then the Soviet soldiers would see what kind of freedom the West had. Secondly, along its frontiers with the East the West should arrange a mammoth sale at give-away prices, or, better still, the free distribution, of all the goods the Soviet people have never even dreamed of. Then they would see what a high standard of living there was in the West! Finally, in the vanguard of the Western armies, the Soviet soldier would find hordes of terrorists fighting for God knows what, plus students and rebellious children. The Soviet people would then see beings who, instead of faces, have ladies' nylon stockings over their heads. And they would give a slight shudder of fear. Then the students would rush to take over the sparsely populated tanks as squats. Whereat the Soviet army would grind to a halt. And when the pack of children, wailing wildly, rushed at the tanks, turning them over and showering them with Molotov cocktails, the Soviet army would flee in a panic to Siberia. And then the Russian émigrés (that is, Jews supported by Latvian riflemen) would restore Monarchy and Orthodoxy on the liberated soil of Russia.

HOW TO SUBJUGATE THE WEST

But on the other hand one could take Western Europe with one's bare hands. For this one needs to expand all types of contacts with the West in every way. The emigration should be stepped up tenfold. Its dissident element should be reinforced. For this, the mass production of Soviet dissidents should be laid on. Special establishments for them, including higher education, should be set up. Popular brochures and books about how to become a dissident should be published. Dissidence should be disseminated in print and on television. Special symposia and congresses and a regular exchange of experience should be organized. Neophyte dissidents should receive free instruction in foreign languages and the techniques of establishing regular contacts with representatives of foreign intelligence services. After passing their final examinations dissidents should be drafted into practical work in strict regime corrective labour camps. On the expiry of their work-sentences, diplomas certifying that the holder is an Accredited Dissident should be awarded; and the recipients should then be banished to Western Europe or the United States. On departure they would be given full freedom of action. The rest would happen automatically. After ten years the West would put its hands up and accept any conditions, provided only that we agreed to cut back our emigration and all the mutually beneficial contacts with the Western world. At this juncture, we will "advise" them to accept our Communist system.

Writer said that these subjects too were fit only for second-grade literature: that is, for satirists and humorists. *He* was writing serious literature. He would have to dig deeper. He had to pierce the deepest secrets of the human heart. He was dreaming of making a profound analysis of the experiences of a brilliant writer who had been forced into leaving his native country and deprived . . .

THE INTELLECTUAL ÉLITE

I'm on my usual way home alongside the river. The water in the river has almost completely disappeared, so the soldiers of the Special Amphibious Battalion will have to put their little dinghies on to wheels. I have the impression that Inspirer is walking beside me, developing his crazy ideas.

"The intelligentsia," he says, "is not homogeneous, because it's a mass phenomenon now. Your Writer is a typical representative of the untalented, vain and grasping mass of intellectuals. As yet, he's better than many of the others. He's not a fool. And, as a Russian, he's gone through difficult patches and suffered. Within the intelligentsia there's a very small section which really does constitute the brains and genius of society; our intellectual élite. If you dig about thoroughly among the mechanisms of our society, you will always uncover the products of the activity of the intellectual élite. The mass of the intelligentsia conceals this fact because *it* exploits its own élite more than anyone else and lives as a parasite at its expense. The majority of the 'intellectuals' appropriates the élite's products and falsifies the overall situation in the culture of society. In this it has a powerful ally—the authorities, the powers-that-be, who also guard this secret carefully because in their capacity as the authorities they usurp the function of the intellect. For power has to appear not only wilful, but wise. What would happen in the army if everyone knew that the plan of the forthcoming conflict was worked out by a group of junior officers headed by a captain who can't even give the command 'Quick March'?

"Take the mechanism of Stalinist repression. Our detractors attribute it all to Stalin himself and his cronies. But in fact it could never have existed without the intelligentsia and, in the last analysis, the intellectual élite. It was planned, elaborated, created and set in motion by sophisticated members of the intelligentsia. I was once on a commission which studied this aspect of the Stalinist repressions. If I were to tell you which members of our intelligentsia had had a hand in them and how they played their hand, you wouldn't believe me. Fortunately for history, all traces of their participation have been eliminated. And our descendants will only be able to guess at the real role of the intelligentsia in the crimes of the Stalinist epoch. Even so, it's too late already to hide the part that the intellectuals played in providing ideological justification for those crimes.

"The Stalinist repressions are a thing of the past. And life goes on. And in such a huge organism as our country there are always Cyclopean mechanisms for resolving questions no less important than the questions of the Stalinist period. Do you think these problems can be solved by the efforts of official institutions? Now the country is preparing for a world war. It's impossible even to imagine what a gigantic amount of brainwork is being expended in connection with this. And who is doing the work? Who is generating the ideas?

"Naturally, the mass of intellectuals come into play as intermediaries between the intellectual élite and the rest of society. We have forced the entire intelligentsia to work for us, the authorities. More than ever before we are using the Western intelligentsia too. Here's a nice little example for you, one out of many thousands of similar ones. A book critical of Soviet society has appeared in the West. Simultaneously the translation of a book by Academician 'N' comes out in the same country. An official of our embassy finds out in advance who will review these books. For this sort of thing we have innumerable and unfailing sources of information which don't cost us any money at all. It also happens that we ourselves recommend suitable people, and the publishers willingly meet us half-way. A meeting, on the face of it accidental, occurs between one of our diplomats and the reviewer-to-be. The diplomat hints that they are intending to translate Reviewer's book into Russian. The rest happens automatically. A bad review appears of the book criticizing the Soviet regime and a splendid one of the book by the Soviet academic. What these books are really worth, you know yourself."

DOUBTS

"I wonder if we are not over-estimating the role of the intellectual élite in our Great Attack on the West?" I say this, turning mentally towards Inspirer. "Contemporary society is intellectually sated. Ordinary people, whom intellectuals consider to be ignoramuses and fools, in fact have intellects quite sufficient to solve all the problems of contemporary life. And when it comes to understanding these problems, intellectuals are not in any way superior to them. Rather the opposite. Intellectuals surpass people who do practical things in their lives only on the plane of logorrhoea. If intellectuals were to replace the present leaders of our society, things would get much worse, because intellectuals don't have any feeling for reality or common sense. For them their verbiage is more important than the real laws and trends of social processes.

"The psychological principle of intellectuals is: 'we could organize everything in the best possible way, but they don't give us the chance'. But the real situation is that they could organize life in the best possible way only in conditions which are in practice unrealizable; and therefore they are incapable of acting even as well as those leaders of society whom they despise. The actual leaders of society do acquiesce in the flow of life, and so they can at least do something. Intellectuals, on the other hand, take umbrage because the flow of life is not under their control. They consider this unjust. They are dangerous because they look clever, when they are really just fools refined by their profession.

"For example, take this problem: can a group of geniuses plan a brilliant long-term policy for the leadership of the country? I say categorically that it can't. Why? The original design and the plan are one thing. The conditions of their fulfilment are another. Geniuses plan in the abstract; that is, well away from the 'petty' circumstances of real life. Without doing that, they wouldn't be geniuses. Do you think, for example, that one of these geniuses on the staff of the head of the KGB can allow for the mundane fact that Soviet spies in a certain region of Western Europe are bound to get drunk, cheat, intrigue and botch their work—in short, behave like normal Soviet people? Of course he can't. No one who takes such factors into consideration will be admitted into the circle of geniuses. It is the practical operator, the head of the relevant division of the KGB, whom all these geniuses regard as a formalist and an idiot, who knows from experience the real value of the espionage network in his bailiwick. He agrees with the intellectuals' brilliant plans but acts as he himself sees fit. And he gets some results at least. So at the end of the day who is the real genius?

"You say the Western intelligentsia works for us? I'm sure that you could provide thousands of examples, like the story about the book reviews. But these are trivial matters. You can't make one elephant out of a thousand mice."

"True," I hear the venomous voice of Inspirer. "You certainly can't. But why try? We don't need elephants. It's precisely mice that we need. And even better, rats. Millions of rats. And I mean educated and intellectual rats."

SUSPICIONS

Any thinking machine deteriorates if it doesn't have real material to cogitate on. This is true of me too. I am losing my points of reference and social orientation. I rush from one fantasy to another without being able to give preference to any of them. Now it's beginning to seem to me that it's all empty talk, while in reality a vile and dirty game is going on. But I'm not one of the players. *They* are playing with me. The players are the Soviet and Western counter-intelligence services. To the latter I seem to be a powerful figure sent by the KGB on a special mission to the West. The former gives the latter to understand that its suspicions are well-founded. For the latter, that is, for Western Intelligence, I am a useful object through which it can demonstrate its professional expertise and so gain the approval of its masters. For the former I am useful as a means of diverting attention from its real operatives. And as a smoke-screen. I'm only a playing card which one side chooses to place before the other side knowing that the latter will trump it and feel satisfied with his apparent victory. For this player it is enough for his victory to be an apparent one, while his opponent is ready to suffer an apparent defeat in order to hide a real victory of another sort. What is important to the opposing sides is not objective truth and justice, but their own activities, which both parties consider to be a success. Nothing in this game depends on me personally. I really could do and say anything I wanted. My fate was preordained by the very fact that I was chosen for this role.

"True," I hear the voice of Inspirer. "That's what a good director is for—to choose the right actor for the role in question."

INTENTIONS

Now I want one thing only: to get out of this alien game and become just a bystander. To see and to understand: that's enough for me. By profession and vocation I am an understander. All my past life can be described in one word: "cogitation". Here in the West hardly any of the normal stuff of everyday life is left to me, just about nil. I had already become an organ of cognition, pure and simple. And it turns out that it is precisely in the role of pure thought that people here need me least of all. Besides, the Homosos is a personality only in the sense that he is a partial function of the collective. My pure-thought role came about as a role within a Soviet collective. And I can exist as an understander only by adhering to a fully-fledged Soviet collective.

"We know this." (I hear the voice of Inspirer.) "Now you are a mere spectator on the side-lines you will understand what's happening better. And when you are absolutely at the end of your tether we shall stretch out to you the hand of brotherly assistance from our Soviet collective. We'll give you some of our very own fraternal aid."

DECISION OF THE FATES

Artist has fixed himself up with a temporary job in a firm which produces Christmas tree decorations. He says he's their "chief artist". It's obvious that he's just showing off and that there's no such Soviet-type job here.

He and his wife quietly collected their meagre belongings and unsold pictures and went away without saying goodbye.

187

Early one morning Inspirer called for me in an official car, as he sometimes did in exceptional circumstances. "In the West," he said, once we had got clear of Moscow, "they like to elevate every nonentity into a great personality. An artist who can't even draw is declared to be the greatest painter of the century; some hideous hag becomes the world's greatest beauty; a dreadful film director is said to be a great innovator; a vacuous scribbler is a tremendous intellect. It's exactly the same in our world of spies. My God, the people they've said were the greatest spy of the century! But if you look into what these spy-geniuses actually achieved, you're simply amazed that anyone paid any attention to them at all. Real geniuses are only uncovered after the passage of centuries. But for *our* epoch to be cleansed of *its* rubbish and reveal *its* genuine geniuses, well, millennia will be needed for that. Too much rubbish has piled up. But that's enough of general chit-chat. Today, I'm going to show you the most insignificant Soviet spy we've ever had in the West."

After an hour we arrived at a settlement of dachas and made our way through the mud to a shack which looked very out of place among the recently constructed chic villas. An unprepossessing little old man came out to meet us. Soon we were sitting on a verandah with rotting floorboards, drinking the vodka and eating the sausage we had brought along with us. Inspirer asked our host to tell us something of his past. Host flapped his arms and said, well, he'd really done nothing worth the telling. "Well, that's what I want you to tell us about," insisted Inspirer. And so, unwillingly, the old man began to speak.

There were many Soviet spies in Germany just before the war, and they produced a flood of information from all spheres of German society. Somebody had to process all this information and send it off to Moscow. In those days there were no electronics. Nor were the means of communication anything like what they are today. Disasters began to happen because of bad organization in processing and transmission. Our whole espionage network was threatened with ruin. And then someone somewhere mentioned a funny young man in a certain research institute in Moscow. This chap was constructing and servicing a very clever piece of apparatus, but at the same time he was solving with lightning speed in his own head mathematical brain-twisters that sometimes defeated doctors of science for months. He was able to commit to memory whole pages of newspapers after a glance; and he did various other "tricks" which amused the scholars at the institute. They transferred this lad to the relevant institution where he got his instructions, and sent him to Germany. There they literally hid him under the ground. For the two years before the war broke out and for the whole of the war itself, he lived in some kind of cellar not far from Berlin. Part of his job was to process, compress and encode in the smallest possible space and shortest possible time the mighty flood of information coming in from all the other spies. After only a few months he had reached such a peak of perfection that he could gauge in a flash the relative value of a document. From many thousands of pages he could extract the passages worthy of attention, sometimes compressing the information into just a few lines.

After the war they wanted to shoot him, just in case, but they decided not to, all the same. Until 1958 he was kept in solitary confinement in the Lubyanka. Then they let him out and gave him a wretched little pension and this horrible little house. He can't remember anything at all of what passed through his head during those years. He doesn't even remember his own system of "packing the information".

"Do they really have in mind a similar role for me?" I thought, as I listened to Old Man's story.

"Your task will be more complex." Inspirer had read my thoughts. "This time we need education, erudition and scientific know-how. And your brains of course. They regard you too as a thinking-machine, you know. But don't count on getting a little house just outside Moscow."

"Our activity in the West is producing results," said Inspirer on the way back to Moscow. "But at what price? It's all lies when people say it doesn't cost us anything. It's just the opposite, it certainly *does* cost us a pretty kopek or two. A bit more, and we shall go bust. We need to change all our work in the West from top to bottom. Our task here is to convince the leadership of this. Your task there is to find out for this purpose what one can't find out from any newspapers, periodicals, books or secret documents. It's a pity we don't have time to discuss the details. . . ."

"But what's the hurry?" I asked.

"Operation Emigration is at an end," he said. "We've been ordered to round it off. And this just at the moment when we could have gained the maximum advantage from it. Well, I've got to be going. Let's say goodbye. I'm sorry to be parted from you. I liked you, and I still love you as a brother. But understand me right. You are my ace of trumps. And perhaps my last trump. Goodbye!"

DECISION OF THE FATES

Writer has found a permanent job in an anti-Soviet publishing house. He's in the seventh heaven of happiness. The pay is wretched, but it's guaranteed. And the work-load is minimal; reading manuscripts and giving opinions on them. Minimal in terms of time and effort, but (in his words) important from the angle of influencing the fate of Russian literature here in the West. Now he can give himself over peacefully to serious literary creativity. Now he will move mountains. In a word, there's no need to sink into the trough of despond. Bad times pass, sooner or later.

"Yes, and something like that is the best that you can hope for too," I thought to myself, as I listened to Writer's exultant bleating. "In due course you'll also land an absolutely pathetic low-grade job and try to persuade those around you, and yourself, that there are no grounds for pessimism, and that bad times will pass, sooner or later."

On the way to the *Pension* an idea came into my head: what if I played a joke on Writer? Suppose I wrote something and sent it to his publishing house? Under a pseudonym, of course. After all, he's a decent chap. I don't want to put him in an awkward position. And in a single night I wrote a novella. The subject was this. A Soviet agent goes to the West pretending to be a dissident. He tries to work well. But to do this he has to become an agent of the Western secret services. In the KGB they suspect him of treachery and want to eliminate him. The Western secret services see a clever KGB ploy here and also decide to eliminate the agent. Now he's down to his last trick: he begins to do sloppy and slip-shod work, to lie, to twist and turn; in short, to behave like a normal Homosos. As a result, all the intelligence agencies of the world recognize him as one of their men. He is promoted in Moscow and he is promoted in the West. As people in the West cannot describe even a meeting of the government, a funeral and acts of terrorism without adding a dollop of sex, I too furnished my story with some spicy scenes of this sort. On almost every page the hero copulates with a beautiful unknown woman (height, 5'6"; waist, 24"; hips, 38" and breasts 38"). Moreover, it isn't he who uses her but she who uses him, in ecstasy over his truly Russian powers of endurance. "Now," she says, "I understand why the Russians finally got the upper hand in the war against Germany."

I sent this story off to the publishing house and began to wait. Days went by. Weeks. Writer went off on one of his "lecture tours". I didn't place any particular hopes on the story. It was more a joke than anything else. The joke didn't come off. It served it right. And I more or less forgot about my foray into literature.

PROBLEMS

The person who is nearest to me now is Landlady. She helps me in my domestic economy (washing, food) and tells me a lot about the life of ordinary people, which is of the first importance from the sociological point of view, although nobody here pays any attention to it. Now she's explaining to me how I ought to save money on public transport. According to her calculations this saving amounts to 50 pfennigs per week, two marks a month, 24 marks a year and 240 marks each decade. "Two thousand four hundred marks in a century," I reckon, finishing her sums for her. "But we Russians have invented an even more effective way of saving money: we walk. This saves us five marks a week and twenty marks a month. In a century it amounts to a huge sum. You can buy a house on it."

Landlady takes my words seriously. Official statistics say that 70 per cent of families here have only one toothbrush; they economize. Here they economize in everything so much that it becomes quite sickening. But we Russians spend all we've got between one pay-day and the next without getting so terribly het up about the future. Which is better? If the Soviet authorities were just that much cleverer they could have raised the standard of living in the USSR in the course of a few years to a point at which all doubts about the advantages of the one way of life over the other would have vanished. Indeed, this is the most powerful Soviet weapon of all; but the Soviet leadership is no longer capable of using it.

DECISION OF THE FATES

Joker has got his residence-permit for the United States. "Now everything will be okay," he said as he bade me farewell. "Come to the States! It's much easier to get a job over there."

"I'm afraid They won't let me out of here," I said.

"Who?" said he, very surprised.

"They," I said.

"Who are They?" he asked.

"I don't know," I said. "But They are They, always and everywhere."

191

The contingent of Pensionnaires has been completely replenished, with the exception of myself, Dissident and his wife. I don't want to make the acquaintance of the new Pensionnaires. And they avoid me. It's clear that somebody has warned them that they ought to be on their guard against me. Nor have I any contacts with Dissident. In the morning the two of them slip silently through the hall to the street, and late in the evening they slink back into their room. That's all. For whole days I lie idly on my bed or look at the television. I go out only for cigarettes and something to eat. And to the interrogation sessions, of course.

I have learned the true value of television for the sociologist who wants to study the West. Look, for instance, at what I learned here in one single day! A church functionary calls for spiritual unity, seeing in this the road to salvation. "Idiot," I say. "If there is a road to salvation it lies not through unity, but through disunity. We need clarity in everything, not muddiness. We need clear-cut forms and not blurred outlines. Better sincere enmity than hypocritical friendship."

Yet another pair of dancers has decided not to return to the USSR. Since non-returners have become a common phenomenon, the Soviet authorities ought to recognize them officially. On the forms Soviet citizens fill in before they go abroad a further question should be added: do you intend to stay in the West or not? If so, state in which country, and why.

Then there was a round-table discussion about a murderer who had killed an entire family of five people. Was he responsible for his actions or not? Luminaries of science, medicine, the law, literature and journalism were all drawn into the discussion. In fact, there's no problem here at all. For 50 years the murderer was a normal man; and now suddenly doubts arise. It's simply that he knew the consequences of his crime in advance. There's no capital punishment; there will be a long delay while his psychiatric condition is clarified (that means a nice long spell in a first-class sanatorium), and so on. And it suits everyone involved that the thing should drag on and on: articles, television appearances, fees.

An old-age pensioner died nearly three years ago in his flat, but they've only just discovered him because of a much-needed repair to the plumbing. For almost three years the man was dead and all that time all his routine business was done for him by his bank. If the sanitation system hadn't broken down perhaps another couple of years might have gone by before they realized he was dead. Again a discussion. Some see in the case the merits of the banking system, others the vices of Capitalism.

A little girl of seven has been kidnapped. They're demanding a ransom of two million marks. A general has been kidnapped too. For some reason or other so far no one has demanded a ransom for *him*.

A bomb explosion in a station. More than 50 dead. It's a curious thing: Western terrorists never seize Soviet embassies or kill Soviet bureaucrats and diplomats; on the whole, terrorists never touch anything connected with the Soviet Union. Why should this be, eh? The Western smart Alecs see in this fact evidence that the terrorists are acting on orders from Moscow. But if this really were so, Moscow would quickly stage an outrage against something Soviet.

School children have started a rebellion. The motive for the revolt was that a girl had killed herself. She thought teacher had reduced her marks by one. The older pupils are demanding the liberalization of the school (although it's Liberty Hall already) and a reduction in the curriculum (although here the curriculum is simply laughable compared with that of Moscow schools). Naturally they are also demanding the demilitarization (!!) of Western Europe and the abolition of military service in general. Pupils from the junior classes are complaining that the price of sweets and cakes has gone up. "If the government spent less money on armaments and more on the real needs of the population," said a seven-year-old mite, "sweets would be cheaper too." A crowd of journalists and other adults talking to the children broke into a tumult of applause.

WE

At night I listen to the conversations in the room where Artist previously lived with his wife. I don't want to reproduce them here. What can Soviet people talk about when, on some pretext or other, they have got out from the hungry, miserable Russian provinces into the fabulously plentiful and brilliant West? But sometimes ominous notes can be detected in their speech.

"It's bad here when one doesn't know the language."

"We'll learn it. And if we don't, we'll get by without it. Ivan hung round here for ten years and didn't even learn how to order a vodka in German."

"Ivan nearly came to grief from not knowing the language; he told me all about it himself. He got hold of some very important secret docu-

193

ments and wanted to send them to Moscow. He packed them up and went to the Post Office. But they wouldn't accept the packet. They shoved some piece of paper at him and told him to fill it in. He looked at the paper and understood one thing; they were asking him to write in his name and address and something else. 'It's a questionnaire,' he suspected, in true Soviet fashion. He thought his cover was about to be blown. He got in a panic and decided to confess. No great harm in that. Many people do it, and later do some very useful jobs for us all the same. He went to the police. He opened the packet and showed them the documents. He pointed his finger at himself and said: *'Ich bin sovietisch Spion'*. They said at the police station that this wasn't their department, sorry. But where was the security service? Nobody knew. A crowd collected. Somebody said there were two security services; one civil, the other military. If the documents were military secrets, he should go to the latter, but if they were industrial secrets, he should go to the former. A heated discussion ensued about political secrets; were they military or civil? Fortunately they found a worthy person who spoke some Russian; he'd been a prisoner-of-war. He explained to Ivan what all the fuss was about and what he should do. The package, it turned out, was too heavy, but one could divide the contents into two parts and send them separately. However, this would cost at least forty pfennigs more. A waste of money. Better send it parcel-post, having first filled in a different type of form. And this would be a good ten pfennigs cheaper. D'you know what the most humiliating thing about all this was? Ivan said that all the time he felt like an utter idiot and that these people were looking down on him as if he were a typical Russian nincompoop."

"Don't you worry, we'll still show them what sort of nincompoops we are."

RÉSUMÉ

I've gone back to devouring the local newspapers. And again I spit in disgust when I look through what they write about the Soviet bloc. They select the facts that fit in with their *a priori* assumptions and interpret these facts in the spirit of the conventional wisdom about socialist society and their wishes for it. If the KGB now demanded from me an instant Report giving them the gist of my observations in a few lines, I would confine myself to the following: the West not only cannot understand the essence of our society, but actively wishes not to do so. The Soviet services which deal with the West can safely accept this judgement as an axiom on which to base their own activities right up to the next world war. All the Western specialists on the Soviet bloc taken together are fundamentally incapable of correctly evaluating the life-expectancy and military potential of the Soviet bloc. They are able only to oscillate between various extremes, occasionally hitting on true ideas by chance. But they cannot evaluate things correctly or make proper use of their own true guesses. Official Soviet ideology comes nearer to the truth in its understanding of social reality in the USSR than anything I have seen here in the West. The ideology is badly formulated, and it's distorted for propaganda purposes; and this allows the bumbling Western verbiage-mongers to regard it with derision. The unvarnished truth often looks monstrous alongside these highly sophisticated misconceptions of the West. Soviet ideology has been subject to Western influence since Stalin's time and it has somewhat improved in its external verbal form. But at the same time it has lost a great deal of its substance. Our views of the West in Moscow are on the whole correct; so we need to go to the West—not to understand it, but to get to know ourselves better and assess our own opportunities in it.

DECISION OF THE FATES

The most inconspicuous people in the *Pension* are Dissident and his wife. One has quite stopped meeting them on the way to the lavatory or the rubbish-bins. And they no longer appear in the hall. I shan't be surprised if it's the unremarkable Dissident who turns out to be that Big Fisher in Troubled Waters about whom I once spoke to Cynic. He is very grey and boring. And so inconspicuous. While counter-intelligence is taking its time to make up its mind about me, Big Fisher has, quietly and inconspicuously, slipped through to wherever it was he needed to go and begun his modest activity as a cancerous cell in the body of Western society. We are crawling into the body of our enemy like graveyard worms. And now I too dream only of becoming a worm that guzzles on its environment and poisons it with its excretions.

MY REAL PROFILE

I said I had had enough of interrogations. They said that my "real profile" was still not yet altogether clear to them. "That," I said, "you will never know. That problem is logically insoluble. If you take a multitude of actions of a mass of people and a mass of internal conditions that correspond to them, then you can reliably judge some of them by the others. The 'true profile' of a mass of people is accurately expressed in the mass of their actions. But when it comes to individual people and their individual actions, usually there is no such coincidence between them. I am a representative of the mass. As an individual I have no face, no profile."

"But you do have some secret goals, don't you?" they said.

"What goals can a worm have when it's attached to a hook? It's the fisherman and the fish who have goals."

"All right," they said. "It really is time—how do you say it in Russian?—to round this off. We have one last request: write us a short description of Soviet man."

To describe the Homosos! What a challenge! In many decades and perhaps even centuries from now the people who cracked this problem will be regarded as outstanding scholars. But what kind of reward will I get in the here and now? Well, never mind. Here, as they say, even half a loaf is better than no bread. I will try to accomplish this epoch-making task for them.

HOMOSOS

The Homosos is *Homo Sovieticus*, or Soviet man, regarded as a type of living being and not as a citizen of the USSR. Not every citizen of the USSR is a Homosos. Not every Homosos is a citizen of the USSR. Occasions on which people behave like Homososes can be found in the most varied epochs and in the most diverse countries. But the man who possesses a more or less full complement of the qualities of the Homosos displays them systematically, transmits them from generation to generation and himself appears as a typical mass-phenomenon in a given society; he is, indeed, the product of history. Such a man is generated by the conditions inseparable from the existence of a Communist (or Socialist) society. He is the carrier of that society's principles of life. He preserves its intra-collective relations by the very way of life he leads. For the first time in history man became Homosos in Moscow and in Moscow's sphere of influence within the Soviet Union; that is to say, in Muscovy.

The Homosos is the product of human adaptation to certain social conditions. That is why he can never be understood outside his normal environment any more than a fish can be understood from its movements when it has been thrown on to the sand or into the frying pan. One cannot judge its characteristics then as one can when it is swimming in the water. One should take the characteristic and typical situations of the normal way of life of the mass of Homososes and then put the question: how will the normal Homosos behave in this or that situation? From the replies to such questions you will get a description of the Homosos as a special type of man adequate to the demands of a special type of society.

Let us take, as an example, the Homososes of today who are living in Muscovy. Food prices have gone up. Will the Homosos arrange a protest demonstration? Of course not. The Homosos has been trained to live in pretty dreadful conditions. He is ready to face hardships. He continually expects something even worse. He is humble before the dispositions of the powers-that-be. How will the Homosos behave if he has to adopt a position in public (that is, at meetings, in his collective) towards the dissidents? Naturally, he will endorse the actions of the authorities and condemn the actions of the dissidents. The Homosos always tries to put a spoke in the wheels of anyone disrupting the customary forms of behaviour; he toadies to the powers-that-be; he is on the side of the majority of his fellow-citizens who are approved by the authorities. How does the Homosos react to the militarization of his country and to the growth of Soviet activity throughout the world, including its interventionist tendencies? He totally supports his leadership because he possesses the standardized consciousness formed by the ideology, a feeling of responsibility for the country as a whole, a readiness for sacrifice and a readiness to sacrifice others. Of course the Homosos is also capable of feeling discontent with his lot: he can even criticize what is going on in the country and the authorities themselves. But only in the appropriate form, in the appropriate place and to the appropriate degree; that is to say, in a way that doesn't appreciably threaten the overall interests of the social organism. Even in this area one can specify the characteristic situations and the characteristic behaviour of the Homosos. From a series of character-revealing questions and their answers, you will get a description of a man adequate to the requirements of Socialist (Communist) society and appropriate to it from the viewpoint of its integrity and its interests as a whole.

The comparison I made above between a Homosos and a fish is one-sided. The Homosos, in contrast to the fish, is himself the bearer and conserver of his environment or social habitat. But this fact derives not from the Homosos's qualities as an individual, but from his qualities as a representative of the mass of Homososes organized into a single whole. Homososes by their common efforts invent, support and accept as reasonable a certain number of absolutely basic principles of their organization. On the basis of these principles the social environment within which they live is formed. To this environment they adapt from generation to generation. As individuals they adapt to one another as they do to the mass of individuals as a whole; which mass forms in its turn a social superindividual. The social environment of the Homosos is as unthinkable without him as he is without it.

The Homosos is not only an agglomeration of shortcomings. He also possesses numerous valuable traits. Or, to be more precise, he possesses qualities which are either good or bad according to the circumstances and depending on the criteria of evaluation applied. One and the same quality will manifest itself as good in some circumstances and as bad in others. For some people the quality will be, or seem to be, a good one; for others, bad. Among the mass of Homososes one can discover all the characteristics known to humanity, but in specifically Socialist (Communist) forms and proportions. While the Homosos reflects in himself the properties of his social entity, he is at the same time only a partial function of that entity. Different functions of the Communist collective are incarnated in different members of it who become preponderantly the bearers of these functions. That is why there are different species of Homosos within the single genus of Homosos.

Homosos society has its own criteria for the evaluation of the qualities and behaviour of its individual members. In many ways these criteria do not coincide with analogous criteria in societies of other types. They are situational. From this viewpoint the Homosos is supple and plastic to a degree that makes him seem quite spineless. He possesses a comparatively large range of fluctuations vis-à-vis social and psychological situations and values, but he also has the ability to revert to a certain average, middling position. The Homosos, for example, can hear you out attentively as you lay bare the ulcers of Soviet society, and he may agree with you one hundred per cent. But do not rush to the conclusion that you have de-programmed him and converted him to your own beliefs. He himself can immediately produce a mass of examples to support what you have said and even express views about his own society that are more critical than yours. But that will not make him cease to be a Homosos. His essence will remain the same. Only a minute percentage of Homososes swallow the bait of such propaganda. We can estimate this percentage in advance: there are marginal deviations of this sort in any mass of people. And the Homosos may, for example, give a sincere undertaking to co-operate with you in your dissident activities. But don't be too quick to congratulate yourself on your success. He can immediately denounce you just as sincerely to the authorities.

198

There are exceptions here too. But we can also predict the number of these exceptions *a priori*. The number of them in Homosos society is virtually nil. This sort of deviation from the norm is quickly spotted by the Homosos collectives and the authorities. Sooner or later it is liquidated. Society is thereby cleansed; and a place is left for the emergence of new deviations of the same kind that are, for the time being, hidden from public view.

If one looks at the behaviour of the Homosos from the viewpoint of some abstract morality, he seems to be a completely immoral being. The Homosos isn't a moral being, that's true, but it isn't true to say that he is positively immoral. In the first instance he is an ideological being. And on that basis he can be either moral or immoral, according to circumstances. Homososes are not villains. Among them there are many good people. But the good Homosos is a man who either doesn't have the opportunity to cause other people harm or who finds no special need to do so. But if he has the opportunity, or is compelled, to do evil, he will do it not less but even more thoroughly than the most inveterate villain.

Up to now the Soviet people who have achieved the qualities of the Homosos of maximum maturity are the ones with a comparatively high level of culture and education and also those in the most socially active part of the population (especially people in management, science, propaganda, culture and education). But that section of highly developed Homososes exerts an influence on all the rest of the country and also on the whole external environment. The virus of Homosossery is spreading apace over the entire globe. It is the gravest disease that can afflict mankind because it reaches to the very essence of the human being. If a man has sensed the Homosos in himself and tasted the poison of Homosossery, it is more difficult to cure him of his disease than it is to return a burnt-out alcoholic or a junkie to a healthy life.

Evolution-wise the Homosos is not decadent. On the contrary, he is the highest product of civilization. He is superman. He is universal. If need be, he can commit any frightfulness. Where it is possible, he can possess every virtue. There are no secrets which he cannot explain. There are no problems which he cannot solve. He is naïve and simple. He is vacuous. He is omniscient and all-pervasive. He is replete with wisdom. He is a particle of the universe that bears the whole universe within itself. He is ready for anything and anyone. He is even ready for the best. He awaits it, although he doesn't believe in it. He hopes for the worst. He is Nothing; that is to say, Everything. He is God, pretending to be the Devil. He is the Devil, pretending to be God. He is in every man.

Gentle reader, look into yourself and you will see there at least the

199

embryo of this crown of creation. For you yourself are human. You yourself are Homosos.

STAYING ALIVE

The West's concern with the Soviet threat is clear from the fact that soldiers are being shown on television more and more frequently. And these soldiers say more and more insistently that they don't want to die, that they want to live and that they are taking part in the activities of the campaigners for peace. The war has not yet begun, but they are already demanding peace. Nobody has died yet (unless you count that blockhead who filled himself up with beer and managed to drown in a dry river-bed), and yet they are already wailing about their thirst for life.

One doesn't need to be taught how to want to live. No mind or courage is required to express this elementary animal urge; an urge now blown up by all the media of mass cretinization into the dimensions of an epoch-making ideology. Hysteria about the fear of death is an ideological method of manipulating people—Western people of course, for it has no effect on Soviet people. And it's a Soviet means of manipulation. It was carefully thought out in all the sections of the Soviet apparatus of power and approved at the very highest level as a general directive for the period right up to the outbreak of the next world war.

"I see nothing bad in the fact that you want to live," I turned in my thoughts to the soldiers who were struggling for peace. "But it isn't dignified for a man to think about this, still less for him to speak about it out loud. It amounts to an intellectual and moral degradation of society when its defenders think only about their own skins. And chattering about peace is the cheapest and least reliable means of preserving peace. The old rule, 'if you want peace, prepare for war', still holds good even in our time. If you want to live, be ready to die."

PREPARING FOR DEATH

In our time this is a problem which concerns everybody. Even if there is a nuclear war, millions of people will have enough time to realize: this is the end. We Homososes have had a rich historical experience here. We have grown used to this finality, and we are ready to meet it as we do the umpteenth Resolution of our very own dear Central Committee of the

Communist Party of the Soviet Union finally to raise our standard of living to a new, completely unattainable level. And we are ready to share our experience with you.

In the Soviet Union we use the following method of curing alcoholics. They are given a special medicine. If, after taking it, a person drinks something alcoholic he is bound to die. Alcoholics are warned about this. Half-way through the course of treatment the specialists arrange an "imitation of death". They give them a little drop of vodka so that they are convinced of the reality of the threat of death. And they actually do begin to die. But the medical authorities don't allow them to die completely. They save them. ("Why bother?" some specialists say.) On completing the full course of treatment a person cannot be saved even if he drinks only a gram of alcohol. Admittedly, there still hasn't been a single case of an alcoholic's being cured by this course of treatment. A few of the patients manage to hold out until the effect of the medicine wears off, and then begin to drink again with redoubled vigour. The majority somehow manage to begin drinking again long before that. But that isn't the point. After their treatment some of these people start to experience the "imitation of death" every time they drink. I am told that in Moscow a secret society has been formed of lovers-of-drinking-to-the-brink-of-death. Sociologists have surveyed a lot of people who've experienced the "imitation of death". Asked whether it wasn't terrifying, they reply with a laugh. The majority affirm that the most unpleasant part of the procedure is returning to life; especially to a life of sobriety.

Western schoolchildren and soldiers could be given a sort of "imitation of death"; and after them the civil servants. Of course, someone would have to teach them how to drink vodka first. But, as the experience of our great country has shown, that's no problem. Instead of another gas pipeline from Siberia to Western Europe one could build a vodka pipeline. And there won't be any protests against this in the West. It will bring in twice as much revenue as the gas, and from the viewpoint of conquering the West it will be twice as effective. All we have to do is cut off the flow, and the West will crawl on all fours all the way to Moscow to get another hair of the dog that had bit them.

As for the theoretical preparation for death, I can offer you some general principles drawn from my personal experience as a Homosos.

Don't worry about the future of humanity. Man is the sort of creature that will survive in any circumstances whatever. In the last 200 years the population of China has grown 20 times; that of Russia ten times. And remember how many of *us* were destroyed! After the next world war the population of the planet, with the exception of white Europeans and white Americans, will double. Rejoice at this! And kick the bucket with the same faith in the radiant future as the Russian alcoholics who are cured (cured?) of our incurable national destiny by the latest discoveries of contemporary science.

Spit at friendship! A close friend of mine used to denounce me, and also denounce others in such a way that everyone suspected that I was the informer. My best friend, Inspirer, sacrificed me for the sake of his manic plans. Remember: the stronger the friendship, the more terrible its betrayal.

Don't love. I have loved and been loved once. It was torture. In our very selves we personified the impossibility of real love, and mutual hatred entered our hearts for ever. Remember: the purer and stronger the love, the more painful the disillusionment.

Get rid of your vanity. Once, on the instructions of the Central Committee, I carried out a very complicated and interesting investigation with a small group of colleagues and very little finance. I conducted this research with great élan. I think it was my greatest contribution to the field of scholarship. A special commission with top academics on it gave it their highest commendation. Academician 'N' said that if this research could be de-classified it would go into all the sociology textbooks as one of the most brilliant investigations in the history of the subject. The results of my research were included in secret documents without mention of my name. I did receive a prize, one month's salary. Later I frequently fulfilled analogous tasks without getting any prize or any praise. Remember: the more you create, the less you keep for yourself.

Don't trust anybody. I have never known a single person who didn't deceive me about something, or who didn't deceive other people in front of my own eyes. Remember: the more you trust people, the more cynically they will deceive you. When you've realized this, you'll see that you are alone. And if you're alone, you won't last all that long.

Learn to lose. The more you lose, the easier it is to meet your death. I have lost everything. I don't walk, I float in the air. I whirl along with the feeling of weightlessness.

Learn not to possess. In that science I have reached perfection. I had so little in life that there was no need for me to learn how not to possess. Look at Enthusiast and shudder at the sight of his fate. He used to have only one pair of trousers which he wore for a good ten years. And he was a courageous fighter against the Soviet regime. Now he has pyjamas, three pairs of trousers and an electric razor. And already he trembles at every rustle, suspecting that it presages Moscow's perfidious intention to deprive him of his precious life.

Don't worry about posterity. Posterity is indifferent to our fate. Our descendants will interpret even our best intentions as attempted coercion and our finest achievements as absurdities and rubbish. Look at Enthusiast again! He's busy persuading a bunch of his own and other people's relatives to come to the West. Remember my words: soon you will see him among the campaigners for turning Western Europe into a "nuclear-free zone". And his snotty-nosed grandchildren will be whooping it up with the junior schoolkids demanding the reduction of the defence budget by a thousand million marks a year so as to get the price of cakes and sweeties down by a pfennig.

Learn to look at yourself from the side, and then it will seem comical to you how such a miserable being ever contrived to develop such a grandiose fear of death. Then you will see that the fear of death has nothing to do with the thirst for life. The man who really has a thirst for life isn't afraid of death. Only the person who sits and waits for death is frightened of it. Know this, that it is a matter of indifference to the dead that life still goes on after they've left.

And do not forget to repeat to yourself, whenever you remember it, that you are ready to die. It is better to do this without tragic pathos, calmly, even with a grin. After all, we shall all turn our toes up in the end. As for myself, I am ready even now. After all, I've known all the main things life can offer. After all, I've nothing much to lose. I've nothing left that's really mine, nothing sacred, nothing mysterious. I am ready to pay for my life in a reasonable exchange. I consider the price to be a fair one. But . . .

It is in this "but" that the essence of our teaching about death consists. One man's readiness to meet death with dignity and another man's submissiveness when it finally faces him are poles apart. In the first case a man fights for his life until the last moment, in the second he panics and capitulates.

I will tell you a short parable which I myself heard in Moscow from an unknown drunkard. "At the beginning of the war," he said, "our unit was smashed and surrounded. We realized we were doomed. 'We'll have to surrender,' some of us said. 'After all, we're *kaput*.' 'We'll have to fight to the last man,' said others. 'After all, we're *kaput*.' We tried to convince the first lot, but in vain. They were paralysed with the fear of death. They threw away their weapons and rushed towards the enemy to give themselves up. We killed some of them ourselves for being cowards and traitors. The rest were finished off by the Germans. Our lot went on fighting God knows, how we fought! How many enemies didn't we send to Kingdom Come! And some of us survived."

"But what did you do it for?" sneered a budding alcoholic of critical bent.

"On principle," replied the drunkard. "We were men then, and we felt it was a matter of our dignity. Or for no reason at all. Simply in order to go out with a bang."

And so, when you have recognized the justice of death and worked out for yourself a readiness to die, say in conclusion this remarkable, life-asserting 'but'. Say to yourself in Russian, *"Pogibat', tak s muzykoi"*; if we have to die, let's go out with the band playing, not like a wimp. Fight for your life. Don't ask for favours, don't beg for mercy, just fight!

DECISION OF THE FATES

Writer came back. In Moscow style I dropped in to see him without warning. There were lots of people there. Eating, drinking and shouting. Then Writer asked for silence and began to read aloud: it was my novella. I watched the reaction of the guests. Sometimes they laughed. At times they grew indignant. At other times they sighed. They asked who the author was. "The author is unknown," said Writer. "Will you print it?" asked somebody. "Not in any circumstances," said Writer. "As literature it's too weak. Its ideational slant doesn't suit us." At this point I recalled the Moscow cliché judgements such as "scientifically [or, artistically] incompetent and ideationally pernicious". I couldn't prevent myself from laughing. People looked at me reproachfully.

"When I got to the West," declaimed Writer, "I realized that the West had fallen behind us. Literature's growth point is not here, but in Russia. Russia will amass new forces and there will be a powerful new literary explosion. It is our duty to prepare it, so we must mercilessly hack off this sort of creativity, if one may use the word (he waved my manuscript about), which lowers the general level of Russian literature. Ladies and gentlemen, we have after all been through the school of the Union of Soviet Writers."

A former Soviet film producer, a veteran of the war, said the sex scenes in the story were very well written. If somebody gave him the money, he could make a sensational film out of them. On the whole, the West underestimated the hidden sexual potential of the Russian people, said Producer. Soon after the war one tipsy Russian sapper in Central Europe wandered into a brothel. (They hadn't yet had time to liquidate the brothels then.) He said he wouldn't leave the place until he had tried every one of the—well, let's say—women there and satisfied the whole lot "in real champion style". What he meant by this expression became evident later when the—well, let's say—women began to rush out of the brothel, wailing and covering their privy parts with both hands. We Russians will show you yet what we are made of! In the end we shall occupy the place in world culture of which we are worthy!

"Should I really begin again to include these people in my list of Soviet agents?" I thought. "No, it isn't worth while. It's impossible to make a good spy ring and fifth column out of these sweepings of Soviet society. For that one must have Homososes of an altogether higher calibre."

THE END OF THE SCREENING

Today my interrogators were unusually welcoming. They gave me coffee and cigarettes. They said the screening was over; now I had only to wait for the decision about my fate. They hoped it would all turn out for the best. It was rather sad. These interrogations had been an important part of my life at this juncture. Before we said goodbye I told them the story of a Western spy who was discovered in Moscow acquiring, for a crazy sum of money, top secret drawings of some bit of military hardware that had long been obsolete in the West, and had been obtained in the West by a Soviet agent who had paid even more for them. They laughed until they cried. They clapped me on the shoulder. They said that we Russians were "really great guys". "What did they do with that Western spy?" they asked. "They exchanged him for the Soviet one," I said.

The soldiers of the Special Amphibious Battalion had let the air out of their dinghies and life-jackets, and put them neatly away. Now they were getting ready for dinner. Soon some of them would be going off, in their own cars, to see their girl-friends or relatives. Others would be driving out to take part in demonstrations of fighters-for-peace. A third lot would collapse into bed in their striped pyjamas. Soldiers in chic pyjamas—a reliable defence for the West.

The screening was over. The hardest part was behind me. No longer need I rack my brains over insoluble problems, prove what can't be proved and refute the irrefutable. What conclusion had their remarkable computers arrived at when they had digested the boundless sum of information they'd received from me and about me? I could have predicted their deduction in advance and without the titanic efforts that had been expended on its acquisition. It's a pity I didn't propose it to Them by way of a scientific experiment. However, They wouldn't have told me the result of the experiment anyway, or said if I'd been mistaken. They couldn't have admitted that some insignificant Homosos was able to compete with their remarkable technology, the embodiment of their great collective intellect. They are certain that in the rivalry between man and machine the future belongs to the machine. They don't know the Homososes. *We* are convinced that in the rivalry between the Homosos and the machine, the future will belong to the Homosos.

What decision are they authorized to take in cases such as mine? Make use of me in grade such-and-such? Leave me to my own devices? Play cat and mouse with me until they're finally ready to finish me off? But that's their business, not mine. I've played out my role.

DELIRIUM

It was late when I returned to the *Pension*. For a long time Landlord didn't want to open the door. I threatened to call the police. He turned nicer, but warned me not to do it again. "This isn't Russia, you know. Here we like having everything in proper order!"

During the night I was tormented by delirious dreams. Inspirer came into my vision. "You've played out your role very well," he said. "Wait just a bit longer and you'll pull through. You'll become a big man. You'll be the plenipotentiary representative of Soviet power in Western Europe."

"And if They also see that as my role," I asked, "what then?" Inspirer faded out without replying.

And it was dawn. I remembered my Edifice and rushed to the window. It glittered in a blue heaven with such unprecedented beauty that it took my breath away. But what is that? In the most prominent place, a gigantic four-letter word shines forth in all its glory: BANK.

Munich, 1981